DRIVE INTO DARKNESS

→ → →

The woman coughed for some time.

Terry said, "You oughtn't to be out. Let's be as quick as we can, so that you can get home. Have you come about the picture?"

"Oh, yes, about the picture."

"Have you got it?"

"Not here. We must drive a little way."

The car began to move. The woman had opened her bag and was fumbling in it. She still coughed.

Then, with the extreme of suddenness, a hand took Terry by the elbow. Not a large hand but a very strong one. It held her rigid and startled. And on that the other hand came up with a stabbing motion. Needle-sharp and deep, something stabbed right into her arm. She cried out and tried to wrench away, but the grip on her elbow held.

The needle that had pricked her was withdrawn. The hand which had held it came around her neck and pressed a pad of something down upon her nose and mouth. She tried to drag herself free...

ROLLING STONE

Also by Patricia Wentworth

THE BLIND SIDE
THE CASE IS CLOSED
BEGGAR'S CHOICE
THE CLOCK STRIKES TWELVE
THE FINGERPRINT
GREY MASK
LONESOME ROAD
PILGRIM'S REST
THE WATERSPLASH
WICKED UNCLE
DEAD OR ALIVE
NOTHING VENTURE
OUTRAGEOUS FORTUNE
RUN!
MR. ZERO
THE LISTENING EYE

Published by
WARNER BOOKS

ROLLING STONE

• • •

PATRICIA WENTWORTH

A Time Warner Company

WARNER BOOKS EDITION

This Warner Books Edition is published by arrangement with Harper-Collins*Publishers*, Inc., 10 East 53rd Street, New York, N.Y. 10022

Cover illustration by Bob Scott
Cover design by Anne Twomey

Warner Books, Inc.
666 Fifth Avenue
New York, N.Y. 10103

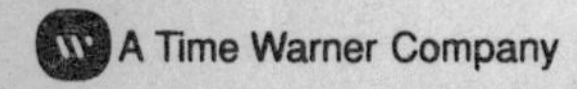

Printed in the United States of America

First Warner Books Printing: August, 1991

10 9 8 7 6 5 4 3 2 1

CHAPTER I

THE rain fell in a fine, steady drizzle. The young man in the armchair looked up from the letter he was writing and glanced with dislike at a prospect where nothing pleased and man appeared viler than usual. It had been raining all day. Everything was very wet. And instead of being the cleaner for this continuous shower-bath, everything, steep tilted roofs, narrow street, small shops, and a wavering, havering, haphazard straggle of men women children and dogs, appeared to be even dirtier than usual.

The room was a bare one, the arm chair dowdy, sagging, but not uncomfortable. The man who occupied it had one leg crossed above the other at a fantastic angle. He brought his eyes back from the window to a writing-block precariously perched against the tilted knee and went on writing. A loosely built young man of indeterminate features, in repose expressionless. But just now when he had looked at the rain they had changed. Something quick, vivid and angry had looked out. Then he was back at his writing, pen running fast, left hand steadying the block.

"I think I've found the man. Wrong expression—as you were—I am on his track. Dictionary for sleuths, use of—don't the department issue it? If not, why not?

All right, all right, I'm coming to the point. You know I didn't ask to be dragged into sleuthing, so you'll just have to take me as you find me. It will, I feel, do you—and the department—a lot of good. Query—is the Foreign Office Secret Service a department? Probably not. That's the sort of moss a rolling stone like me doesn't gather. Yes, I'm really coming to it—the point, *cher maître*, the point."

Here the young man grinned suddenly, showing good teeth. He was ready to bet that no one had ever called Colonel Garrett *cher maître* before, and he had a clear and pleasant picture of what Garrett's reactions would be. Then he went on writing.

"He calls himself Pierre Riel. I am told he is Spike Reilly. I think he may be the goods. Someone told a girl, who told a man, who told a girl, who told another man, who told me that Mr. Spike had once talked in his cups. Moral of this—all criminals should join their local Band of Hope. I go now to take a room in the same pub as Spike. Viewed from the outside it presents every appearance of being about as low in the social scale as you can get. If I fall a victim to dirt, drains or bugs, I presume that a grateful government will pay for my obsequies.

Yours unofficially,
J.P.T.

P.S. I shall post this on my way. Another thrilling installment tomorrow.

P.P.S. Brussels has some fine architectural features and a lot of bells. I like it better when it doesn't rain.

P.P.P.S., or what comes next. It's been raining ever since I got here.

N.B. That is all, *cher maître*."

The grin showed again for a fleeting moment. Then, with the letter enveloped and stamped, suit-case in hand and raincoat on back, Mr. Peter Talbot clattered down a steep and rickety stair and sallied reluctantly forth into the rain.

He posted the letter, and pursued a damp and devious course through a number of mean and narrow streets. The odd thing was that his spirits kept on rising. And, paradoxically, this was a depressing circumstance. He even groaned over it slightly himself, because, on his own private barometer, that sudden lift was a certain indication of cyclones ahead, and at this stage of the proceedings while the blood mounted to Peter's head, he could still be aware that his feet were cold.

He was whistling between his teeth when he came to the Hotel Dupin and pushed through into its narrow, dingy hall.

A room? But certainly m'sieu could have a room. If m'sieu would register. And the suit-case of m'sieu would be taken up, *o bien sur*.

Peter Talbot stood with the pen in his hand and looked at the register. Five—no, six names up, illegibly scrawled, the name of Pierre Riel. Something sang in his ears. He bent down and signed the good old-fashioned name of John Smith.

CHAPTER II

PETER looked presently from a third-floor window, and beheld a back yard under rain—very literally under rain, because the water stood in pools amongst a jumble of old barrels, broken crockery, a mouldering dog kennel, and other odds and ends. There were logs of wood, a perambulator with only one wheel, something that looked like the wreck of a bicycle, and a hip bath with a hole in it. He was wondering where all these things had come from, and wondering too about the odd muttering sound which seemed to come from the room on the right. He had taken it at first for the murmur of voices in conversation, but there were not two voices, there was only one, and it went on, and on, and on.

There was a communicating door. The first thing you do about a communicating door in a place like this is to find out whether it is locked, and whether there is a bolt on your own side. Well, it was locked all right, but there was no sign of a key, and there wasn't any bolt. Not so good. Behind that door was M. Pierre Riel, alias Mr. Spike Reilly, and Peter would have preferred that there should be a bolt.

With his hand on the jamb he listened to the muttering voice. Either Mr. Spike Reilly was drunk, or—or—he saw again very vividly the scrawled name in the register—the very illegible scrawled name. If he hadn't known what name to look for, the odds would have been against his making head or tail of it.

The mutter on the other side of the door died down, and then rose again waveringly to a kind of scream. The scream broke off in a gasp. Peter walked down the stairs he had just come up and routed out M. Dupin—small, dark, sallow, with eyes as bright and beady as a rat's. Rather ratlike about the teeth, Peter thought. The way he had of half cupping his hands too—

"Who's the fellow in the room next to mine?" he said. "And what's the matter with him? Is he ill, or only drunk?"

M. Dupin cupped his hands and showed his teeth apologetically. Madame Dupin, at the desk, shrugged tightly upholstered shoulders and sent a glance to the ceiling.

"It is M'sieu Riel."

Dupin shrugged too.

"It is only last night that he arrives and we notice nothing. We think he is a little drunk perhaps. But this morning he does not get up, he does not move. He has a fever, he talks all the time. And what can I do? I say to him, 'Will you send for your friends—will you send for a doctor—will you tell me of someone to whom I can send?' And does he answer me? No. He has a delirium. He goes on talking, and there is not a single word of sense in all he says—not one. It is English, English. English all the time. And he calls himself Pierre Riel. Without a doubt that is not his name. Who knows whether we shall not find ourselves in trouble with the police?"

"Have you sent for a doctor?" said Peter.

"Assuredly not! Who knows that he can pay for one?" Madame Dupin's voice was indignant. It was one of those husky voices with no breath behind it.

Dupin showed his teeth in an ingratiating smile.

"Now if m'sieu, who is also English, would like to arrange for his compatriot—"

Peter looked blankly from one to the other. His heart

sang. His face showed nothing. He said in a stupid voice,

"I'll go up and see him."

As he climbed the dark, musty stair, something said in a warning voice, "What a damned fool you are. No one ever gets luck like this if it isn't to land him into the hell of a mess. You take my advice and get out." To which he replied rudely, "Who's getting out?" and walked in upon M. Pierre Riel.

He shut the door behind him and stood a yard or two inside it and a yard or two from the bed.

The bed-clothes were tumbled beyond belief. The man on the bed was undoubtedly very ill. He neither saw Peter nor answered him. He talked in that incessant hoarse mutter which had come droning through the door. There was a wash-stand and some water in a jug. An empty glass was tipped over and lay on its side unbroken. Peter half filled it. He knelt by Pierre Riel and held it to his lips. The man gulped the water down, choked on the last of it, and said with his first coherent words,

"What's the good of water? Give me brandy."

Peter said, "I'll get you a doctor." But the man shook his head.

"No good. Who are you? If you're a doctor, I don't want you. Go away. I don't want anyone—want brandy—cognac—order bottle—" He dropped to the muttering again.

Peter set down the glass and stood looking at him. "Better get him a doctor. I think he's going to die. Not much loss to anyone but me. You can't begin with luck like this and expect it to last. Well, better get on with today's good deed." He turned to the door, but before he reached it the muttering voice arrested him. Words were emerging, many at a time, quite clear. Then panting breaths and an unintelligible murmur of sound. Then words again.

"The money's—not—enough. I say—it's not enough. You say there's no risk—no risk—" He gave a wild, unsteady laugh. "You're telling me—and perhaps—there's something I can tell." There was a blaze of fever in the eyes. The words came tumbling out. "I said—I'd find out—who you were—didn't I? And I will. And when I do—you'll have to pay me something more than—a postman's wages. And if you think I can't—find out—why then you can think again—do you hear? Because I know—I know—" He stared at Peter with the blazing eyes which saw some shape from his delirium, and said in a clear voice of triumph, "Maud Millicent—what have you got to say to that? Maud Millicent Simpson—what have you got to say to that? If I can find her, I can find you—can't I? And I'm going to find you—if it takes me from here to—to—" He groaned, flung out an arm, and said vaguely, "Ah now, what was I saying?" The flare had died. The voice dropped to a whisper. "Mind you, it's hundreds of thousands for you. What do I get? Postman's wages—I'm nothing but a postman. And I'm through, I tell you—" The voice broke and changed. "Where's that brandy? Look sharp about it, can't you!"

When Peter came back he was lying on his side watching the door, but the eyes had no sense in them and the muttering had begun again.

Peter went over to the window and stood there with his back to the room listening. This was Spike Reilly whom he had been following, and he thought he was a dying man. What he ought to do, what he had every opportunity of doing, was to pick up that suit-case and go through it. He had only to open the connecting door—there was a key on this side all right—and step into his own room with the suit-case in his hand. Whatever papers there were, he could go through them at his leisure.

He could—well, he just couldn't. Irrational thing, one's code. If Spike had been drunk—oh, yes. If Spike had been dead—why certainly. But since Spike was dying—devil take it, it couldn't be done. Not if Garrett, the Foreign Office, and Scotland Yard all stood in a row and yelped. This pleasing picture occupied him for a space.

He wondered how soon the doctor would come, and became aware that the voice had died down. Turning, he saw that the man was looking at him. The look, at first blank, became intent. In a whisper Spike Reilly said, "Who are you?" and even as he asked the question, the eyes went blank again, and the voice failed on a gasp.

There was no more sound or movement. Nothing. Peter stood where he was and listened. Not a breath. Nothing. Neither Pierre Riel nor Spike Reilly any more. Just a dead man lying there on the tumbled bed.

Peter picked up the suit-case and went through the communicating door into his own room.

CHAPTER III

HE would have to be quick. And yet perhaps not so very quick. Their client's condition had obviously aroused no passionate interest in either M. or Mme. Dupin. He did not think it likely that they would hurry themselves over sending for a doctor. On the other hand, not safe to count on that. Get on with the job, and get on with it quick.

There was, as a matter of fact, very little in the suit-case. Pyjamas and washing things had been taken out, and had left a good-sized gap. There remained a pair of black laced shoes, a pair of pants, a woollen undervest, a packet of cigarettes, a brand new pair of braces, a small writing-block, a packet of envelopes, and a battered paper-covered novel entitled *Her Great Romance*. And that was all. He shook the novel and flicked through the pages—just in case. It wasn't a likely receptacle for papers of a private and particular nature, but you never could tell.

He repacked the suit-case, took it back into the next room, and turned his attention to the garments which had been flung down anyhow, half on a chair, half trailing to the ground. There was a rain-coat—nothing in the pockets. Trousers—a key-ring and a handful of loose change. Waist-coat pocket—a cheap cigarette-lighter. He took up the coat—handkerchief and cigarette case in the breast pocket on the left, pocket-book on the right. Peter let everything fall and grabbed the pocket-book. He took it over to the window.

The first thing that came out was a folded letter. It fell right out on to the floor, and he had to stoop down to pick it up—two sheets, torn from one of the cheaper blocks, and the top one began, "Dear Jimmy—"

He stood there frowning at the sheet. There was no address, no date. "Dear Jimmy" . . . He couldn't remember that he had ever read a private letter belonging to someone else before, and he didn't like doing it now. But he supposed he had to. Well, it might be a private letter, or it might not. He would just have to see. By the cold, rainy light at the window he read:

"Dear Jimmy,

It's no use your going on asking me to tell you things about Mrs. Simpson, because it wouldn't be safe for you and it wouldn't be safe for me—at least that's the idea I've got about it. You've never seen her, and she's never seen you, and I don't see why you can't leave her alone. I'm sure I'm sorry I ever mentioned her name, and if it hadn't been for getting into the same bus like I told you, I don't suppose I should ever have thought about her again. She didn't think I'd recognise her either, and I don't suppose hardly anyone would, because of course it's fifteen or sixteen years, and she's aged a lot more than that and everything about her different. But there's one thing that won't ever change about her, not if she was a hundred, and when I'd spotted that, sitting opposite her in the bus, well, I was quite sure and I spoke to her. And of course she said I was making a mistake and it was no such thing, so I waited till she got off, and I followed her. And I said, 'Well, Mrs. Simpson, if you don't want me to know you, that's one thing, but if you think you can persuade me that you're someone else, well, that's another.' So then she came off it and we had a talk, and she said she'd got her reasons for keeping quiet, and better for everyone if I didn't talk. I didn't like the way she looked at me when she said that, and I told her I'd hold my tongue. And that's just what I mean to do, so it's no use your asking me about when I knew her before, or how I knew her again, or where she is, because, as I said to start with, I think we'll both be a lot safer if I hold my tongue. I've got my own ideas, and I'm keeping them to myself, and if you'll take my advice you'll clear out of this job you're in and keep clear, because I don't like the sound of it.

Yours affectionately,
Louie."

This was queer stuff if you like. What was it Spike Reilly had said in his voice of delirious triumph? "I know—I know—Maud Millicent Simpson—what have you got to say to that? If I can find her, I can find you—can't I? And I'm going to find you—" Maud Millicent Simpson—Mrs. Simpson—encountered in a bus sixteen years after some unspecified event—a person whom it was safer not to know—"If I can find her, I can find you—can't I?"

Peter thought Garrett would be interested. He put the letter away carefully and went on turning out the pocket-book.

Notes. Spike Reilly carried quite a lot of money—a great deal more than one would have expected—enough for a long journey. That made you think a bit. . . . A passport made out the name of James Peter Reilly. So wherever he was bound for with that bulging pocket-book, it was under his own name. . . .

But Pierre Reil *here*. Why? . . . Protective colouring—a most natural desire to melt into the landscape. Riel in Belgium. Reilly—well, where would one be Reilly? England, Scotland, Ireland, or the United States of America. Quite a nice wide field for speculation, but Peter had a hunch that the first and nearest of these countries would fill the bill. He reflected in passing that the photograph on the passport wasn't very much like the man on the bed. Of course he was dead. . . . His own passport photograph would have fitted a dozen people he knew.

The thought just slid over the surface of his mind and was forgotten, because the next thing that came out of the pocket-book was a sheet of cheap greyish paper with lines of figures written across it—

10. 16. 27. 1. 103. 8. 9. . . . They went on like that, row after row of them, all down one side of the sheet and all down the other. Peter's finger-tips tingled. He slipped the pocket-book back into the pocket from which it had come and threw the coat across the chair, because this, most unmistakably, was the goods. A cipher, and Mr. Spike Reilly's marching orders no doubt. His eye travelled down the paper, looking for repetitions of the same number or group of numbers—something which might stand for the commonest letter E, or for such words as *a, and,* or *the*.

When he had turned the page and come to the bottom of it, he whistled softly. There was no help that way. He began to wonder—and then with extreme suddenness he stopped wondering.

A pencil mark—a thing which he had seen without noticing, and which came up now as invisible writing comes up when you hold it to the fire. A pencil mark. . . . He had the suit-case open and the paper-covered novel out of it in a flash. A well thumbed book. That ought to have attracted his attention at the very outset. Read and re-read by the look of it, the pages dog-eared and thumbed—dirty pages, with here and there a pencil mark, and here and there a smear as if indiarubber had been used. He called himself a dull fool for having seen no more than a dirty trashy novel, because now he was prepared to eat the pages if they did not hold the key to the cipher.

He went through into his own room again and sat down to *Her Great Romance*, the sheetful of figures propped before him.

10. 16. 27. 1. 103. 8. 9. . . . On the simplest plan this would be page 10 line 16, page 27 line 1, page 103 line 8. But then how did you know which word or letter of line 16 to pick? If it was a letter, perhaps the third number gave

it—say the twenty-seventh letter of the sixteenth line on the tenth page. No, that was a wash-out, because in the next group it would give you page 1 line 103, which was absurd. . . . Come back to page 10 line 16.

He flicked the pages over and found the place. Round about line 16 a girl called Gloria was putting on a yellow hat. The Y of yellow had a faint pencil mark under it. It was the second letter in the line, the first being A—"a yellow hat"—just like that.

Peter wrote the Y down on a slip of paper and turned to page 27 line 1. The first letter of line 1 had a just visible pencil mark under it. It was an O—" 'One life, one love, one fate,' said Lord St. Maur." Peter said "Well, well," and wrote the O down after the Y.

On page 103 line 8 the ninth letter was marked, and it was a U. Peter said "Eureka!" He had a perfectly whole possible word on his paper, and he saw how the thing was worked. The first number, 10, was a page number, and the second, 16, was a line number, and the next number, 27, was a page number; but to get the letter number of page 10 line 16, you took the 2 from 27, which was the next page number. The next group gave page 27 line 1, and the 1 from the next page number, 103, as the letter number. And so forth and so on. Simplicity itself, and a quite unbreakable cipher if Spike Reilly hadn't been so free with his pencil marks, and so careless as to carry only one novel in his suit-case.

If *Her Great Romance* had been unmarked and lost in a crowd of other similar romances, a lot of things might have happened differently. One man might have lived, and more than one might have died. Terry Clive would probably have come to a sticky end.

As it was, it took Peter no more than a quarter of an hour to collect the dotted letters and arrange them in words and sentences. He tried to hold his mind back from making sense of them, because something kept telling him to hurry, but some of the meaning got through and he finished the job in a state of tingling excitement. The deciphered message ran:

"You are to come over here. I have work for you. Double pay and bonuses. Cross Thursday. Go Preedo Library Archmount Street. S.W. noon Friday. Say you expect call. Await instructions."

There was no signature.

Peter sat and looked at the words. This was Tuesday. If one crossed on Thursday as the note suggested, one would naturally make a point of being on hand to take that call in Preedo's Library, wherever that might be. And someone could be told off to find out who was at the other end of the line. A word to Garrett would fix that all right. These thoughts moved on the surface. They fell into place and made a neat picture. But underneath something disturbed and disturbing took shape and came blundering into view.

Peter got to his feet, got to the door, got to the head of the stairs, and stood there listening. . . . Nothing. Nobody. He went back to his own room, half drew out his pocket-book, and slid it back again.

Crazy—that's what it was.

Well, with a strong enough motive you took a crazy risk.

In this case just how strong was the motive?

And the answer to that was, ask Garrett.

For his own part, he had an idea that Garrett was fussed—and Garrett didn't fuss easily.

He thought about Garrett's last letter: "The thing is a snowball. I don't know where it's going to roll or what it's going to pick up on the way. It started with picture-lifting, fairly plastered itself with blackmail from the insurance companies, and has now added a murder. No knowing where it'll stop—" Well, he had been roped in because he had stumbled on something odd, and because he wasn't a regular agent. The novelist is a privileged Nosey Parker. It is his job to watch people and listen to them. It flatters some, and flutters some but no one suspects him of being in with Scotland Yard or the Foreign Office.

Peter contemplated the impossible—the plan which had come surging up in the middle of his neat picture—and found angles from which the impossible began to look possible. Of course if the doctor were to come butting in, the whole thing blew up. But there didn't seem to be any sign of the doctor. The Dupins didn't hurry, hadn't hurried, wouldn't hurry. There would be time enough and to spare.

No harm in having a look at the passports anyhow. He went through into the next room. Took out Reilly's pocket-book, extracted Reilly's passport. Took out his own pocket-book, extracted his own passport.

Well, here they were, side by side.

James Peter Reilly.

Accompanied by his wife? (Apparently and most fortunately not. Children ditto.)

National status—British subject by birth.

He turned the page.

Place and date of birth—Glasgow, 1907. (Glasgow Irish, was he?)

Domicile—Glasgow.

Colour of eyes—grey.

Colour of hair—brown.

Special peculiarities—scar on back of right hand.

Peter laughed suddenly.

"And that settles it," he said, "because—" He lifted his own right hand and made a fine wide gesture. The impossible, thus warmly invited, advanced and made itself at home. Peter's hand with the long white scar across the knuckles came down on his own passport.

John Peter Carmichael Talbot. (Also, thank heaven, without a wife or any other encumbrances.)

National status—British subject by birth.

And over page:

Place and date of birth—Harrogate, 1910.

Domicile—Europe, but the passport said London.

Colour of eyes—grey.

Colour of hair—brown.

Special peculiarities—scar on back of right hand.

"And a very nice usual place to have a scar. Mine was old Ellen Updale's cat—the time Peggy and I did her up in red white and blue streamers on Armistice Night. I wonder what his was. One of life's unsolved mysteries. Not my fault if the doings at Preedo's Library are another of them. Well now, what about the photographs? They're the real snag."

He stared at the two passport photographs. Spike Reilly had a good bit more hair on him than Peter Talbot. The photograph showed no parting, and a sort of all-over, brushed-back appearance.

Peter went into his own room, tousled his hair, damped it, and slicked it back. The effect was quite revolting, but a good deal more like the photograph of Mr. Reilly. Spike Reilly was clean shaven, and so was Peter Talbot. He went over to the glass and experimented. He could get that sulky twist of the mouth and the frown between the eyes well enough. With chewing-gum to bulge the cheeks, he ought to be able to scrape past anyone who hadn't an unnaturally suspicious mind. The trouble was that Suspicion was that sort of bloke's first, last, and middle name.

All the same he could do it. He felt the sort of certainty with which a leap is measured and accomplished before the muscles tense and the body rises. He could get away with Spike Reilly's passport.

But what about Spike Reilly getting away with his? The Dupins had seen them both. Well, it had been very, very dark in the office—rain outside and thrift within—one didn't waste good electricity at four o'clock in the afternoon. The Dupins had seen precious little of Peter Talbot—a hat, a raincoat and a muffler. As for Spike Reilly, no one is surprised if a dead man looks a bit different from his photograph when alive.

Of course he mustn't let the Dupins see him again—not to say see him. He must leave at once while the light was bad—pay something, not too much, and get out. A corpse in the next room would be a good enough excuse. Yes, that was it. He'd march down with his suit-case, call for a drink—he could do with one—say he hadn't bargained for corpses, and clear out. They couldn't stop him.

"Anyhow, here goes!"

He had plumped for the crazy adventure, and the next thing to do was to set about it with the same careful attention to detail as if this were chapter one of a thriller, and he villain or hero with a crime to conceal. Not murder, thank heaven. But he would certainly be in a nasty mess with the local police if he was found out trying to pass off the man on the bed as the corpse of John Peter Carmichael Talbot.

None of his own clothes were marked. He didn't suppose Spike Reilly went round labelled, but he would have to make sure.

He made sure.

The next thing was to change pocket-books. He emptied both and made a thoughtful redistribution of the contents. There must be plenty to identify the dead man. Half a dozen cards inscribed Mr. Peter Talbot made a good start. Then the notes—Spike Reilly could keep his own money to bury him. And he had better have a letter or two as well as the cards. An invitation from Marion von Stein—"Oh, Peter, I think your poems are great. No, really I mean it. Do come and read me some more..." And Aunt Fanny's last weekly budget—"And, my dear boy, I do wish you would give up this roving life and settle down. And I haven't even a proper photograph. You have always been so obstinate about being taken. I am sure that snapshot on my mantelpiece isn't a bit like you. I was showing it to Terry yesterday, and she said it might be anyone, and Miss Hollinger said so too. But of course Terry hasn't ever seen you, as I've only just got to know her. And I don't think Miss Hollinger had ever met you either, but she says she did once, when you brought me home after that matinee I enjoyed so much. We met her at the gate, and it was nearly dark. So she couldn't really give an opinion about the photograph, because she didn't really see you. And I told her it wasn't a bit like you, and it isn't. And now I must tell you about Terry. I have made a new friend—you will laugh, but I feel she really is a friend—a most charming girl called Terry Clive, I believe it is short for Theresa. I missed the step coming down off a number nineteen bus, and she very kindly picked me up and brought me home. I should so much like you to meet her...."

Peter showed all his teeth in a grin. Miss Fanny Talbot's

nets were so perseveringly and so artlessly spread. Her letter went in on top of Marion von Stein's, and the pocket-book into the pocket of Spike Reilly's coat. Peter added his own cigarette-case with the initials J.P.T. and took in reluctant exchange a much more ornate affair without initials at all.

"Well, that's that!" he said.

There was a sound of footsteps on the stair. He went through into his own room and shut the door.

CHAPTER IV

COLONEL Garrett sat at an office table and drove a spluttering pen. He was a little sandy man with bottle-brush hair and small grey eyes which could sharpen until they looked like two points of polished steel. A scarlet bandana with a lively blue and magenta pattern bulged from the over-full pocket of a really outrageous tweed jacket, in colour ginger with an over-check of maroon and green, in cut quite indescribable. It was a moot point among Garrett's friends whether he had an unnaturally depraving effect upon his clothes, or was the subject of some subtle revenge on the part of a criminal mind which evolved these nightmares as a punishment for having been at some time or other landed by one of Garrett's nets.

The pen drove. There was a knock at the door. Garrett scowled, cast his pen at the blotting-paper, where it stuck quivering, and snapped, "Come in!"

The man who came in was a long, lazy person, most beautifully dressed. He had a single eyeglass, and fair hair in process of receding from a brow already high. He was, in fact, Mr. Fabian Roxley, and he was a good deal more intelligent than he looked.

Garrett's scowl departed.

"Yes, yes, I wanted to see you. Come in and shut the

door. Always a damned lot of draughts in this damned place. Sit down!''

Mr. Roxley was careful with the knees of his trousers as he sat.

''Everyone is yapping,'' said Garrett. ''I've had the *Sureté* on the line over the last picture that was lifted from the Louvre.'' He grinned rather like a terrier who sees a rat. ''I told 'em I wasn't Scotland Yard—said 'Try Whitehall 1212,' and rang off. They've got a bee in their bonnets—a whole hive of bees—think there's something political behind it. Odd how that keeps on cropping up.''

''I can't see anything political in it myself,'' said Fabian Roxley in his cultured voice. ''As long as insurance companies will pay to get a picture back, it's a profitable job to steal a famous picture and hold it to ransom. They paid out five thousand on that little Romney, and, I believe, as much as thirty thousand on the Gainsborough.''

''No affair of ours,'' said Colonel Garrett. ''I've said so all along. We get dragged into it because every time Scotland Yard gets flummoxed they think the Vulture has cropped up again, and because the Vulture was our pigeon they come down on us. And I tell 'em—'' Colonel Garrett banged the table ''—I tell 'em they can catch their own picture thieves. At least that's what I ought to tell 'em.''

''Instead of which?''

Garrett scowled.

''I put my young cousin Peter Talbot on to trailing a fellow who had a pal on the outskirts of the Vulture's gang—name of Grey.''

''And your man's name?'' enquired Mr. Roxley.

''Fellow called Spike Reilly. I got something about him from Munich. The letter to the Earth Insurance was posted in Munich. The letter about the Gainsborough was posted in Vienna on the fifteenth of September. I told Peter to see if he could pick up any trace of Spike there about that time. He got that—Spike was there all right. And he got something else. I told him to follow Spike round and see what he did. This is what I got from him yesterday.'' He pulled a letter out of a drawer and tossed it over.

Mr. Roxley read it attentively, from the *Cher maître* with which it began to the *Cher maître* with which it closed. Then he said,

"What was the other thing he got?"

"He's a damned insolent young pup!" said Garrett.

Fabian Roxley retained his lazy calm.

"You said he got something else about Spike Reilly. What was it?"

"I didn't say it was about Reilly—it wasn't. Remember the Fragonard that was taken out of Medstow Hall in July? Peter was in a café, and he heard a man say the name Medstow, and the man who was with him hushed him up. The first man was English, and a bit tight. He may have been Spike Reilly. The other man was French. He tried to shut him up. The Englishman said, 'Some day I shall find out who he is, and then I'll have a lot of money in my pocket.' The Frenchman said, 'Money's no good if you're dead, my friend—and I think you would be dead.' And after that they kept their voices too low for him to hear any more. He couldn't find out who they were. There was a demonstration going on outside, and when they went away he lost them in the crowd."

"Not very much to go on," said Mr. Roxley in a dubious tone.

Garrett glared.

"Who's going on it?" he said rudely. "You can go over and see Scotland Yard and tell 'em to catch their own picture-thieves! What are they for?"

"It's not only picture-thieving since last Saturday—it's murder. You know, that's funny. This fellow—this picture-thief—he's in a big way of business, making pots of money out of the insurance companies and getting away with it every time. What's he doing messing about with fire-arms and shooting butlers? It's all wrong—most inartistic. What's he want shooting Solly Oppenstein's butler? The thing's ludicrous."

"Go and tell all that to Scotland Yard," said Garrett. "Murder's their job. Tell 'em about Spike Reilly. You can give me Peter's letter back, and I'll scrag you if you let on about his impudence. Oh, and you can tell 'em I've had another line from him—it's just come in. It says to look out for all telephone calls to Preedo's Library, Archmount Street, S.W., round about noon tomorrow, Friday. The person who calls up will probably be the man they're looking for, and if they look lively they may get him. They are not on any account to interfere with the person who is waiting for the call. It may be Peter, or it may be Spike Reilly shadowed by Peter. In either case the police had better stand clear. Here—read for yourself." He tossed a single sheet of paper over to Mr. Roxley, who read in Peter Talbot's small, legible hand:

> "*Very important*. Spike warned to be at Preedo's Library, Archmount Street, S.W., to get his instructions by telephone. I suppose you can arrange to have all calls traced. Spike's appointment is for twelve noon, Friday. I shall be there. J.P.T."

The lazy eyebrows lifted a trifle.

"Can I take this along?"

"If you like."

Mr. Roxley got gracefully to his feet.

"I should like to know why the fellow shot the butler," he said in a lazy voice.

Garrett gave his terrier grin.

"Perhaps the butler knew too much. Butlers sometimes do."

"It doesn't always pay to know too much," said Fabian Roxley, and took his leisured way out of the room.

Garrett watched him go with impatience, yet when the door had been softly closed he continued to stare in that direction. His expression changed. He looked uneasy, uncertain. Then with a jerk flung round to the table again, plucked his pen from the blotting paper, and began to write.

It was perhaps ten minutes later that the telephone bell interrupted him. He picked up the receiver, jammed it against his ear, and snapped.

"What is it?"

A voice said, ''Miss Talbot on the line, sir. Will you speak to her?'' and Garrett snapped again.

''Oh Lord—I suppose so! Put her through!''

There was a click against his ear, and then his cousin Fanny Talbot's voice, breathless and tearful:

''Frank! Oh, is it Frank—''

Garrett snorted.

''Yes, it's me! I'm supposed to be working—I'm paid to work, you know. What is it, Fanny?''

He heard her gulp down a sob.

''Oh, Frank—such dreadful news—oh, Frank! I felt I must ring you up and tell you.''

''You're not telling me anything, Fanny.''

''It doesn't seem possible—''

Garrett groaned.

''What is it this time? Cook given notice? Vicar leaving? Parrot dead?''

Each of these tragic events had been the occasion of a tearful call from Fanny.

There was another and a more emotional sob.

''Oh, no. Oh, Frank—oh, I know you don't mean to be unkind, but—oh, Frank, it's Peter!''

''*Peter?* For the Lord's sake, Fanny, come to the point!''

Fanny Talbot stopped sobbing and said quite simply,

''He's dead.''

''Who's dead?''

''Peter,'' said Miss Talbot in a quivering voice. Garrett said, ''Nonsense!'' The line vibrated with the word. He heard Fanny gasp and say ''Oh dear!'' and repeated his remark—''Nonsense!''

''Oh, no, Frank, it isn't. Oh, if it only were! But I've had a letter—oh, Frank, it's so dreadful—he died in Brussels all alone on Tuesday afternoon. And I was having tea with Miss Hollinger, and I little thought—oh, Frank, I felt I must tell you at once!''

Colonel Garrett scowled and banged the table.

''You're talking nonsense, I tell you! I had a letter from Peter this morning—two letters, one by the first post and one by the second. They were both dated Tuesday.''

Miss Fanny gulped down another sob.

"They must have been written before. There is a letter from the doctor—oh, Frank, they didn't call him in in time—Peter was dead when he got there. They found my last letter in his pocket-book, and he wrote—it was very kind of him, and I can read French quite easily of course, but I don't know how I'm going to answer it, because that's much more difficult—perhaps Miss Hollinger—oh, I don't know what I'd do without her—my dear friend Miss Hollinger, you know—or perhaps you don't, because I don't suppose you've ever met her—she hasn't been here so very long, but such an acquisition as a next-door neighbour, and perhaps she can help me with the French—I know she has travelled abroad—and so very kind about dear Peter, though she didn't know him—"

Garrett was staring hard at the wall in front of him. Peter had written him two letters on the Tuesday—two letters. . . . Not a word about being ill. He wasn't ill when he wrote those letters. Damned impudent letters. Not the letters of a sick man. Certainly not the letters of a man who is so sick that he is going to die. . . . Unless—unless—there had been foul play— He turned sharply to the telephone, cutting across Miss Fanny's flow of words.

"All right, all right, all right! I'll be round. I want to see that letter."

CHAPTER V

PETER emerged from an unfamiliar Tube station upon the traffic of a main suburban road. A boy who was selling papers informed him that Archmount Street was the third turning on the left. He bought a paper and pursued his way. The poster was a staring WHO KILLED THE BUTLER? Not being interested in butlers as a race, and being without any particular information about this one, the buying of the paper had been a mere *quid pro quo* for the information about Archmount Street. But by the time he had turned out of the main road his eye had been caught by three other posters, and every one of them mentioned the butler—BUTLER CASE CLUE—BUTLER CASE NO CLUE—BUTLER CASE INQUEST. He began to feel a certain curiosity. Anyhow, if he had got to hang about in Preedo's Library, it would be just as well to have something to read.

He reserved the butler, and began to look about him for the library. It was about half way down Archmount Street on the right, between a hat-shop and a cleaner's. Picture postcards and fancy goods in the window, horrible china book-ends, pseudo-eighteenth-century shepherdesses in pink smirking over their shoulders at imitation shepherds in blue, Scotch terriers very fiercely black and white, gnomes with red noses and long white beards, pink and gold vases, lamp-shades painted like Jezebel, objects in poker-work, objects in fancy leather. Peter was reminded of the bazaars beloved by his Aunt Fanny. He wondered who bought this sort of truck and what they did with it, and why no one started a mission to wean them from the vice. S.P.P.T.—Society for the Prevention of the Production of Truck. Or just S.S.T.—Society for the Suppression of Truck. The whole of the front part of the shop appeared to be given up to it.

At the back the place widened out and returned to sobriety. Walls covered with books from ceiling to floor. People, mostly women, standing with their backs to the room and gazing with varying degrees of hopefulness at the crowded shelves. In one corner a sort of counter where an elderly woman with a fuzzy grey fringe was trying to listen to two people at once. For the first time it occurred to Peter that it was going to want some nerve to go up to the fringe and say, "Good morning— I'm expecting a telephone call," because after all he wasn't a subscriber, she didn't know him from Adam, and he really hadn't any business to be here. Suppose she said so. Suppose she told him to clear out. Suppose she wouldn't let him take the call when it came through.

He advanced to the counter and waited apprehensively behind a stout, determined woman who wanted *Love-nest for Two* and kept on saying so, and a thin little dreep with pale flaxen hair and a lisp who was having an argument about the date on which she had taken out her subscription. The fringe dealt firmly with both of them—"No, Mrs. Waters, we haven't a copy in, but you're next on the list. . . . Oh, no, we wouldn't do a thing like that—I'm most particular about taking everyone in turn. . . . Well, Miss Margetson, I've got the date written down, and I don't see how there can possibly be any mistake about it, but if you like to go on to the end of the week, you can—that is, of course, if you intend to renew. . . . Yes, sir?"

Peter produced an apologetic smile which was not without charm.

"I don't think I've got any business here," he said—"in fact I know I haven't. But a friend of mine sent me a message to say he was going to ring me up here, and—and—"

"There'll be a charge of threepence," said the lady briskly. "It's not a thing we want to make a practice of, but of course if it's just once in a way—what name will it be?"

There was a horrible breath-taking moment while Peter wrestled with the answer. He said "Reilly," but he wasn't sure whether he had said the right thing. Was Spike Reilly to have been Spike Reilly over here, or had he an alias handy? Since his passport was made out in his own name, Peter inclined to the belief that no alias had been considered necessary. Which meant that the late Mr. Reilly's copy-book was not seriously blotted as far as the British police were concerned. A cheering thought.

The lady wrote the name down, spelling it in the English fashion—Riley. She indicated a group of chairs about a table littered with magazines.

"I will let you know when the call comes through."

Peter found a vacant chair between a little old man with a beard, a cough and tinted glasses, and the stout lady who had demanded a Love-nest. He unfolded the paper he had bought at the station and bent his mind to the case of the murdered butler. Quite a simple story, but if anyone had been watching Peter he would have seen a bored, casual look become suddenly intent. So that was it, was it?

He read three columns with interest, and then tried to sort them out. Mr. Solomon Oppenstein's house in Park Lane had been entered on the previous Saturday night, and an attempt had been made to steal his famous Gainsborough, *The Girl with the Lamb*. The picture had been half cut from its frame, and the body of Francis Bird, Mr. Oppenstein's butler, was lying on the floor a yard or two away. He had been shot through the heart at close range.

Garrett's last letter sprang into Peter's mind. Blackmail had been added to picture-lifting, and murder to blackmail. And this, beyond any doubt, was the murder. Peter stared at a smudgy picture of Francis Bird and wondered if his murderer was at this moment preparing to ring up Preedo's Library. The police should be able to trace the call. He had warned Garrett, and Garrett would put them on to it. He wished the call would come through. He wished—

The old gentleman on his right was having a very bad fit of coughing, so bad that the book on his knee slipped down and fell at Peter's feet. Peter stooped to pick it up, got his hand on it, and felt the blood run tingling to his face. The book was *Her Great Romance*.

He came up in good order with the volume in his hand and proffered it politely. The old man stopped coughing, stuffed an outsize in white silk handkerchiefs back into his pocket, and said in a weak, asthmatic voice,

"Oh dear me, yes— I dropped it. Most kind of you, I'm sure. I'm changing it, you know."

"The mischief you are!" said Peter to himself. "And I wonder what that means." He thought he had better find out.

He looked the book over and enquired,

"Is it any good, sir?"

The old man shook his head.

"Oh, no," he said—"not now. Oh dear me, no—quite out of date—oh, yes, quite. I'm changing it—got a much better one—one I can really recommend, if you're looking for something." He produced from his coat pocket a mustard-coloured book with an arresting title, *The Corpse in the Copper*. "A very ingenious work really—oh, highly ingenious—I can really recommend it. Ah well, I must be going."

He produced the handkerchief again and blew his nose. A fit of coughing supervened. *The Corpse in the Copper* slid under the table. He finished coughing and drifted over to the counter, and from the counter to the shop and the street beyond.

"He has dropped his book," said the stout lady who had demanded a Love-nest.

She spoke accusingly, but Peter could have embraced her, because he had been on the point of making the remark himself, and it certainly came better from her. He retrieved the Corpse with a swoop, ejaculated "I'll see if I can catch him," and sped in the old man's wake.

Nothing doing. Not a trace, not a sign, not a mark. The old man with his rain-coat, his soft hat, his muffler, his spectacles and his cough was nowhere to be seen. Not that Peter really desired to see him. He did not think that his further acquaintance would be welcome. What he had wanted was an opportunity of bestowing the Corpse in his own rain-coat pocket.

This accomplished, he returned to the library and enquired whether his call had come through. The lady with the fringe was now at leisure. She smiled graciously upon him and said she was afraid it hadn't.

"What time were you expecting it, Mr. Riley?"

"Well, he said round about twelve."

"And it's ten minutes past. But some people are so unpunctual. You wouldn't believe, Mr. Riley, the people that come in just as we're closing. Most inconsiderate, I'm sure."

Peter agreed. He bent a little nearer and asked,

"Who is the old man who went out just now?"

The lady shook her head.

"Quite a stranger to me, Mr. Riley."

"Isn't he one of your subscribers? I thought he was changing a book."

"Oh, no, Mr. Riley. He just came up and asked about our subscription rates, and off he went. He's quite a stranger to me. Are you waiting any longer for that call?"

"I think I'll have to."

Peter went back to his seat and resumed the paper. It made an excellent screen. Behind it he was thinking, "Deep—aren't they? And who do they trust?" Not Spike Reilly—that was sure enough. Spike is tipped off to wait for a call, but in case he has the bright idea of tipping anyone else off, the plan is changed, there isn't any call. There is only a prattling old gentleman who drops his library book and does a vanishing trick. Peter felt as sure as he had ever felt about anything in all his life that there wasn't going to be any call.

He sat where he was until the clock on the counter struck one. It was a cheap Swiss clock in a case encrusted with edelweiss. There wasn't going to be any call.

He got up and walked out into Archmount Street.

CHAPTER VI

OVER what he considered to be a well earned lunch Peter toyed with *The Corpse in the Copper*. When he had turned half a dozen pages a slip of paper fell out and narrowly escaped his soup. He retrieved it, found it covered with figures, and put it away in his pocket. He had undoubtedly received his instructions, and the next thing was to find himself a room where he could get down to decoding them. All his old haunts were barred of course, but he remembered a quiet private hotel where Vincent used to stay—he had written to him there. And Vincent was in Kenya, so there could be no danger of running into him. The Edenbridge—yes, that was the name. Well enough out of Aunt Fanny's way too.

He called up, and found he could have a room.

Half an hour later he was sitting down to his instructions. Same cipher. Quick and easy to read when you got the hang of it. He wrote the message down letter by letter, and then sat back to read it over. It was a long one this time. He frowned at it and read:

"Go Preedo's Library. Take out subscription and leave address. Funds will reach you. Go Pratt's garage, Lemming Street. Buy second-hand Austin, fifty pounds. Pay cash. Tomorrow Saturday go Heathacres, Firshot, Surrey. Leave car edge of heath. Enter drive two A.M., proceed terrace, and wait. If no development, leave not later than half past three."

He put in the punctuation as he read, and when he had finished he went over it again, and then sat a long time with his elbow on the table and his chin in his hand.

They wanted his address.

He was to buy a car.

He was to repair to Heathacres, wherever that might be, at the sort of hour when burglars yawn and safes give up their loot.

He wondered whether the late Spike Reilly had been a good man with his hands at a safe, and whether safe-breaking was the job he had been destined for. Because if so, it was going to be a quite considerable flop. It struck him that the paths of crime were full of pitfalls for an unpractised foot. The fact was, he hadn't really looked beyond that telephone call which Spike was to have waited for in Preedo's Library. He had taken Spike's place. He had rolled up to take the call. And left it up to the police *via* Garrett to get a line on anyone who happened to be ringing up Preedo's Library with a message for Mr. Reilly. Well, there hadn't been any call—only an old boy with a cough and a string of instructions for Spike in a brand-new book. Nothing to arouse the slightest suspicion in the most suspicious copper's mind.

That was where they had got to. And now what next? Did he go on, or didn't he? Oh well—futile to come as far as this and then throw up the sponge. One heartening fact emerged. He had been accepted as Spike Reilly, and that meant that Spike Reilly wasn't personally known to the old boy who had passed him the book. Because, though he had got through all right on Spike's passport, he couldn't expect to deceive anyone who knew him in the flesh.

Back again to what next.

Three courses open.

(1) Cut loose.

(2) Obey the instructions just decoded.

(3) Report to Garrett.

He considered a combination of 2 and 3. He could tell

Garrett what he had done and what he was going to do, and then get along and do it.

He frowned, bit the end of his pencil, and considered reporting to Garrett. . . . Lots of reasons against it—masses of them. First and foremost—nothing much to report except the sort of thing which was pretty well bound to plunge him into official hot water. He had engineered a false death certificate, he had travelled under a false passport. And what had he got to show for it? An ingenious cipher, some instructions which might portend a burglary.

Not really good enough.

On the other side. . . . He considered very seriously the possibility that he might be shadowed. He thought he was dealing with very careful, painstaking people. The affair of the telephone call which hadn't materialized was proof of that. They were running him round from pillar to post, sending him here, there, and to Heathacres. He had an idea that they were testing him. If he did just what he was told, they might begin to trust him. If this was correct, an approach to Garrett would be fatal. He made up his mind to obey the instructions to the letter.

CHAPTER VII

HEATHACRES stands amidst pine and heather and looks across to Hindhead. It is modern enough to be comfortable, and old enough to have acquired a certain mellow charm and what house agents describe as well matured grounds. The pines stand round them. A long terrace faces south. Where the garden ends heather and bracken begin to clothe the slopes at first in green and then in a brightening glory of purple and gold.

Mr. James Cresswell is an ardent gardener. Rare shrubs, rare trees, rare plants, the things that other people haven't got, the museum pieces of the horticulturist—these are his fancy out of doors. Inside the house he has a second vice. The walls are hung with pictures of price. The English school—no foreigners here, though he will entertain them in the garden. A Lawrence, a Turner, a Gainsborough over which there has been some controversy, a Romney—the usual Lady Hamilton—and, imposing but certainly spurious, the portrait of a *Lady in Blue* which he maintains is a Sir Joshua.

In person Mr. Cresswell is one of those small, spare, grey men who make themselves felt. If it was not he who had founded the family fortunes, this is merely because his father had done so already. An atrocious portrait of Joshua Cresswell in Sunday broadcloth, with his hand on the family

Bible, hangs over the dining-room mantelpiece and testifies to the obstinate filial piety of his son.

On the Saturday evening a party of eight was dining under the old gentleman's rather sardonic gaze. It rested upon the daughter-in-law whom he had invariably addressed as Mrs. James until the moment when, from a patriarchal death-bed, he had administered a parting blessing—"Good-bye, Emily. You're a good wife to James, but you'd be the better for plucking up a bit of spirit with him. God bless you."

Emily sat at the foot of the table in the dress for which she had paid a great deal, and which looked, as her clothes invariably looked, as if she had plucked it from a bargain basement in Tooting. Her grey hair straggled a little, and inclined to the shedding of hairpins. Some lovely and valuable pearls showed up the lines on a thin, discoloured neck. She wore spectacles of the old-fashioned gold-rimmed kind, and talked in a flurried, nervous manner to Mr. Basil Ridgefield who had taken her in to dinner—tall, thin, point device, with distinguished grey hair, a monocle, and the easy manners of a man of the world."

"You see, I like primroses, and—and things like that," said Emily in a nervous whisper.

"My dear Mrs. Cresswell, why shouldn't you? I adore them myself. We're in good company, you know—there is Primrose Day. Don't take any notice of your husband. He's a collector, and they are not human, you know. Come now, you had better make a full confession. I am probably a fellow low-brow. What other pleasant common flowers would you like to have if your husband were just an ordinary human being?"

Emily looked nervously up the table, saw James engrossed with Pearla Yorke, and said in a hurried, uneven voice,

"Well, you know, I really do like hen-and-chicken daisies, but James says they seed all over the garden—and columbines—and marigolds—and sweet alyssum—and London pride—"

"And he won't let you have them? Too bad."

"Oh, they wouldn't be at all suitable." She tripped over the words. "Of course I know that. James is a collector, as you say."

"Everyone collects something," said Basil Ridgefield.

His monocle surveyed the table. On Mrs. Cresswell's other side was Mr. Joseph Applegarth, a tall, rotund person with a florid face and a jolly laugh. On his own left Miss Margesson in shiny blue sequins which twinkled with every movement of her thin body. Black hair, dark languishing eyes, a good deal of eye-shadow, a lavish use of cream, powder and lipstick, a blood-red mouth and blood-red nails. James Cresswell beyond her. Then Pearla Yorke ethereal in grey, Fabian Roxley, and his young ward Terry Clive.

Terry was looking well tonight. Her rather childishly round face, fresh colour, and curly brown hair were pleasant to look at. Norah Margesson had been a beauty, and Pearla Yorke was one. But he thought Terry looked very well tonight. Fabian Roxley obviously thought so too. His lazy eyes had a pleased look as he bent to Terry in her pink frock.

The monocle approved. Yes, that might be a very good thing—if it came off. There was no certainty—girls were incalculable creatures—

Terry caught his eyes and laughed.

"Oh, Uncle Basil—how intriguing! Do tell us what we all collect. Stamps for you, plants and pictures for Mr. Cresswell. But what about the rest of us? What about Fabian?"

Basil lifted a deprecating hand.

"Fabian? Oh, criminals of course—the political crook, the master spy, the international menace."

Pearla Yorke leaned an elbow on the table, looked at him with her eyes of a dreaming angel, and said in her wistful voice,

"What do I collect, Mr. Ridgefield?"

"Oh hearts, Mrs. Yorke, without a doubt."

She gave him a lovely smile.

"Dear Mr. Ridgefield, how charming."

"And I?" said Norah Margesson.

Basil said, but not aloud, "Scalps, my dear Norah." He would have liked to say it aloud, but a civilized dining-table is no place for home truths. He therefore smiled, lifted his glass, and said,

"Toasts, my dear Norah."

She was not so pleased. She may have divined the word which he had not spoken. She threw him a dark glance and drank from her own glass.

"I'm sure I don't collect anything," said Emily in a hurry.

James Cresswell laughed, not very pleasantly.

"Why, you're the worst collector of junk I've ever come across in my life." He turned to Pearla again. "You wouldn't believe the stuff she keeps hoarded up—old clothes, old books, old letters."

Emily's lip trembled. She flushed unbecomingly. The hand in her lap clenched upon itself. Yes, it was true. Old clothes—her wedding dress—baby clothes. Old letters—James's letters when he was courting her and all the world was young. No use keeping them—no use—

Terry's voice broke in. Terry's colour was high.

"And what do I collect, Uncle Basil? You mustn't leave me out."

But it was Fabian Roxley who answered her in his slow, pleasant voice.

"Oh, you collect friends."

"Well, I don't know that I've ever collected anything—not since I traded a job lot of silkworms for a pair of skates when I was ten years old," said Joseph Applegarth.

Terry turned to Fabian Roxley. She had a pretty dimple.

"That was nice of you. I like my collection best of all. I like having lots, and lots, and lots of friends."

Fabian smiled down at her.

"You pick them up in trains, and buses and places. It's not too safe, you know."

Terry said, "Pooh!" A shadow went over her eyes. "Oh, Fabian, my old lady who I picked up in the bus is so unhappy. Her nephew is dead—Peter Talbot, who wrote books and wandered round on the Continent. Poor old pet, she'd got it all fixed up in her own mind that he would come home and fall passionately in love with me and live happily ever after, just round the corner so that we could come to supper on Sundays. But now he's gone and died suddenly in Brussels, and it's simply knocked her flat. Why should horrid things like that happen?"

Everyone else was talking. Fabian said in a slow, almost inaudible voice,

"What do you expect me to say—that I wanted him to survive and come home, and go out to supper with you on Sunday evenings for the rest of his life?"

Terry's grey eyes acquired a sparkle.

"And why not?"

"Do you really want me to tell you—here and now?"

The sparkle became an angry one. It threatened and commanded. Fabian met it mildly. He said,

"I will if you like. I don't mind who knows as far as I am concerned."

Terry's chin came up. She opened her mouth to speak, but the movement of Emily Cresswell's chair checked whatever it was she had been going to say. Everyone stopped talking at once. Emily's fluttered voice was heard in an indistinguishable murmur, and eight people got to their feet.

"Just as well," thought Terry to herself, as she followed the other three women out of the room. "Because it cramps one's style quite frightfully being under Uncle Basil's eye, and a host on one side and a hostess on the other. But just you wait!"

CHAPTER VIII

THE drawing-room at Heathacres is a long room facing south with windows almost to the floor and a glass door opening upon the terrace. All were curtained now with heavy hand-woven linen. The deep couches and the many chairs were covered with the same weave. There was very little colour. The linen was of the palest shade of green, the carpet a pearly grey, the cushions faint blue, pale straw-colour and the shade which used to be called philamot—*feuille morte*—dead leaf.

The *Blue Lady* gazed down the length of the room at a quite authentic Lely on the opposite wall. Even a spurious Reynolds may look haughtily at a Restoration beauty. The *Blue Lady* had an extremely haughty look. In her heart of hearts Emily Cresswell sympathized with her. Over the light stone mantelpiece hung the Turner. It was a cherished belief that the picture had been painted from the very spot on which this room now stood—that here Turner had planted his easel and set thumb to palette. No evidence could be adduced to substantiate or deny the claim, since the painter had seen and transferred to his canvas not the earthly beauty of hill and sky, but some strange apocalypse of his own.

In this pale room, under this presentment of a burning glory, Emily Cresswell, faded and angular in black, had the air of an incongruous visitor. She drew Terry to the fire and cast a worried look at the other two. She ought perhaps to be talking to Pearla Yorke or to Norah Margesson, but Pearla always gazed past her as if she wasn't there, and Norah—no, she couldn't, she really couldn't think of anything safe to talk about. And Norah wouldn't want to either— She gave a sigh of relief, because they had crossed to the other side of the room and were talking to each other.

She turned with gratitude to Terry, whom she loved.

"Do you know Miss Margesson well?"

"Uncle Basil has known her a long time," said Terry soberly.

Mrs. Cresswell's voice hesitated, and went on only just audibly.

"He doesn't like her very much, does he? I thought at dinner—oh, I am afraid he hurt her feelings."

"What he said was a compliment."

Emily shook her head.

"You didn't really think so, nor did she. And I am sure he did not mean it that way—you can always tell."

Terry nodded.

"I know what you mean. He doesn't like her, I don't know why."

"Oh dear," said Emily—"and that does spoil a party so."

Terry said, a little warmly. "He hasn't any business to spoil your party. I'll tell him so. But I think he was just teasing."

Emily flushed.

"Oh, my dear, if you could. I mean, I'm so anxious that there shouldn't be anything to upset her, because—well, it doesn't matter what I say to you, does it?"

Terry dimpled.

"I don't know, darling."

"Such a relief," said Emily Cresswell. "Because you're everyone's friend and so it's quite safe, and there isn't anyone I can talk to about things, you know."

"Oh, I'm safe," said Terry. She didn't know about being Norah Margesson's friend. She was sorry for her, but friendship—

Emily dropped her voice still lower.

"She asked me to have her, you know—because of

Joseph Applegarth. A little while ago I did think—because it is time he married if he is ever going to. He and James were at school together, you know. And there's all that money. But of course money isn't everything, and she must be quite twenty years younger—"

Terry thought privately that Mr. Applegarth deserved better of fate.

"He looks kind and jolly," she said.

Emily Cresswell nodded.

"Oh, yes, he is. And oh, my dear, I'm afraid there's nothing in it—at least not on his side, because when he heard she was going to be here he said she would be a handsome girl if she had a little more flesh to cover her bones with. And do you think he would have talked like that if he had any idea of proposing?"

"I don't suppose he would, darling. But cheer up, she can't be in love with him. I mean, he's an uncle-ish sort of person. He couldn't inspire a fatal passion."

"Oh, no, my dear. But I'm afraid—" She hesitated, and then said in a hurried whisper, "It's the money. It's dreadful not to be settled in life— I don't think she knows where to turn. Oh, I don't think I ought to have said that."

Terry laid a hand on her arm.

"Has she been borrowing from you?"

The dull colour mounted to the roots of Emily's hair.

"Oh, my dear, you won't tell anyone, will you? Poor thing, she was so upset. But of course I couldn't, because James would have been dreadfully angry. You know I haven't any money of my own, and he's generous to me, but he always sees my pass-book, and I couldn't. She was dreadfully upset, so I am afraid it will be a great disappointment—about Joseph, I mean—" She broke off, looked at Terry with simplicity, and said, "Money doesn't make people happy, my dear."

All at once Terry felt dreadfully sorry for her. She was a great deal sorrier than she could manage to feel for Norah Margesson, who borrowed from everyone she knew and had been running after one rich man after another for the last ten years by all accounts. She said,

"I know, darling."

And with that Pearla Yorke came drifting over to the fire.

"What a marvelous room this is," she said, in a voice whose sweetness matched her angel gaze. "If I could plan a room for myself, it would be just like this. It really is the most divine background."

Terry's eyes danced.

"For you?" she said.

Pearla smiled upon her.

"Oh, yes, it's quite, quite perfect. I shall tell Mr. Cresswell that he must, must, *must* let me be painted in this room. Sorgenson is doing me for the Salon, and this room is so divinely right. I shall tell him that he simply must come down and do me here."

Emily gazed dumbly. If James said yes to this, she would go and stay with old Aunt Emily Leconfield at Harrogate. There were limits to what one could stand, and if Mrs. Yorke was coming here to stay—perhaps for weeks, and a foreign painter coming in and out, or perhaps staying too, and paints all over the drawing-room—well, she would have reached her limit, and even James couldn't stop her going to stay with Aunt Emily. The thought heartened her. She cut across Pearla's indecision as to whether pearl-grey or a very faint blue would be most becoming, and said in a flat, mild voice,

"I don't think I should care about it."

Pearla actually looked at her, eyes wide, lips parted.

"But they are my best colours," she said with wistful surprise. "Everyone thinks so." She turned appealingly to Terry. "I hardly ever wear anything else."

Terry's eyes had a sparkle in them.

"I don't think Mrs. Cresswell was bothering about that. You meant, didn't you, darling, that you didn't feel frightfully keen on turning your drawing-room into a studio?"

But the courage had run out of Emily. She said, "Oh, I don't know," and was glad when the door opened and the coffee came in.

Norah Margesson took her cup to the glass door that opened upon the terrace. She jerked the curtain back and stood there looking out. Emily, though sorry for her, was annoyed. In her young days a girl didn't show so openly that she was waiting for the men to come in. The continual restless shimmer of the blue sequins hinted at the fact that Miss Margesson was not waiting very patiently. And really it wasn't any use. Emily was quite sure that Joe Applegarth hadn't any intentions at all.

The men came in quite soon—much sooner than usual. Emily thought, "James can't stay away from her," and then was horrified, because this was just what she had been refusing to admit, even to herself. Pearla was going to meet him now. He was taking her off to the end of the room, pretending to talk to her about the Lely which hung there, a picture she didn't really like to have in her drawing-room—one of those brazen Charles II women with about forty yards of pale satin slipping off her everywhere and showing a great deal more than was decent. Emily's conscience pricked her suddenly and hard. "Oh, I'm wicked! How do I know they're not talking about the picture? It cost enough."

Actually, they had begun by talking about the picture, because Pearla looked up at it and said in a sighing voice,

"Oh, how lovely her pearls are!"

"They ought to be," said James Cresswell, "seeing that King Charles gave them to her."

Pearla said "Oh!" as if he had shocked her. And then, "I wonder what happened to them. You know, I can't help having a very special feeling about pearls because of my name. And I haven't got any—"

He looked at her bare exquisite neck, and then they both looked across at Emily.

"Your wife's pearls are lovely," said Pearla, only just above her breath.

James said, "Pretty fair." His sharp glance dwelt on them, appraising them. Emily couldn't set them off, never had been able to set them off. He had given them to her when the boy was born. His mind winced away from that. A sickly child that had lived no more than half a year—that was the best she could do. And no second child. The Cresswells had never run to big families, but they had been healthy enough. He felt the old resentment as he turned to meet Pearla's wistful gaze.

Joseph Applegarth had joined Norah Margesson. He was a kindly man, and he thought she looked lonely over there by herself, but no man of his age and figure wants to stand about and talk after a good dinner. He liked his rubber, and if the bridge tables were not brought out soon, he would take it on himself to give James a jog. Good thing too, if it stopped him making a fool of himself with that Mrs. Yorke. Very pretty woman of course, but not the thing—no, no, decidedly not the thing, in his own house and right under poor Emily's nose.

Norah Margesson pulled the linen curtain between them and the room.

"There ought to be a moon," she said. "Isn't it the Hunter's moon in October? It ought to be rising about now. You can't see it from here. Let's go to the end of the terrace and look. It's quite warm tonight." She turned the key as she spoke and pushed the door.

Joe Applegarth took fright. He hadn't been a rich bachelor for more than fifty years for nothing. He was hearty, but he wasn't simple. He laughed his jolly laugh and stepped back a pace into the lighted room.

"No, no, no—not at my time of life. My moon-gazing days are over—if I ever had them. It's so long ago, I don't remember. No, no, what suits me now is a good fire and a lighted room, and a rubber or two of bridge in pleasant company." He sent his voice cheerfully down the room. "Hi, James—what about some bridge?"

No one was really sorry for the diversion except Norah Margesson. James Cresswell had gone as far as he meant to go for the moment. He might be giving Pearla Yorke a string of pearls for Christmas, or he might not. That would depend on circumstances. Pearla herself was relieved. The idea of the pearls had been planted, and that was enough.

On the other side of the room Fabian Roxley was finding it increasingly difficult to make indifferent conversation. Under a calm exterior he felt a clamorous hatred for these people—for Applegarth's loud voice and Emily's foolish one, for Pearla's airs, and all their silly faces. He wanted to be alone with Terry.

Emily looked round with gratitude.

''We're just two tables,'' she said quite brightly. ''Mr. Ridgefield and I, and Mr. Roxley and Terry—oh, no, that won't do—we mustn't have two of a family. Terry, you and Mr. Roxley had better go to James's table, and Mr. Ridgefield and I will have Joseph and Norah. Oh dear me—where is Norah?''

Terry said, ''She went out on to the terrace. I'll fetch her.'' She ran off.

Emily shivered.

''Oh dear, I thought there was a draught. How could she be so foolish? It is much too cold, and she hasn't even got a wrap—and Terry hasn't either.''

Terry ran along the terrace in her pink frock. There was no moon yet, only a brightness where the moon would be. And, at the end of the terrace against the brightness, a dark unmoving shape.

Terry came up to it, slackening her pace.

''Norah—they want you to make up a four for bridge. Ouf! Aren't you petrified out here?''

Norah flung round. Her sequins clashed.

''Why should I come in? What have any of them done for me that I should put myself out for them?'' Her voice panted with anger.

Terry was appalled. Everyone knew that Norah had a temper—but really! She said in rather a dry little voice,

''Well, of course you can do just as you like. Uncle Basil hates cut-throat, so you'd be one up on him. The others won't mind, except that darling Emily is quite sure you are catching your death of cold, and the benevolent uncle will think he has offended you.''

Just for a moment Terry wondered if Miss Margesson was going to strike her. There was that sort of feeling in the air. Then she said,

''Full of common sense—aren't you, Terry? There's no moon anyhow, so I might as well come in.''

CHAPTER IX

PETER Talbot drove his newly acquired Austin along a dark and apparently endless road. Not that he minded about its being endless, or dark either for the matter of that. It was a pleasant October night, and presently the moon would be up. He wondered whether the people whose instructions he was obeying had taken the moon into their reckoning. It would be bad enough to lurk burglariously about Heathacres in the dark, but a very bright full moon would impart an indecent air of melodrama to the proceedings. Country house set. Spotlight on hero who is about to break into tenor solo—high C, *vibrato*, and *con amore*. Lord, no, I'm the villain—a villain on the right side of thirty is a baritone, on the wrong side a bass. Afraid I can't manage either.

He began to compose a tenor solo to be sung at the window of the burglaree whilst waiting for an accomplice to hand over the loot. It came out rather well, and distracted his mind from the fact that he was beginning to get cold feet.

All the instructions had been followed up to date. In the name of James Reilly he had taken out a subscription at Preedo's Library and given his address as the Edenbridge Hotel, Minden Avenue. No more than a couple of hours later a messenger-boy had delivered a package addressed to

Mr. James Reilly, which package contained the gratifying sum of 80 in one-pound Treasury notes.

In pursuance of his instructions he had then visited Pratt's garage, Lemming Street, inspected, haggled over, and finally purchased for 50 an elderly but organically sound Austin 14. He was not driving her without enthusiasm in the direction of Heathacres. He continued to divert himself with his tenor solo.

He reached Firshot at a little after midnight. A large-scale map of Surrey had informed him that Heathacres lay half a mile beyond the village on the left-hand side of the road. There did not seem to be any other houses near it, and the right-hand side of the road was bordered by the heath mentioned in his instructions.

He found the place easily enough, ran the car off the road behind a convenient clump of thorn and holly, and began to think what he would do next. The luminous dial of his wrist-watch told him that it was five-and-twenty to one. He was therefore nearly an hour and a half ahead of his instructions, which said, "Enter drive at two A.M." There was something peremptory and precise about this which got his goat. He thought he would enter drive when he found it convenient, and he thought there was no time like the present, because for the moment the moon was behind the bank of cloud and he had no real wish to tread an illuminated stage.

It was a longish drive, winding at first over the open heath and then taking to itself marching ranks of tall, dark cypresses. He hoped that he would not be obliged to make a hurried exit, since for quite a third of the way there would be no cover at all. The cypresses stopped. Other and lower shrubs took their place. They ceased too. He came out upon a gravel sweep, and saw the black bulk of the house between him and the sky.

No terrace this side. A canopied porch, pillars, steps going up. The terrace must be on the other side of the house. He got in amongst shrubs again, scratched a groping hand on a tall clipped holly, and smelt the smoky, resinous tang of *arbor vitae*. Then by good fortune he blundered on to a path and came out of the shrubs to an open space where his feet met grass. He could see the house again now, long and low, with the terrace running the whole length of it. His path had brought him out upon a lawn at the terrace foot. There were steps going up quite near to where he stood.

His instructions said, "Proceed terrace and wait." If that meant that he was to climb those steps and wait for the rising moon to emerge from its bank of cloud and floodlight him, well, he was off. There were some very nice convenient bushes to hand, and he intended to use them as cover. Anyhow there would still be well over an hour to wait.

He got between a prickly bush, not holly, and a dark smothery one with a queer aromatic smell and waited. The moon came slowly up out of the cloud-bank. The dark sky brightened. His bushes stood out black against it. High over head the great dark boughs of a cedar stretched over the lawn. The front of the house began to shine. A white house, or cream-washed; creepers like a shadow pattern on the wall; every window that was shut beginning to glitter; every open window mysteriously empty—black, blank, and empty. It was rather like looking at a person who is asleep. There is only a shell—no life, no awareness; the sleeper does not know that you are there at all.

The house stood in the moonlight, and did not know anything about Spike Reilly and his instructions.

And then all at once the blank emptiness of one of those open windows was filled. Something moved in the dark room behind it. Peter saw the movement first—something light, something white. Then a girl came to the window in her nightgown and looked out. Her neck and arms were bare. Her hair looked dark and her eyes, but everything else was white. She stood there quite still for a while and looked up. Then she turned suddenly and was gone, and the window blank again.

Peter stood and looked at it. It was the nearest of all the windows. If he had stepped out upon the lawn, she would have seen him. He could have struck a romantic attitude and got off with his tenor solo. What a wasted opportunity.

He was still looking up, when away to the right something flashed. He looked down and along the terrace, and saw what it was. Someone had opened a long glass door. It led down to the terrace by a couple of steps. At the top of these steps a dark wrapped figure stood and held the door in a not very steady hand. The door opened outwards. There was a trembling reflection from the glass, the kind of shifting light which moves on moving water. The figure stood there hesitating, and then came out upon the steps and down them into the moonlight, pushing the door to behind her.

It was a woman in a long black coat which covered her to her feet. She was bare-headed, her black hair ruffling in the breeze. She came quickly along the terrace, and he saw her face quite plainly—a handsome haggard face, eyes deeply shadowed, lips apart. At the top of the steps she stopped and looked back across her shoulder. She had both hands together at her breast, half clutching at her coat, half holding something. Before Peter had time to wonder what it was she had run down the steps and stood peering into the shadows.

"Jimmy—are you there?" Her voice, a naturally vibrant one, was hushed to the very edge of audibility. She paused, drew a quick breath, and said the name again, a little louder, "Jimmy—"

Peter stood uncertain between his bushes. Was it his cue, or wasn't it? If it was, something had gone wrong with the timing, because it couldn't be more than one o'clock, and he wasn't supposed to be entering the drive until two. If it wasn't his cue, then who was Jimmy—and was he butting in on an assignation? Well, to his mind this girl didn't look as if she had come to meet a lover. She had the air of being in a kind of terrified hurry. She stood just beyond the bottom step and called again,

"Jimmy—are you there?"

Bearing in mind that he was Spike Reilly, and that Reilly's baptismal name was James, Peter concluded that he had better be there. He said, "Yes," and moved forward, but not so far forward as to risk identification.

Just as he took that step, the glass door flashed again. A girl looked out. Peter saw that, and thought "Hullo!" He had no time to think anything else, because the first girl came running at him. She said, "Quick, quick—take them!" Then she half turned, looked back, and saw the swinging door and someone coming down the steps to the terrace, someone coming out of the door which she had left ajar behind her. With a terrified gasp she pushed what felt like a heavy string of beads into Peter's hands and ran away past him and down the path which skirted the house.

CHAPTER X

TERRY Clive woke up and found the moonlight in her room. She jumped out of bed and ran to the open window. She had no idea what had waked her, but she wanted to see those heather and bracken slopes under the moon. There had been a bank of cloud when she came up to bed. It was there still, but for the moment the moon rose clear. Nice to have a view like this hanging there in the window-frame day in day out, under the sun and the moon and the stars. She thought, "I hope it's a comfort to Emily," and thought, "It would be to me." And then wondered whether anything would really comfort you if you had lost your baby and never had another, but only a husband who was rude to you in front of people.

She leaned out of the window and saw how the moonlight bleached the bracken and the heather. But the pines were too dark for it. They stood up black and strange and dreamed their own dreams.

She had been looking for only a minute or two, when she heard a sound, and the moment she heard it she knew she had heard it before, and that it had waked her. It was the sound of Emily Cresswell's door closing just along the passage, and it was queer that it should have waked her, because it was such a soft brushing sound. There was a strip of plushy stuff on the bottom edge of the door to keep out draughts, and it made a soft shush-shush against the thick pile of Emily's carpet whenever the door was opened.

She wondered if Emily was ill. It must be quite late. They had come up at eleven. She thought it must be one o'clock or past by the moon. She opened her own door and looked out. Emily's door was shut, and someone who wasn't Emily was walking away down the passage. There was no light in the corridor itself, but a light burned all night long in the hall. Against the glow which came up from the well of the stairs Terry saw a tall shape move as, just a few hours ago, she had seen out on the terrace a dark shape stand against the brightening sky. She thought it was the same shape. She thought—no, she didn't stop to think. She snatched a rough warm coat from the cupboard and padded barefoot after the person who had come out of Emily's room. What business had anyone to be in Emily Cresswell's room in the middle of the night, and to go sliding off along the passage and down the stairs like a black ghost? It was in Terry's mind that she would find out.

She came to the top of the stairs and looked over. There was a flight, and a landing, and another flight that turned. The bottom step was under Terry where she looked over—right under her. The light shone on it. She looked down, and saw Norah Margesson in a black satin coat that hid her to her feet. Her hair hung loose over the collar of the coat. Her face without make-up had a desperate pallor. Her hands were out before her, the right pressed down upon the left. But what she carried could not be hidden. Milk-white and lovely, Emily Cresswell's pearls were heaped between her palms. Here and there they escaped, dripped down, and caught the light. The clasp with its brilliants dazzled. Before Terry had time to draw her breath in a gasp, Miss Margesson was gone out of sight, and Emily Cresswell's necklace with her.

Just for a moment Terry felt absolutely petrified. She couldn't think, and she couldn't move. She just felt cold to her bones and rather sick. That lasted for about half a minute. Then a hot, restorative anger surged over her. Her mind raced, and her feet. If Norah was walking in her sleep she must be brought back. If she was stealing Emily's pearls she must be made to give them back. Terry didn't believe she was sleep-walking. She believed she was stealing.

She arrived at the bottom of the stairs and looked about her under the light. The drawing-room door stood open a hand's breath. All the other doors were shut. She pushed the partly open door and found the drawing-room dark beyond it—all dark except for one tall bright panel where a green linen curtain had been pulled aside from the glass door which opened upon the terrace. The curtain had been drawn when they left the room two hours ago. A cold draught met her, and she saw that the door itself was ajar. She opened it wide and looked out.

The moonlight was flooding the terrace, and there was no one there. But away to the right where the steps went down and the shadows began—tree shadows, making a black pattern on the grass and merging into the black formlessness of crowding shrubs—there something moved. Some thing or some one.

She reached the terrace and ran along it to the steps. And down them without check or pause to what she had seen amongst the shadows.

Peter stood his ground and watched her come. He felt some pardonable interest as to what this was all about. If he ran for it he would probably brain himself against a tree trunk or be tripped and flung sprawling. He didn't fancy the prospect. He thought he would stay put and see what was to be seen. He didn't think that the girl could see him. The other one hadn't until he moved.

He was full of a lively curiosity. This girl was barefoot. She had a rough coat hanging open over her nightgown. She ran straight down the steps and right up to him. She caught him by the arm and shook it. She said in a breathless tone of rage,

"Give them back at once!"

When she shook him his handful of beads rattled. She let go of his arm and took him by the wrist. Her hand was small, and strong, and icy cold. She said, still in that furious whisper,

"Give them back at once!"

Peter grinned, but of course she couldn't see him. They were in the darkest of the shadows. She couldn't see anything. But he had seen *her*, and she was the girl who had looked out the window—the one to whom he ought to have been singing his tenor solo. Well, he wouldn't have minded. But instead here she was, trying to shake him. He gave her marks for courage, because if he had really been Spike Reilly, or the Jimmy whom the first girl was expecting, she was running a rather unpleasant risk. He said mildly,

"Do you mind telling me what you want?"

She stamped a bare foot.

"Mrs. Cresswell's pearls—you've got them in your hand! If you don't give them back at once, I shall scream."

Peter certainly didn't want her to scream. He rather fancied that this would have been the cue for Spike Reilly to take her by the throat. As he was not prepared to do this, he said with all the social charm he could muster,

"Oh, I shouldn't do that."

"Then give me the pearls—at once!"

"Pearls, are they? Well, well!"

"As if you didn't know!" Her whisper was edged with contempt.

"Actually, I didn't. Believe it or not, that haggard female just ran down the steps and shoved them at me, after which she ran away. And if you know what it's all about, I don't."

"And you expect me to believe that?"

Peter shook his head.

"Oh, no—it's a wicked, unbelieving world. Why, if anyone came along and found us here, do you suppose they would believe that you were doing a bit of private sleuthing? Oh, no, they would see you clasping me affectionately by the wrist, and like you they would immediately believe the worst."

Her cold, tight grip relaxed, and then tightened again resolutely.

"What are you doing here if you didn't come for the pearls?"

"You've no delicacy," said Peter. "But if you want to know, I had an assignation."

She gave a little angry laugh.

"Oh, yes—with Norah—to take the pearls!"

"Any good offering you my word of honour that I've never seen Norah before—didn't know her name, and hadn't any idea what it was she was pushing at me?"

She stamped again, really hard. It must have hurt. She said in that edged voice,

"Not the slightest. Give me the pearls!"

"All right, all right, don't get excited." He moved forward a step or two, stretched his right hand, and set the pearls dangling in a patch of moonlight.

Terry, discovering that she was holding the wrong wrist, let go of it and sprang back. They both looked at the pearls. She made a snatch and missed them, because a long arm shot up and held them, still dangling, out of reach.

She was out of the shadow now, and he could see her face. She looked young and angry, and her eyes were very bright. Her hair curled all over her head like a child's. She had a soft round face and a soft red mouth. Peter Talbot felt a dangerous desire to pick her up and kiss her. He wondered what she would do if he did.

His hand came down and offered her the pearls politely on an open palm.

"Here you are. I'm not really a thief, you know. And if I were, there's something I'd rather have than pearls."

Terry had held his wrist, but she took care not to touch his hand. She picked up Emily Cresswell's necklace, whisked round, and ran up the steps and into the house. Peter watched to see if she would shut the door, but she left it ajar.

He went back to his place, and wondered what was going to happen next.

CHAPTER XI

THE first thing that happened was the reappearance of the haggard female, whose name he now knew to be Norah. She came up the steps at the other end of the terrace, stood there for a moment, and then went quickly to the door, which still stood ajar. She opened it, went in, and shut it after her. Peter thought he heard the click of a turning key. A curtain was drawn across the glass. The moonlight struck on its pale folds. Nothing else happened.

The question was, did this close tonight's performance, or was it only the end of the first act? Peter had a look at his watch. It was not quite half past one. His instructions had said definitely, "Enter drive at 2 A.M." That meant either that he had not been intended to come on until the second act, or that the scene in which he had just played an unrehearsed part didn't belong to his play at all, but to a highly dramatic curtain-raiser by some other hand. It was, of course, possible that he had been sent here to meet Norah and take over Mrs. Cresswell's pearls from her. If this was the case, it would account for the fact that no one else seemed to be on hand to do so. If he was not the Jimmy Norah expected, well, where was that other James? He was to know later, but at this time it puzzled him a good deal.

The interval between the acts lasted a long time. He

reflected that even if nothing else happened, he was bound to wait here until half past three, and it seemed an extraordinarily flat, cold, and unprofitable way of spending the night. The wind was rising, and was now definitely in the east. Cloud was rising too, and the moon was veiled, though not yet darkened.

It was about ten minutes to two when he became aware that there was going to be a second act after all, and that the curtain was rising. Literally and physically, the curtain behind the glass door had once more been drawn aside. Its pale folds, which had caught what faint diffusion of light there was, stirred and withdrew, leaving a darkness in their place. He heard the click of a key again, and just perceived the movement of the opening door. Someone came out on to the steps and descended to the terrace. It got suddenly darker. In the close dusk it was impossible to see who it was that came. Peter could distinguish neither shape nor contour, only a moving shadow. If it had not moved, he would hardly have known it was there. When it ceased to move, he only made it out because he knew that it was there. His eye had not had to follow it very far. It had come towards him for a yard or two and stopped where the next window fronted on the terrace, a window which the moonlight had shown to be closed and curtained. And here the shadow stayed. There were faint sounds—oh, very faint. But Peter's hearing, at all times acute, was now strained to the utmost. He came out from his cover, and foot by foot crept nearer until he stood by the steps which led to the terrace.

It was just there that he caught the unmistakable tinkle of broken glass. The sound set his thoughts racing. Broken glass in this connection could mean only one possible thing. Someone was cutting a pane of glass from the window next to the long glass door. All the sounds he had caught corroborated this. But the person who was cutting out the pane had come from inside the house to do it. Why? There was an easy answer to that, and Peter had no difficulty in supplying it. Act II was going to stage a burglary, and a burglary had got to be an outside job. The stage manager was a careful soul. Nothing would be left to chance, and very little to Spike Reilly. Afterwards he was to wonder what would have happened if he had run in then and there and caught the shadow *in flagrante delicto* with his treacled paper, and his professionally smashed-in pane of glass. It wouldn't have been very easy to explain away. At the time, it simply never occurred to him to do anything of the sort. All that was in his mind was to play his part right through. He wanted to do that—to meet his fellow actors, to get the hang of the plot.

He stood where he was and waited.

The thing took a little time. He heard a clock strike inside the house, two faint strokes, and again the tinkle of falling glass. The shadow moved from the window and went back by the way that it had come. The glass door shimmered vaguely and fell to. He heard the key turn in the lock.

Ten minutes went by. They passed at an intolerable slow, dragging pace. He looked at his watch and found that they had really gone. It was ten minutes past two, and Spike Reilly was now officially here.

He walked up the steps and made his way along the terrace to where he had seen the shadow at his work, and he had no sooner reached the spot than he knew that the curtain was sliding back. Someone looked at him. Not a face, nor eyes, but someone there—aware of him—watching. A voice soft and muttering said, not in a whisper but also without sound,

"Give your name."

He said, "Spike Reilly," and immediately something was pushed at him through the square which had been robbed of its glass. It was a long roll—a canvas roll tied up with string at either end. The ends were about three feet apart—that was how he thought of it, feeling for it in the dark. An awkward thing to carry, an awkward thing to be seen with.

He said, "What am I to do with it?" and the faint mutter from inside said,

"Put it in the boot of your car. You will receive instructions."

Peter thought, "If I was really Spike Reilly, I'm hanged if

I'd keep the corpse in my car.'' As it was, it might lead to a useful contact. He left that vague, and said,

''All right. Anything else?''

The voice said, ''No—hurry!''

He went away down the steps and into his cover again, because he wanted time to think. It was the devil and all playing a part like this in the dark.

He waited to see if anything more would happen, but there was not so much as a flicker of light from behind any of those curtained or uncurtained windows. After the first few minutes he knew that that was what he was waiting for. If a light went on anywhere, he could mark the window, and it would be a clue. Man or woman, whoever was awake in that house with a light burning, it was to him or to her that the finger of certainty would be pointing.

But there was nothing to point at—not so much as the flicker of a match. The house slept under its eaves in the shadow of the cloud-bank, and every window was black, and blank, and secret.

CHAPTER XII

THE morning broke upon discovery. A housemaid shrieked and scurried. The butler arrived—a thin, intelligent man, as efficient as he looked. Whilst reporting in person to Mr. Cresswell, he sent Robert the footman to telephone to the police.

Descent of James Cresswell in a dressing-gown. Descent of Emily. Highly regrettable language on James's part. Ineffectual tears from Emily. Descent of guests—Joseph Applegarth, Fabian Roxley, Basil Ridgefield—a male chorus of horror and sympathy.

Because the Turner had gone.

The frame leaned against one of the green linen chairs, but the canvas, very neatly cut, was missing, and a glance at the other side of the room showed how it had gone. A pane had been removed from the window on the right of the long glass door—quite professionally and noiselessly taken out by sticking a piece of treacled paper over the glass before breaking it. The sticky mess encrusted with splinters lay there upon the pearl-coloured carpet.

It was Barnes, the efficient butler, who insisted that no one should touch it, or in fact come near the window at all—"in case of finger-marks and footprints." There were no visible footprints, but then, of course, it had been a dry night.

Terry Clive, coming down next, found two groups of people all staring at a broken window, with an open lane between them. She saw at once that the picture was gone, and ran to Emily, who allowed herself to be supported to a chair. Terry was very fond of Emily Cresswell, but she had never expected to find her a comfort, yet at this moment what she would have done without her she could not think. It was all right to be Terry Clive on her knees by a weeping hostess, murmuring "Darling, don't cry," but the idea of being Terry Clive just standing there for everyone to see that she looked like a ghost, and a guilty ghost at that—no, that wasn't so good.

The police arrived.

Norah Margesson looked around the door in a flame-coloured dressing-gown, said irritably, "A burglary? What's gone? One of the pictures? I thought someone had been murdered," and trailed away up the stairs again.

Mrs. Yorke kept her room. Not for anything the world could offer would she leave it until every rite that served her beauty had been fulfilled. These took time, and could by no means be hurried. What was a dead picture on canvas to the living one which she daily presented to the world?

Downstairs the police inspected everything. And discovered nothing except that there were no finger-marks on frame or window. The burglar must be supposed to have worn gloves.

"Not the slightest doubt about what sort of job it is. Daring lot, I must say. You'd have thought they'd have lain low a bit after the Oppenstein affair. Bad business that poor chap of a butler being murdered there. 'Tisn't often a burglar carries arms either these days. And a lucky thing none were used here, Mr. Cresswell, because there's no doubt about it's being the same lot. The ordinary criminal—well, it stands to reason he wouldn't know how to handle this high-class picture business. No, it's a line by itself. We'll be communicating with Scotland Yard at once, and they'll be sending someone down. You see, it's murder now, not just this picture racket."

James Cresswell listened with an air of abstracted gloom.

He didn't care who had been murdered so long as he got his Turner back. He had no opinion of the local police, and a fairly low one of Scotland Yard. This picture-stealing game had been going on for a year, and they hadn't caught anyone yet. As a considerable contributor to the country's taxes, he wanted to know what they did with the money. If an employee in his business was not efficient he got the sack. The police were there to catch criminals and restore stolen property. If they couldn't do their job they should be replaced by others who could. He judged by results, and he wanted his Turner back. These feelings, though not put into words, were plainly discernible.

The police did not linger. They removed the treacled paper, and Barnes instructed the housemaid who had screamed to sweep up the splinters of glass. The guests retired to their rooms to dress. Emily Cresswell stopped weeping, and reflected that it might have been worse. She said so to Terry as they went upstairs.

"You know, it might have been my pearls. And wouldn't that have been dreadful, because they were just there on my dressing-table, and once pearls are gone you can never trace them—you've only got to cut the string, and of course no one can swear to them—and I don't really think I could bear it."

She shut her bedroom door upon the two of them and went across to the dressing-table. The pearls lay there in a heap just as Terry had dropped them down in the darkness and the fear of the night which had gone. The sun was shining in at the windows now. It showed up the veins of Emily's thin hands, and it showed up the sheen on the pearls. They really were too beautiful. Emily looked down at them.

"James gave them to me when our little boy was born. It's all gone, you know."

Terry's eyes stung. She said,

"Oh, no, darling!"

Emily shook her head.

"He stopped loving me a long time ago. I shouldn't like the pearls to go too."

Terry kissed her and ran out of the room.

All through breakfast she was wondering what she was going to do. She had never had a secret before, not one that mattered, and this one might be going to matter terribly. Norah Margesson had taken Emily Cresswell's pearls and given them to a man who was waiting at the foot of the terrace. Norah had called him Jimmy, and he was waiting there for the pearls. . . . *Was he?* Of course he was. And if it hadn't been for Terry Clive, he would have got away with them, and poor darling Emily would never have seen them again, because she was quite right—you can't trace pearls.

Terry had saved them and put them back. And then someone had cut the Turner from its frame and got away with it. Well, what did Terry know about that?

She sat at the breakfast table between Joseph Applegarth and Fabian Roxley, and drank Barnes's admirable coffee, and thought miserably about what she knew. She had taken the pearls and put them down on Emily's dressing-table. And then she had gone into her own room, but she hadn't been able to sleep. She really had tried, but it was no good at all. She had tried for quite a long time, but it wasn't any good, so she had gone and looked out of the window again.

Why had she done it? Oh, why, why, *why* had she done it?

Fabian Roxley said, "Terry, you look like a ghost," and something shuddered inside her, because that had been her own thought. *And ghosts walk in the night.*

She made a gallant attempt at an impudent grin and said, "No time to make up—that's all. The natural face isn't too good, is it? The old lady I was telling you about last night is always saying, 'But, my dear, why can't you girls just leave yourselves to nature?' So if I go and see her like this, she'll know."

On her other side, Mr. Applegarth chuckled.

"We used to say 'As pretty as paint' when I was a young man, but a girl couldn't paint then unless she was going in for private theatricals. I remember my sister taking a poppy out of her Sunday hat and rubbing her cheeks with it before she went to a dance, and my mother made her go upstairs and wash her face with soap and water. She's got granddaughters now—she's older than I—and last time I saw the eldest one she'd got lips the colour of orange-peel, and her eyebrows plucked, and stuff on her eyelashes." He made a comical grimace. "Well, I don't like it, I must say, but I suppose that shows I'm getting on."

"Plucked eyebrows have gone out," said Norah Margesson. Her own had never needed plucking. They grew in a fine and delicate arch, and she was perhaps not sorry to draw attention to them.

Terry, looking at her across the table, wondered that she could be and look so like herself. How could you be a thief in the dead of night, and take Emily's pearls and run out with them to an accomplice who was all ready and waiting so that one couldn't even think it had been a sudden frightful temptation, and then come down to breakfast as if nothing had happened?

It shook Terry a lot. If Norah could do that—and Norah had done that—why then, shouldn't it have been Norah who had cut the Turner from its frame? She felt her cheeks grow suddenly hot. It didn't fit—she couldn't make it fit. Something inside her said, "Please let it be Norah." Because she knew already that Norah was a thief, and it would be horrible to have to know a thing like that about anyone else.

The thoughts went on in her mind. She passed Mr. Applegarth the marmalade, and she spoke when she was spoken to, but the thoughts went on.

She was very glad when breakfast was over, because by that time she knew what she was going to do. She followed Emily out of the room, put an arm round her waist, and got her away from the others. There was a cold north-looking room behind the dining-room where nobody ever came. She took Emily there and said,

"Darling, I want to speak to you."

Mrs. Cresswell looked at her with surprise and concern.

"My dear, what is it? You look so pale."

"I feel pale," said Terry. "Darling, listen. I got up in the night, and I looked out of my window, and I saw something.

And I don't want to tell the police, so I thought I had better tell you."

Emily Cresswell looked alarmed. She said "Oh, Terry!" in her nervous, fluttered way; and then, "What did you see?"

"You'd better sit down," said Terry. She put Emily into a chair and knelt beside her. "Now, darling, brace up, because it's no good our both going at the knees."

"Oh, my dear—what did you see?"

Terry patted her.

"Well, that's just it— I don't want to say—not yet—not unless I'm obliged to. Because, you see, that burglary wasn't really a burglary at all. That is to say, it wasn't an outside job like the police think it was."

"Terry!" gasped Mrs. Cresswell.

"I'm sorry, darling, but it wasn't. It was someone in the house. You've got to brace up, because I've got a most lovely plan. I know just what you feel, because I've been feeling like it myself ever since the middle of last night. But I really have got a plan. I was getting greener and greener all through breakfast, and then suddenly when I was passing Mr. Applegarth's cup for a third go of tea I had a brainwave and I saw how Mr. Cresswell could get his picture back, and no horrible scandal."

Emily blinked at her.

"Oh, my dear—it sounds too dreadful! Are you sure?"

"It's a very good plan," said Terry in her most earnest voice. "It just dropped on me from heaven. Listen, darling. I'll go round having heart-to-hearts with everybody, like we're having now. I shall tell them—one at a time of course, and in the most deadly confidence—that I was looking out of my window last night, and that I saw something. *But I shan't tell them what I saw.* And I shall say that I don't want to tell the police or anyone because of the horrid scandal, and you and Mr. Cresswell hating it. And if the picture was returned, well, then I wouldn't ever say what I'd seen, but if it wasn't back by the day after tomorrow, then I should have to tell the police."

"Oh!" said Emily Cresswell in a shaking voice. A

hairpin fell into her lap and she picked it up and put it back again. ''Oh!'' she said again. ''Terry, I can't believe it—I can't! What did you see?''

Terry got to her feet. Talking about the plan had made her feel much better. There was colour in her cheeks and a sparkle in her eye.

''I'm not telling,'' she said.

CHAPTER XIII

TERRY'S first heart-to-heart talk was with Mrs. Yorke. She couldn't really push her imagination to the point of seeing the lovely Pearla wandering about a dark house in the dead of night cutting pictures out of their frames. Pearla liked a warm, comfortable bed with a pale blue eiderdown, and lots of beauty sleep with her face all nicely creamed and her wave beautifully set and covered with the latest thing in boudoir caps. All the same, you couldn't leave her out—you couldn't even count her out. The only thing to do was to go ahead and get her over.

Pearla received her with pleasure. She was doing her face, and she rather liked someone to talk to. The eighteenth-century fashion of receiving admirers at the dressing-table would have appealed to her. She was young enough to have nothing to conceal, and was so much interested in herself that she took the interest of others for granted.

Terry sat down, and watched the removal of one cream and the patting-in of another. The room was very warm and full of delicate blended scents. Even with her face shiny and with nun-like swathings to protect her fair hair from any possible touch of cream or powder, Pearla looked extremely lovely. She gazed earnestly at her own reflection, and thought so herself. She thought how much lovelier she would look if she had pearls like Emily's. She wondered whether James Cresswell would rise to giving her pearls, and how far it would be necessary to go if he did. Business men were apt to demand value for money—

Terry's voice broke in.

"Mrs. Yorke, I'm so worried. Can I tell you something?"

"Me?" There was genuine surprise in the angel voice. Girls were not apt to confide in Pearla Yorke.

Terry said, "I'm so worried," and proceeded to tell her why.

Pearla, still gazing at her reflection, gave the greater part of her mind to a cream she was trying for the first time. Mona Lasalle swore by it, but her skin wasn't nearly so delicate. She wondered if it was really wise, but there was no doubt that Mona's complexion had cheered up quite a lot lately. And it might be the cream. It was certainly a scandalous price.

With the small balance of attention left over she considered Terry's story. And really it all seemed a ridiculous thing to be worried about, because if the girl really had seen anything, well, the police were the people to confide in, and actually she had probably imagined the whole thing. Pearla didn't say so, but she hinted at it.

"Of course it's all terribly sordid, and I'm so glad it was all over before I knew anything about it. And one feels for poor Mr. Cresswell losing his lovely picture like that, but I suppose the police will get it back for him, and if you can help them, I truly think you ought to. So if you want my advice, there it is."

Pearla leaned forward and began to apply just the very faintest trace of eye-shadow. A thought too much and it put five years on to your age. It must be no more than the merest hint to give depth and mystery to her eyes. She heard Terry's voice, but without giving any attention to it. And then suddenly she was shocked, because the girl was actually saying,

"I won't go to the police unless I have to."

Pearla Yorke turned from the charming picture in the glass.

"Oh, but you ought to. Poor Mr. Cresswell—he does love his pictures so much."

Terry said, "Yes." And then, "Perhaps it will be found, or—" she hesitated—"returned. I don't think I'll do anything about the police for a day or two. Of course if nothing happens by the day after tomorrow—" She got up and went to the door. "I really do think your advice is good, only I don't think I can take it—at least not before Tuesday."

She had meant her next conversation to be with one of the men, but when she emerged upon the passage she saw Norah Margesson look round the door of her room and draw back again. After all, Norah was going to be the worst, and it would be better to get her over. When you hate doing a thing very much, the only way is to do it quickly. She ran along the passage, knocked without giving herself time to think, and went straight in upon her knock.

Miss Margesson was looking out of the window. She appeared surprised, and Terry thought that stupid, because if Norah had seen her, she might have been supposed to have seen Norah. Miss Margesson's eyebrows went up. She said "Well?" and Terry found herself suddenly angry. This helped a lot, because it is almost impossible to be embarrassed and angry at the same time. She found herself looking Norah straight in the face and saying quite loudly and clearly,

"You know I followed you last night."

Miss Margesson had the light behind her. She was always pale. It was impossible to say that she was any paler now. Her voice was casual as she said,

"Oh, did you? May I ask why?"

Terry's cheeks burned.

"To get Emily's pearls back of course."

Norah said, "Oh?" and then, "Did you get them?"

"Yes, I did."

"What a good thing. She'd hate to lose them—wouldn't she? But I don't quite know why you're talking to me about it."

"Don't you?"

"No, my good child, I don't."

Terry was glad she was so angry. She said,

"It's no use—I saw you. You came out of Emily's room and went downstairs. It was about one o'clock. I looked over the banisters and saw you in the hall. You had the pearls in your hand. You went through the drawing-room and out on to the terrace, and I followed you."

"Did you? I must have been walking in my sleep—I do sometimes."

Terry said, "Rubbish! You went down the steps and called, 'Jimmy!' You pushed the pearls at someone, and then you looked around and saw me and ran away."

Norah said, "Have you told the Cresswells this peculiar story?"

Terry shook her head. She wasn't so angry as she had been, and she was beginning to think what Norah Margesson must be feeling like.

"Are you going to tell them?"

Terry found her voice.

"I don't know."

"And what do you mean by that?"

"Look here, Norah," said Terry, "this is all perfectly horrid. I got Emily's pearls back, and I don't want her to know you ever took them—she'd hate it frightfully. But if they ever went again, I should have to tell her. And then there's something else. After I put the pearls back I couldn't sleep, and just before two o'clock I was looking out the window and I saw something. I'm not telling anyone what I saw—not yet—but if Mr. Cresswell hasn't got his picture back by the day after tomorrow, I shall tell the police, and if I have to do that, there's no saying what else may come out, whether I want it to or not."

Norah looked at her. The skin of her face seemed to have tightened. There was a terrifying cold anger in her eyes. She said in her husky voice,

"So I took the picture—and if I don't give it back, you'll tell the police about the pearls—"

Terry shook her head.

"I didn't say that. I don't want to tell anyone about the

pearls, but if Mr. Cresswell doesn't get his picture back by Tuesday, I shall tell the police what I saw when I was looking out of my window just before two o'clock. And if they start asking questions and making enquiries they may come across your friend Jimmy, and they may find out about the pearls. It would be much better if the picture came back—it really would."

Norah Margesson made a step towards her. It was only one step, but her voice seemed to spring at Terry.

"Get out of my room! Get out, I say—get out!"

Terry was extraordinarily glad to find herself in the passage again.

CHAPTER XIV

SHE found Joseph Applegarth in the garden. He was god-fatherly, kind, and emphatic. Terry ought without the slightest delay to place the police in possession of any evidence which she might have. Very nice feeling on her part to want to give a thief the chance of restoring the stolen property, but actually what she would be doing was to give him just what he wanted, time to cover up his tracks and get away with it. And then he laughed, and said it wasn't very flattering of her to jump to the conclusion that one of her fellow guests had a hand in the matter.

Terry found herself feeling young and confused, and the plan not quite so clever as it had seemed when she was talking to Emily.

Joseph Applegarth's eyes twinkled at her embarrassment.

"Come, come—I won't tell them you've been suspecting them. But I'd dearly like to know which of us you thought was the most likely to be getting up in the night and stealing Turners. I'm afraid you must knock me out, because I sleep from the moment my head touches the pillow, and I couldn't wake at two in the morning if my life depended on it."

Terry coloured brightly.

"Oh, but I didn't say I suspected anyone in the house. Why should I?"

Behind the twinkle his eyes were very shrewd.

"I don't know why you should, but you do. If you have got a reason, you ought to give it to the police, and if you haven't, my dear young lady, I don't think you ought to come round telling us what you'll do if James doesn't get his picture back within forty-eight hours."

Terry felt miserably abashed. Put like that, it sounded dreadful. And it had seemed such a bright idea. She raised candid eyes to Joseph Applegarth's and said so.

In a way it was a relief to hear him laugh, but it made her feel foolish too.

"Well, we're none of us very likely picture-thieves, I'm afraid," he said with a chuckle in his voice. "There's James himself—he might have done it for the insurance, you know. And Emily—well, you may be able to think up a reason for Emily stealing one of their own pictures, but I can't. And your uncle—now if it had been a rare stamp, I don't know that I should trust him. These collectors are all alike—no morals at all when it comes to their own especial hobby. And that long fellow Roxley—he's some sort of Foreign Office policeman—intelligence or something of that sort. Were you suspecting him? I should have said he was a bit lazy for getting up in the middle of the night myself. And then there are the two ladies. Just between you and me and the garden roller, I could imagine that pretty Mrs. Yorke being tempted by a diamond ring or a string of pearls, but I don't think she'd take any stock in paint unless she was going to put it on her face. And that leaves Miss Margesson to the last, and I'm going to ask you straight out—what makes you think it was she?"

The blood rushed violently to Terry's face. She said,

"I don't. Oh, Mr. Applegarth, *please*. You see, I don't know."

"You know something," said Joseph Applegarth drily, "or you think you do, and what you think you know has given you the idea that the job was done by someone inside the house—and that means one of the guests, because nothing would ever persuade me or anyone with a head on his shoulders that Barnes and his wife had any hand in it. I employ his brother, and I know the stock they come from—Yorkshire, and honest as the day."

"Oh, yes," said Terry.

"And none of the others sleep in, so that brings us back to the guests again—unless you're going to put it on James and Emily." He laughed with obvious enjoyment, and then was suddenly grave. "Look here, my dear, if you'll take my advice—which I don't suppose you will—you'll leave the police to do the job they're paid for and forget whatever it was you thought you saw last night."

Terry said, "I can't," found nothing more to say, and ran away from him across the lawn to the rose garden, where the October roses wore pale copies of their brilliant summer petals. They were still sweet, and they were still lovely, but the departing glory had left them faint and fragile.

Terry walked among the roses, and tried to feel clever and grown-up and practical again. Mr. Applegarth had put her back to ten years old and her first day at a new school. He had called her my dear, and she felt that for twopence he would have patted her on the head. She was very glad indeed to see Fabian Roxley coming towards her, because she was practically sure that Fabian was in love with her, and if anything could make you feel grown-up after being talked to in the most shattering way as if you were a little girl, it would be the company of someone who was at least thirty, and who might propose to you at any moment.

Just what she would say if Fabian Roxley did propose to her Terry didn't know. She hadn't got past the agreeable fact that he admired her and quite obviously wished her to know it. He got a welcoming look, and the whole poured-out story of the plan, to which he listened with admirable if rather lazy attention.

"Emily and I really did think it was a clever plan," said Terry with mournful zest, "but so far everyone has either told me to go to the police or else got frightfully angry."

"Which am I going to do?" said Fabian, looking at her with half closed eyes.

"Well, I hope you won't do either."

"I shall probably tell you to go to the police, Terry."

Terry shook her head.

"It's no good—I won't—not until day after tomorrow."

"And why day after tomorrow?"

They were sitting on a bench recessed into the hedge which surrounded the rose garden, Fabian Roxley lounging as was his wont, Terry sitting bolt upright and rather flushed with her hands in her lap. She had on a blue tweed skirt and a periwinkle jumper which made her eyes look blue. Her head was bare, and the bright brown curls stood up all over it. The hands in her lap were small, and square and brown, and she had put on a new bright cherry-coloured nail-polish which she thought might be exciting. Now that it was on, she didn't really like it very much. She had not used either lipstick or rouge, so there was nothing, as it were, to take your mind off the nail-polish. Mr. Roxley thought she looked like a little girl who had been dressing up. Like Peter Talbot he felt an urge to pick her up and kiss her, and like Peter he restrained himself.

He said, "Why the day after tomorrow?" and Terry said firmly, "To give the picture time to come back."

"I see. And suppose it doesn't come back?"

"Then I shall go to the police."

"And tell them that you were looking out of your window in the night and you saw—well, what did you see?"

"I'm not telling."

He smiled, dropped his voice, and said,

"Not even me?"

Terry shook her head.

"Not anybody at all. Why, I didn't even tell Emily."

"So young and so secretive," sighed Fabian. "I thought you were going to confide in me. Rather nice to have a secret together—what do you think?"

Terry shook her head again.

"Not till the day after tomorrow."

"And then it won't be a secret at all. What's the good of a confidence which I shall have to share with the village policeman and the whole of Scotland Yard?"

"Perhaps it won't be quite the whole of Scotland Yard," said Terry kindly.

She was rewarded by seeing Mr. Roxley assume a more or less upright position.

"I don't believe you saw anything at all."

"Well then, I *did*," said Terry with energy.

"Just as you like. But since, I gather, you didn't actually recognize anyone—" There was a slightest questioning inflection in the lazy voice.

"I didn't say so."

Fabian Roxley laughed.

"If you had, you would have gone to that person and tackled him—or her. There would have been no need to go the round. No, if you did see someone, you were not sure who it was—that it quite clear. But I should like to know why you are so sure it was one of the Cresswells' guests. Why cut out the servants?"

Terry hesitated. Then she said,

"It couldn't have been any of the servants."

"Why couldn't it?"

"There are only the Barnes who sleep in the house. The footman and the housemaid are brother and sister and they come up from the village, and the between maid comes and goes with them. Her mother is cook at the Vicarage and she sleeps there."

"But the Barnes sleep in the house," said Fabian Roxley.

"It wasn't the Barnes," said Terry. "Mr. Applegarth said at once it couldn't be they, because they come from Yorkshire like he does, and he knows all about them and they're as honest as the day. But the police mightn't take any notice of that."

Fabian Roxley smiled.

"For the matter of that, most of us have known each other for years, and if we're not all as honest as the day—rather an archaic expression, don't you think?—we have presumably paid our income tax, our rates, and our card debts up to date, and none of us has been in prison so far as I know."

"But it couldn't have been the Barnes," said Terry earnestly, "because—well, do you know Mrs. Barnes?"

"I'm afraid not."

Terry spread out her arms to encircle an imaginary bulk. "Vast," she said—"immense. Honestly, she has to be seen to be believed. She's older than Barnes, you know, and a perfectly angel cook. And if I'd seen her, I couldn't possibly have thought it was anyone else. No, it wasn't Mrs. Barnes."

"And why wasn't it Barnes?" said Fabian gently.

Terry leaned forward.

"Because he's left-handed. You couldn't have stayed in the house without noticing that."

Fabian's eyes opened suddenly.

"You're not telling what you saw—but you saw quite a lot, didn't you? Enough to be sure it wasn't a fat woman or a left-handed man." He dropped his voice to a low persuasive tone. "Terry, what *did* you see?"

There was a pause. She had an impulse to tell him—she had an impulse to tell no one. The two impulses pushed at her. It was like being caught between two doors—she couldn't go back, and she couldn't go on. She didn't know that she had turned very pale. She got to her feet and stood looking at him strangely.

He said "Terry!"

And she said, "No, no—I'm not going to tell anyone," and turned and ran away from him as she had run away from Joseph Applegarth.

CHAPTER XV

"A LITTLE quiet, Terry?" said Basil Ridgefield.

It was Sunday evening, and they were driving back to London with Terry at the wheel.

She said, "Am I?" and hoped she hadn't blushed.

Of all words in the language she thought that "quiet" least described her feelings. The sky overhead was quiet, a low grey sky drawing down into a dusk that might presently turn to fog, and all the country under this dusk was quiet too—very tame, and grey, and quiet, and dull; no colour, no life, no light and shade. But Terry's mind wasn't quiet. It was full of rushing thoughts, hopes, fears, and suppositions. It was full of things she had said to Emily, Pearla, Norah, Mr. Applegarth, and Fabian, and the things that they had said to her. And the things she might have said if she had thought of them in time, and the things they might have said if they had all been living in the Palace of Truth. None of these thoughts was quiet company. Some of them shouted at the tops of their voices, and then she had to try and shout them down. She kept her eyes on the long grey road under the dusk and said,

"Am I quiet?"

Mr. Ridgefield turned a little in his seat, surveyed her through his monocle, and said in solicitous tone,

"Yes, my dear. What is the matter—didn't you enjoy yourself?"

Terry looked round at him quickly, and then back again at the road. How extraordinarily like Uncle Basil to be surprised if you hadn't enjoyed yourself, when there had been a burglary, and policemen all over the place. That sort of thing didn't disturb anyone else. He would be sorry that the Cresswells should lose a picture they valued, and he had displayed a charming sympathy, but being sorry and sympathetic was just as much a part of his social manner as saying good-morning or how do you do, and it meant as little. Terry had a feeling that it wouldn't have meant much more if the Cresswells had lost a child instead of a picture. Uncle Basil had lovely manners for every occasion, but she had sometimes wondered what would happen if you could strip the lovely manners off. Was there anything underneath that could laugh, and cry, and feel, and love and hate as Terry herself could, or would there be only a little grey, dry, shrivelled thing like the withered kernel of a nut?

Terry wondered, and was smitten with compunction, because he was always so kind to her, and when people got over fifty perhaps you couldn't expect them to have real feelings any more. Perhaps when Terry Clive was fifty—(help!)—all the living, tumultuous feelings which were her would be withered away to something all grey and quiet—"And one might just as well be dead!" said Terry passionately to herself.

Her eyes sparkled, but she didn't look round again.

"Do you enjoy burglaries and policemen, Uncle Basil?"

Mr. Ridgefield laughed.

"Well, my dear, you will think it very shocking of me, but in a way I do—I should say I *did*. But I beg that you will not tell the Cresswells. You see, I was afraid that I was going to be bored. Norah Margesson bores me. She expects me to make love to her. You have probably noticed that she expects every man to make love to her, and a dozen years ago a good many of us were quite willing to oblige. Now—" he shrugged his shoulders—"I am quite determined to remain young, and I find that exceptionally boring. And as for the rest of the party, Pearla Yorke is a lovely creature, but James Cresswell really should not allow her to play bridge. She revoked three times when she was playing with me, and only once with James, which I consider unfair. It would bore me to play bridge with Helen of Troy if she revoked. And James Cresswell is in a frame of mind in which he would bore anyone. So, you see, I feared the worst. The burglary was really quite a god-send, but it seems to have disturbed you—rather unduly, I think. May I ask why?"

Terry said, "Yes"; and then, "I was going to tell you, Uncle Basil."

Mr. Ridgefield said, "Dear me, this sounds very portentous."

"Oh," said Terry, "it's horrid. I didn't think anything could be so horrid."

"My dear child—"

Terry looked round for a moment, and he saw that there were tears in her eyes.

"You see, I really do love Emily. I know she bores you, but I love her. I wouldn't mind if it was only Mr. Cresswell, because I don't think he treats her at all nicely, and he's got lots of money, so he could buy another picture."

Basil Ridgefield gazed at her in mild horror.

"My dear Terry, you can't just go out and buy Turners."

"Well, I don't care," said Terry. "It's Emily I'm thinking about, and she'd hate to have a scandal and one of her guests dragged in—and having to go into a witness-box and swear things, and so should I. So we thought it was a beautiful plan, and I thought it would be quite easy. But it wasn't—it was quite frightfully horrid."

Mr. Ridgefield took out his eyeglass, polished it carefully, and put it back again.

"Do you mind being a little more lucid? I don't really seem to know what you are talking about."

"That's because it's so horrid," said Terry in a drooping voice. "It's easy enough to say things when they're nice, but the horrid ones seem to get all tangled up."

"I've noticed that. You had better try and disentangle them."

"I am trying. The trouble is that there's a bit at the beginning I don't want to tell anyone ever—" she saw a small, vivid picture in her own mind of Norah Margesson under the hall lamp with Emily's pearls in her hands—"and there's a bit at the end that I don't want to tell anyone till Tuesday, so I have to begin right in the middle, and that's what makes it difficult."

"I can see that. Well, suppose you begin wherever you want to and tell me as much as you can."

Terry nodded.

"Yes. I woke up in the night—"

"Last night?"

"Yes. I woke up and I couldn't go to sleep again, so I went and looked out of the window. It must have been somewhere round about two, because a clock struck afterwards. And I looked out of the window, and I saw something."

Mr. Ridgefield looked at her curiously.

"What did you see?"

Terry flashed him a glance.

"That's what I'm not telling—not to anyone—not till Tuesday."

"Dear me," said Mr. Ridgefield. "Not very lucid—are you? I suppose you couldn't make it all a little clearer?"

Terry blinked fiercely. You can't drive a car and cry at the same time. Anyhow, what was there to cry about? She didn't know, but it would have been very comforting to weep on a kind shoulder. She said despising things to herself and blinked again.

"That was the plan," she said. "You see, I saw something—out of the window—and I thought if I told everyone, then the person who had taken the picture would know that I knew, and if the picture came back, I wouldn't say anything ever, but if it didn't come back, then I should have to go to the police on Tuesday."

"Tuesday?"

"Tuesday."

"Day after tomorrow?"

"Day after tomorrow."

"Really—my dear child! May one ask why day after tomorrow?"

"To give the person who took the picture the chance of sending it back."

Mr. Ridgefield gazed with astonishment.

"Terry—are you serious?"

"Oh *yes*," said Terry, in a tone of heartfelt unhappiness.

"You really saw something?"

"I really saw something."

Mr. Ridgefield assumed a brisk matter-of-fact tone.

"Well, my dear, what did you see?"

Terry shook her head.

"I can't tell anyone—not till Tuesday. You see, it wouldn't be fair, because I've told them all I wouldn't."

"You have told them all?"

"Yes—Emily, Norah, Mrs. Yorke, Fabian, and Mr. Applegarth."

"But, my dear child, this is monstrous! It amounts to saying that one of these people took the picture."

"Someone did."

"A burglar, my dear. The police said at once it was an outside job."

Terry shook her head.

"No."

Mr. Ridgefield leaned back in his corner. He said coldly, "I find all this a little fantastic—a little, shall we say, hysterical. If you really think you saw something you should make a statement to the police. They might, or might not, attach importance to it. If you would honour me with your confidence, I should feel better able to advise you."

Terry choked down a sob.

"Oh, Uncle Basil, I can't!"

CHAPTER XVI

AT half past twelve on Sunday night Colonel Garrett switched out his bedside light, put his head on his pillow, and prepared to plunge into the deep, unbroken slumber which would last until seven o'clock on Monday morning. But scarcely had he closed his eyes, when the telephone bell rang.

Garrett looked forward to a period of retirement in which the telephone would ring itself black in the face and he could tell it to go to blazes. That time had not yet arrived. He flung back the bed-clothes, snapped on the light, and padded barefoot across the hall into the glorified cupboard which he called his study. It had a loud-patterned linoleum on the floor, and contained an office chair, an office table, and the telephone.

The bell rang again as he came in and slammed the door. Garrett scowled at it, jammed the receiver against his ear, and barked "Hullo!"

A voice from the grave answered him. It said,

"Needless to ask if it is you, *cher maître*."

Garrett stared. Both voice and language belonged to Peter Talbot who had been buried three days ago in Brussels. Fanny Talbot had sent a wreath, Garrett himself had sent a wreath. Fanny Talbot had with difficulty been dissuaded from going to the funeral. Her solicitor had attended instead.

"Who's that?" said Garrett in a voice with a very sharp edge to it.

The voice of Mr. Peter Talbot sounded pained.

"Is this the way to receive a call from the Other Side? A little decent joy is indicated, *cher maître*."

The gritting of Garrett's teeth was plainly audible. He rapped out an unparliamentary word.

"If you're Peter Talbot you've got something to explain."

"Oh, no, we never mention him, his name is never heard, our lips are now forbidden to speak that once familiar word. But you are quite right, I have lots to explain. Can I come along and do it?"

"Now?" said Garrett.

"I am afraid so. I'd like my beauty-sleep too, but I really think we'll both have to cut it out. You see, I'm not in a position to come and see you by day."

Garrett scowled again.

"All right, come along. I'll let you in."

He went back to his room and put on a luridly checked coat over his pink and orange striped pyjamas.

It was exactly seven minutes before the knock he was waiting for fell gently on the outer door of the flat. He opened it with a jerk, and saw Peter Talbot with a soft black hat on his head and a voluminous dark muffler about his neck. He was unwinding it as he stepped inside the hall. He slipped out of a Burberry, took off his hat with a flourish, and said,

"Well, well, it isn't every day you get me back from the grave—is it?"

Garrett had closed the door—gently for once.

"What have you been up to?" he growled.

"What have I not been up to! Produce a drink and a decent chair and you shall hear all. Honestly, Frank, it's about time somebody did hear all, because I'm beginning to have a horrid suspicion that the people who are running this show have cast me for the part of a scapegoat. I don't know, you know, but there's just the horrid possibility, so I took a risk and rang you up."

Garrett gave him a hard, frowning look, turned his back,

and marched into the sitting room, where he threw a log on a fire that still had some life in it and produced the required drink. The chairs were shabby but comfortable. The room smelt of books and shag and wood smoke.

Garrett got out a frightful old pipe and lighted it. Then he shot his first question at Peter.

"Whose funeral have you been getting away with?"

"Oh, Spike Reilly's. I hope you sent a wreath."

Garrett glowered.

"Your Aunt Fanny did. Fanny is a good deal more cut up than you deserve."

"Yes—I'm sorry about that. But think how she'll enjoy getting me back. Now listen. You got my letter saying I was just moving over to Spike Reilly's pub?"

"Yes, I got it."

"Well, I went there, and I got the room next to his. And there he was, in a high fever, delirious and obviously going to peg out. I told the people in the hotel to get him a doctor, and then I went through his things. Well, I found the cipher he was using and his last lot of instructions. He was to go to England. Well, the more I thought about it, the more I felt like taking his place. He talked all the time, and said some funny things. And then he died before any doctor came, and I swopped his papers with mine and came over here as Spike Reilly."

"A bit of a risk," said Garrett with a lift of the eyebrows.

"So so. But he was working under orders from a king-pin over here. Hadn't ever seen him—didn't know who he was. That came out from what he said. He'd no end of a grouse on about only being used as a postman and not getting enough pay. He seemed to think the king-pin was making the hell of a lot of money, and he wanted a better rake-off for himself. The instructions I got hold of promised him better pay and bonuses, and they told him to go to Preedo's Library on Friday at twelve noon and wait for a telephone call. You got my note about that?"

Garrett nodded.

"Yes—passed it to Scotland Yard. Their pigeon. They couldn't trace any likely call."

Peter grinned.

"There wasn't one. They're leery, you know. I had to tell the woman at the desk I was expecting a call and give her my name, and she told me to sit down and wait. Well, there was an old boy next to me, all beard and eyebrows. He dropped a book—I picked it up. And what was it? *Her Great Romance*, no less. And that was the book Spike Reilly had for decoding his instructions. Boy—did I jump! I gave it back to him, and he said it wasn't any good and he was changing it, and he trickled up to the desk, palavered there for a bit, and then went out of the shop. And I picked up the book he had left in his chair and hared after him, but there wasn't a sign. I came back, and they didn't know anything about him—said he'd only been asking about subscription rates. So there I was, with a thing called *The Corpse in the Copper*, and a new lot of instructions inside it."

Peter continued his story, brought it down to Saturday night, and gave a lively and detailed account of the doings at Heathacres.

Garrett snapped out an occasional question, but sat for the most part in silence, not smoking, but with his pipe sometimes in his hand, sometimes clenched between strong, discoloured teeth. When Peter had finished, the gimlet eyes took a prodding glance at him.

"A nice mess of hot water you've got yourself into, I must say."

"Out of the frying-pan into the fire, *and* a pretty kettle of fish," responded Peter affably. "And whilst we are playing proverbs, here's another—'A burnt child dreads the fire.' Which is why I'm here."

Colonel Garrett scowled and said bitterly,

"You got buried under a false death certificate, you travelled on a fraudulent passport, you've been a receiver of stolen pearls, and you are actually at this moment in possession of a burgled picture which has entirely destroyed the week-end repose of Scotland Yard."

Peter smiled engagingly.

"All with the best of motives, *cher maître*."

"And if you call me that again, I'll throw you to them!"

"Well, it makes quite a good password, don't you think? None genuine without this label. So look out for it if I have to call you up. I've a feeling we'll do better without names." His voice took a sudden serious tone. "You know, Frank, there's something uncommon nasty about this. If you don't mind listening to what may be pure fancy on my part, I'd rather like to tell you what I think."

"Go ahead," growled Garrett.

Peter took out a pocket-book, opened it, and extracted Mr. Spike Reilly's passport. He handed it to Garrett and said,

"Just take a look at the visas, will you—the last three. I came over on Thursday, so that one's mine. But Spike Reilly was over here on his own passport the week before, and he went back to Belgium via France last Sunday, which was when I picked him up. Now Solly Oppenstein's picture was attempted, and Solly Oppenstein's butler was shot, on that Saturday night. I'm not saying that Spike Reilly started to lift the picture or shot the butler—I don't think he did. All his complaint when he was delirious was that they only used him as a postman, and that he didn't get paid enough. I think I'm prepared to say that I'm certain he hadn't any active part in the Oppenstein affair. But he was in England at the time—I think you will find he hadn't got an alibi for the time. I've got an idea that the reason he was over here was because someone thought he would do nicely for a scapegoat if anything went wrong. Or he may have come over on his postman's job just in the ordinary way of business, and the scapegoat idea may have cropped up later when something *had* gone wrong and they found themselves with a murder on their hands. How does that seem to you?"

Garrett's face was frowningly intent. He jerked a hand and said,

"Possible. Anything's possible in crime. Any more?"

Peter said, "Lots." He laughed, reached for his drink, and finished it. "When I was waiting for the show to begin at Heathacres I had the nasty thought that, Spike Reilly being no more, I was now public scapegoat number one. If I had really been a criminal I should have legged it back to my car and gone away in a hurry, because what hit me right between the eyes was this. Here was the whole country humming over the Oppenstein business—was it sense to stage another picture theft so soon, knowing as they must know perfectly well that to be found out, or even to be suspected over the Cresswell affair must mean being involved right up to the neck in the Oppenstein murder. And right there I began to see a lot of horrid cold daylight. Spike Reilly was in England when Solly Oppenstein's butler was shot. If Spike Reilly was pinched a week later with another valuable picture in the boot of his car, don't you think it would be apt to result in Mr. Reilly standing his trial for murder? Mind you, he couldn't give anyone away, because he didn't know who he was working for—that came out quite clearly. He was all set to do a spot of mole work and find out. Now what do you think of that?''

Garrett gave a sardonic grin.

''That you'd better shift Cresswell's Turner out of the boot of your car.''

''Lord! Is it a Turner? I call that doing things in style!''

''Yes, it's a Turner, and Cresswell's hopping mad. Now you'd better listen to me. What do you know about the Cresswells and their week-end party?''

Peter said, ''Nothing.'' And then, ''The woman who gave me the pearls was called Norah. She thought I was someone called Jimmy. The other girl was quite young—seventeen, eighteen, nineteen—something like that. That's all I know.''

''All right, then you can sit up and listen. James Cresswell has pots of money. He collects pictures and bullies his wife—name of Emily—quiet, nice woman—don't drink, paint, flirt, or think. Guests in the house on Saturday night. Joseph Applegarth—old family friend—even more money that Cresswell—Yorkshire—bachelor—hearty—no known vices. Mrs. Yorke—Christian name Pearla—late husband rather indistinct army officer—good-looker—small income—rich friends. Miss Norah Margesson—not as young as she was, and not as well off as she'd like to be. I suppose she couldn't keep her hands off Emily Cresswell's pearls, but it don't sound to me as if she would be in on the picture racket. But you can't tell. The Jimmy she took you for was probably one Jimmy Duluth, at present lying in Guildford hospital with a broken leg. Ran head on into a bus at eleven o'clock on Saturday night, having drink taken, which accounts for his not keeping his date with Miss Margesson. They've been about a good deal together. To continue. Remaining guests. Basil Ridgefield—elderly gentleman with pretty ward and what is said to be the finest stamp collection in the world. Ward's name Terry Clive, short for Theresa—nice kid, just out—''

Peter leaned forward.

''No! Not really!''

Garrett glared.

''How do you mean, not really?''

''Because it's too odd. Aunt Fanny's last letter was all about this Terry Clive.''

''Yes. Fanny knows her—swears by her. So does Fabian Roxley. Well, he's the last guest. He's by way of being my secretary—lazy young devil, but brains. I got all this dope from him. He's been dining with me. Well, that's the house-party. Now spot the criminal. Fabian's beat. I'm beat. But of course you'll have us both beat.''

''I don't know.'' Peter got up and stood with his back to the fire. ''All I know is, someone came out of the glass door and faked a burglarious entry.''

Garrett's frown became alarming.

''You're sure of that?''

''Absolutely.''

''In the dark?''

''It wasn't dark. Full moon behind a bank of clouds, which is a very different thing. When I first got there it was clear moonlight. I'd recognize the Norah woman and Terry Clive anywhere. But when it came to the picture business best part of an hour later, there was a great deal of thick cloud and visibility was bad—no detail, no features—nothing to recognize anyone by—just a black figure moving in a thick dusk. But whoever it was certainly came out of the glass door—I'll swear to that—and went to the window on the left and cut a pane out of it, and went back through the door into the house and shut the door again. I'll swear to the whole of that."

Garrett jumped up from his chair and began to walk about in the room with a short, jerky stride.

"What's the good of that if you can't say who it was? Was it a man or a woman?"

"I don't know," said Peter slowly. "I thought of it as a man, but he must have had a long coat or a dressing-gown—and it might have been a woman quite easily."

"Height?" snapped Garrett.

Peter stretched an arm along the mantlepiece.

"Nothing to go by," he said despondently. "It might have been someone tall with a stoop, or it might have been someone just ordinary. Heights are very misleading in a strange place with bad visibility. No, I shouldn't like to say. But look here—what about the servants? Isn't it much more likely that somebody should have been planted in the house? Isn't that the way these things are done?"

"This one wasn't. At least it doesn't look as if it was." Garrett glared suddenly. "You know, you're damned inconvenient, Peter—you and Miss Terry Clive. Here's the police and everyone else quite sure it was an outside job, and you two come along and upset the apple-cart."

Peter laughed.

"My dear Frank, the only way it could have been an outside job would be for me to have done it, and I'm afraid you must just accept my word that I didn't."

Garrett showed his terrier teeth in an angry grin.

"You only went off with the swag."

"Exactly," said Peter. "But what's this about Terry Clive? What did she say?"

In a dangerous voice Colonel Garrett explained the position of Miss Terry Clive as reported by Fabian Roxley.

"She says it wasn't an outside job. She says it wasn't the servants. She says she looked out of the window and saw something. She says she won't say what she saw—not until day after tomorrow, which is Tuesday. She says this is to give the thief a chance to return the picture."

"I expect she saw the same as I did," said Peter cheerfully. "She must have done. Her window was over the one that was burgled. I saw her looking out of it earlier on—a nice romantic scene. But why does she say it wasn't one of the servants?"

"The cook's too fat. The man's left-handed. And the other three sleep out." Garrett's tone was one of wrath and gloom.

"Then," said Peter equably, "it was either Mrs. Cresswell, Mr. Cresswell, Mrs. Yorke, Miss Margesson, Mr. Applegarth, Mr. Ridgefield, Fabian Roxley, or Terry Clive."

CHAPTER XVII

"ANYHOW it's none of my business," said Garrett explosively. "Burglaries and murders and picture thieves, they've none of them got anything to do with me." He thrust with the heel of his slipper at the smouldering log. A sliver caught and went up in a shower of sparks. "You said this man Reilly talked. What did he say?"

Peter was reminded of a terrier who has been called to heel and sneaks back to have another smell at the forbidden rat hole. Frank knew he was poaching—had known it all along—but he couldn't for the life of him help nosing a trail.

"What did the fellow say?" growled Garrett.

Peter shut his eyes for a moment. He was calling up the shabby, frowsy room; the tumbled bed; the muttered delirium of the dying man—words that ran into one another and made no sense, sentences which came tumbling out; and then that low incoherent muttering again. He said,

"Wait a minute—get a pencil and paper and write it down."

"I'm getting it."

"There's not much."

Garrett crossed the room, came back, and said,

"Carry on."

Peter spoke—quite low, so as not to disturb the picture or drown that muttering voice.

"He was pretty far gone. It was this sort of thing—'The money's not enough.' He kept on saying that, and that they told him there wasn't any risk but he didn't believe it. He said, 'You're telling me—and perhaps there's something I can tell. I said I'd find out who you were—didn't I? And I will. And when I do, you'll have to pay me more than a postman's wages. And if you think I can't find out, why, then you can think again.'" Peter gave out the words slowly, a few at a time, and heard the scribble of a hard-driven pencil. He went on. "Then he said, 'I know—I know.' And then, 'Maud Millicent.'"

Garrett said, "Good Lord!" in a voice exactly like the terrier's bark.

Peter put up a hand.

"Go on—get it down. 'Maud Millicent,' and, 'What have you got to say to that? Maud Millicent Simpson. What have you got to say to that? If I could find her, I could find you—and I'm going to find you.' And then he broke off and wanted to know what he'd been saying, and wanted me to get him brandy. And that's about all."

He looked round and saw Garrett's eyes like points of steel.

"Maud Millicent Simpson. He said that? You're sure?"

"Quite sure. Why?"

"Because," sald Garrett grimly, "if she's in this, I'm in it too."

The terrier had caught sight of his rat, and there was no holding him. Peter felt just a little sorry for the rat. He thought he would hate to have Garrett on his trail. He asked with some curiosity,

"Who is the lady—an old flame?"

Garrett used a regrettable expression about Maud Millicent Simpson.

"She's beaten me twice, and I suppose she thinks she can do it again."

"Who is she?"

Garrett showed his teeth.

"Maud Millicent Deane—that's how she started—parson's daughter, and the cleverest criminal alive. She worked with the Vulture, and when we got him, she carried on with what was left of the organization. She married first a bloke called Simpson, and then that gasbag Bernard Mannister. Took her brother's place as his secretary, and took everyone in. Used Mannister as a catspaw. Ran a blackmailing racket, with herself in the middle of it as a medium—called herself Asphodel. That was the Denny affair.[1] You won't remember it."

"Yes, I do," he said—"vaguely."

"She got away that time by the skin of her teeth. Then she cropped up again, impersonating Henry Postlethwaite.[2] He's a distinguished professor. She went to him as his secretary, managed to isolate him from his family, and was caught out on the edge of murdering him and a niece. Well, she got away that time too. If she's in this business, she won't get away again if I can help it. But if she's in it, you're up against something—all of us are. She can write any hand, use any voice, impersonate a dozen different types. In these two affairs I've been telling you about she passed unquestioned as Mannister's secretary, a correct and colourless young man—as Asphodel, an exotic type of medium—as Della Delorne, an ex-chorus girl—as Miss Cannock, an old maid secretary—and as Henry Postlethwaite himself. Nobody suspected her in any of these roles. Whatever part she's playing now, nobody's suspecting her—you may take that for gospel. She's a damned sight too clever."

"How old is she?" said Peter.

Garrett shook himself.

"Thirty-eight—thirty-nine—something like that. Mannister died a couple of years ago, so she's a widow again. You're sure Spike Reilly said Maud Millicent Simpson?"

"Absolutely certain. He'd got a letter about her too."

"*What!*" Garrett fairly shouted the word. "Why didn't you say so?"

"*Cher maître*, I am saying so. Anyhow it was in his

[1] *Walk with Care, by Patricia Wentworth.*
[2] *Dead or Alive, by Patricia Wentworth.*

pocket-book, and in case you're interested, here it is." He extracted two flimsy sheets and passed them over.

Garrett glared at him and at them, snorted, read at a furious rate, and then turned back again to the beginning.

"Who the devil's Louie?"

"I'm afraid I can't help you."

Garrett made the sound which is usually written "Pshaw!"

"What's the good of educating the masses? Here's a woman who's had some sort of an education, probably at the country's expense—doesn't put her address, doesn't put a date, and she signs herself Louie!"

Peter chuckled.

"She didn't know that the Foreign Office was going to be interested. The late Spike obviously knew her surname, and where she lived."

"Then I wish he could change places with you," said Garrett brutally.

Peter burst out laughing.

"My dear Frank, you overwhelm me—a little more than kin and less than kind, and blood's thicker than water, and all that! In fact a live Spike Reilly is what you want, and if you could consign me to his cemetery and have him here instead, it would be O.K. by you."

Garrett actually betrayed an irritable but distinctly human feeling.

"Don't be more of a damned fool than you can help," he growled. He banged the sheets with his fist. "Don't you see, this woman knew Maud Millicent sixteen years ago or so when she was married to Simpson. She knew her then, and she knows her now. Whenever this letter was written, it wasn't more than a week or two ago. The ink's quite fresh, the creases in the paper are quite fresh. It mayn't have been written more than a few days ago. And I'm prepared to eat my boots if Maud Millicent Simpson isn't behind this picture racket and the whole bag of tricks. They're tricks she's used before, and there's nothing she don't know about them. Intrigue, blackmail, murder—she's used them all. And here we've got someone who knows Maud Millicent—

knows *who* she is and *where* she is—and we've got to find her."

Peter lifted a hand and let it fall again.

"Well, you can always try. A pity I'm not Spike Reilly—he knew."

Garrett kicked the log again viciously. This time it broke into a blaze and scorched his coat. A reek of burning wool joined the shag and the smell of leather.

"What did he want to die for when he might have been useful?"

Peter laughed.

"You know, I very gravely doubt whether he had any urge to be useful—especially to you. He was all set for a little quiet blackmail, I think. And in any case if he was alive instead of me, he wouldn't be sitting here talking to you, and you wouldn't know that he'd ever heard of Maud Millicent Simpson."

Garrett gave his short barking laugh.

"Well, that's true enough."

"And now," said Peter, straightening up and taking his arm from the mantelpiece—"now, Frank, what do I do next? There's a stolen Turner in my car. What about it? Do I turn it over to the police and tell them what I know, or do I go on standing in with my criminal employers in the hope of finding out who they are?"

Garrett said, "You go on standing in."

"And if I'm arrested with the Turner on me—what happens then? For all I know, it may be part of the plan to have me arrested and put the Oppenstein murder on me too."

Garrett shook his head.

"You're all right about that—you weren't in England."

"True, *cher maître*. The real Sherlock touch! You know, I keep on forgetting I'm not Spike Reilly—and he would have been for it, because he *was* in England."

"Of course I could tell them about you at the Yard," said Garrett in a reluctant voice.

Peter turned a determined face on him.

"No, you don't, Frank! You don't tell anyone, or I'm off. The job's quite dangerous enough without making it any worse. You don't know, and I don't know who it is we're up against, and if a whisper of what I'm doing gets to him, or to her, or to them, well, I'd be for it. You wouldn't get stung for a wreath this time. No fuss, no flowers, no drums, no funeral notes—just a particularly inconspicuous grave, or perhaps not even that. An unknown body fished up out of the Thames a good deal the worse for wear. Somehow I don't fancy it, and if you're going to open your mouth to a single solitary soul, I'm off."

Garrett looked at him in silence. For once his face was expressionless. Then he said,

"Mean that literally?"

"Quite."

"Roxley saw your letters."

"Both of them?"

Garrett jerked his head in an affirmative nod.

Peter tried to remember what he had said. In the first letter he had spoken of Spike Reilly and said he was following him to his pub. In the second, the short note written after he had changed passports, he had said to watch Preedo's Library on the Friday morning, and—"I shall be there." But Roxley wouldn't have expected him to be there, because Roxley must have been told that Peter Talbot was dead. Roxley must have believed that Peter Talbot was dead. Roxley must go on believing that. Everyone must go on believing that. He said in a decided voice,

"Roxley's got to think I'm dead. You're certainly not to tell Roxley."

"Why, you damned young fool, he's my secretary. What have you got in your head?"

"Your own list of suspects," said Peter coolly. He proceeded to recite the list in a perfectly level voice. "James Cresswell, Emily Cresswell, Joseph Applegarth, Mrs. Yorke, Norah Margesson, Terry Clive, and Fabian Roxley."

CHAPTER XVIII

AT ten o'clock on Monday morning Miss Blanche Hollinger opened her front door and stood for a moment looking up at the sky. Was it going to rain, or was it not? And if it was going to rain, would she have time to go round the corner to that nice flower shop and get back before the rain began? Or would it be better to take an umbrella? She had on her second-best shoes, quite stout with laces—they would not matter. And her black cloth coat was no longer new, but the fur collar would get damp, and when it was damp the worn places looked a great deal worse than they really were. And then of course a hat, however old, was not improved by a shower.

Miss Hollinger's hat was a summer hat which she was wearing out. With care it might do for rainy days in the spring. It was black like her coat, with a straw crown and a brim of alternate bands of ribbon and straw. There was a round paste ornament on the right-hand side, and a bunch of mixed clover on the left. The clover had an extremely fatigued appearance, but Miss Hollinger thought it did very well. She had a scarf which combined the clover colours about her neck, and she thought the effect highly successful.

She was of middle height and rather indeterminate colouring. Her hair might once have been brown and have lost its colour preparatory to turning grey, or it might from childhood have straggled about her neck in these same mouse-coloured wisps. She did her best with a crimp, with pins, with combs, and a controlling net, but odd pieces and ends were prone to escape, and even in church Miss Hollinger could be seen adjusting them. In feature she was as indeterminate as in colouring. Her expression was mild and hesitant. Her eyes peered through slightly tinted glasses.

Perhaps the glasses made the sky seem greyer than it really was. She went back into the house and came out with her umbrella on her wrist and an old drab raincoat over her arm.

In the flower shop she asked the price of everything.

"I want a few flowers for a friend—a bereaved friend. Those lovely roses now. . . . Oh, no, I'm afraid—not six shillings a dozen, much as I should like to. Orchids would not be suitable—and of course very expensive. But what about those beautiful carnations? . . . Six-pence each! Oh well, I am afraid—you see it would take so many to make a bunch. Now those are really very beautiful chrysanthemums. . . . Oh, yes, of course—specimen blooms, and perhaps not really appropriate—in the circumstances. I think perhaps something simpler—just a simple bunch. Now what about these?"

"Those are two shillings, madam—all except the pink ones."

Miss Hollinger put her head on one side and peered at a slightly dashed bunch of magenta chrysanthemums.

"And these?"

"Ninepence, madam. As you see, they are not quite fresh."

Miss Hollinger beamed.

"I will take them. I am sure they are very nice—very nice indeed—just what I wanted—such a sweet shade."

It was not raining when she came out of the shop. She might have left her umbrella at home. She had a way of walking as if she might trip over her bunchy skirt. She tittuped back past her own door and ascended the steps of the next house, where she rang the bell. The elderly maid who answered the door stood aside for her to enter, but she shook her head.

"I am afraid not, Miller—not this morning. I have to go and see a friend. Perhaps this afternoon—but better not tell her in case I am prevented. My friend is coming to town on purpose to see me, and I do not yet know her plans. But how is dear Miss Talbot today? I could not go out without enquiring and bringing these few flowers. With my love please, Miller, and if I can come in later I will. And how did you say she was?"

Miller's large, pleasant face was unresponsive. "She don't give you time to say nothing, and that's the truth." She took the flowers, sized them up as left-overs, and said,

"Miss Talbot is about the same."

Miss Hollinger coughed sympathetically.

"Ah, yes—a heavy blow. We must do all we can. And you will give her my love, and—oh, yes, I shall make a point of looking in later on if I can possibly manage it."

CHAPTER XIX

WHILST Miss Hollinger was buying flowers and enquiring after his aunt, Peter Talbot was engaged in the unsatifactory occupation of kicking his heels. At ten o'clock he did not feel like kicking them in the hotel any longer, so he walked round to the garage and kicked them there. There are always things that you can do to a car. He did some of them, and felt better, until the fact that he was practically within touching distance of a stolen Turner which the whole of Scotland Yard was looking for began to bore its way painfully into his consciousness. By about a quarter to eleven he was beginning to get hot behind the ears every time anyone looked his side of the garage. He decided to knock off before he got to the point of falling upon the nearest mechanic's neck and proclaiming his guilt.

He walked back to the hotel, and wondered when he would get any more instructions, and what they were likely to be. If he could have guessed, then it is on the cards that he would have gone round to Colonel Garrett and thrown in his hand. But he didn't know, and he didn't guess, so he walked up the steps and into the hall of the hotel in a bored but not particularly apprehensive frame of mind.

The hall was the sort of hall which is made by throwing a small front sitting-room into the original passage entrance of a London house. The office was in the back sitting-room, with a sliding glass shutter behind which sat a bored sallow girl who used a magenta lipstick.

Peter stood just inside the door, and beheld his Aunt Fanny's bosom friend Miss Hollinger in converse with the bored sallow girl. He was petrified with horror. What in the name of all that was improbable could Blanche Hollinger be doing at the Edenbridge Hotel? She lived next door to Aunt Fanny, so she couldn't possibly be wanting to book a room, and if she wasn't booking a room, what was she doing? Yes, that was it—*what was she doing?* Was it a case of "Fly—all is discovered," or was it not? His immediate impulse was to fly. But if he flew or, alternatively, fled, how was he to find out whether flight was a necessity or merely a chucking up of the sponge?

Besides, *was* he absolutely sure that it was the Hollinger? They had only met once, and then in semi-darkness. If he had encountered her face to face in the street he would probably have passed her by, but this back view was just what he had seen on more than one occasion when he had lurked behind Aunt Fanny's drawing-room curtains and beheld Miss Hollinger trip down the next-door steps. He couldn't, of course, have sworn to her features, but he could have sworn to that battered hat, and that ghastly bunch of clover, and the scarf with its drabbled shades of cyclamen and fuchsia. The voice too. No one who had ever heard that voice would forget it—rather high, with a faintly tinny sound and just the suspicion of a lisp. And the flow of words. Oh, it was certainly the Hollinger, and as certainly he meant to find out what had brought her to his hotel.

The thoughts passed in a flash. Her back was towards him. He reached a chair on the right of the door, snatched up somebody's discarded newspaper, and spread it widely between him and danger.

The bored damsel said in an extinguished voice,

"I couldn't say, I'm sure."

Miss Hollinger was brightly insistent.

"But my friend intended to come here—I am quite sure of it. I think you had a Mr. Vincent staying here some time ago. It may have been a year or two ago—I am not quite sure on that point."

"I couldn't say, I'm sure," said the damsel at the desk.

"Not that it matters," pursued Miss Hollinger. "But he was a friend of the nephew of a great friend of mine—not the friend I am enquiring about—oh, no, quite a different person—a Miss Talbot."

Peter groaned behind his paper. He had come to the Edenbridge because he remembered that Vincent had stayed there. It appeared that the Hollinger was here for the same reason.

She went on explaining herself.

"So I wrote to my friend—not Miss Talbot, but the friend I was expecting to find here—and told her she could not do better than book a room at the Edenbridge Hotel—because I am sure any recommendation of my dear friend Miss Talbot's. . . . And so then she wrote and said she would—"

The damsel gazed at her magenta finger-nails.

"We have no one of that name."

Miss Hollinger became a trifle flustered.

"I can't understand it at all. The name is Clephane—rather unusual—Scotch, I believe. Perhaps if I might just look at the register—"

A perfectly awful stab of apprehension went right through Peter. He knew his Aunt Fanny's fatal habit of handing round letters. How many of his letters had she handed on to her dear friend Blanche Hollinger, and would dearest Blanche be sufficiently familiar with his writing to recognize it when she saw it in the Edenbridge register? There wouldn't be much to go on. James Reilly—British; and, for his last address, Brussels. It was the Brussels that might give him away—he had written to Fanny Talbot from Brussels. His conscience made a coward of him. Of all the ignominious ways of being caught out! And then he was blessing the sallow girl in his heart because she wasn't making any move to hand over the register.

"There's no name like that in the book, and no correspondence from anyone of that name."

"I can't understand it at all," said Miss Hollinger in a

distressed voice. "I certainly understood—in fact I made quite sure. I really should be obliged if you would let me look for myself."

The girl threw her an exasperated glance.

"I'm sorry, but there's no one of that name in the hotel."

Miss Hollinger drooped and turned away. As she passed him, Peter could hear her making small distressed sounds and murmuring, "Oh dear, I can't understand it at all."

He went thankfully up to his room and waited to see what would happen next. Something was certainly due to happen. You don't just steal a Turner and leave it at that. You have to dispose of the corpse. Perhaps someone would come and remove it from the car without dragging him any farther in. Perhaps they wouldn't. . . .

Peter sat in one of those rigidly uncomfortable chairs of which hotels appear to have the monopoly and read the two newspapers he had brought in with him and the one he had picked up downstairs. They all had large headlines about the theft of the Turner. Two of them said the police were following up a clue, and the third believed an arrest was expected at any moment. That, of course, made pleasant reading. All three linked the theft of the Turner with the attempted theft of Mr. Oppenstein's Gainsborough and the murder of his butler, Francis Bird. One headline said, "Two crimes in a week," and proceeded further to enquire what the police were doing.

The most enterprising of the three papers had photographs of the Cresswells and their guests. Peter studied them with considerable interest. James Cresswell—a frowning snapshot, curiously balanced by Emily in a tiara which had slipped a little to one side. Joseph Applegarth—unjustly rendered rather smug in a top hat and a morning coat, assumed possibly for a funeral, as he had a dark waistcoat and wore no buttonhole. Miss Norah Margesson in tweeds. The lovely Mrs. Yorke in evening dress. Fabian Roxley in flannels with a tennis-racket. Mr. Basil Ridgefield, slim and monocled, coming out of his own front door with his ward Miss Terry Clive behind him. Well, one of these people had cut the Turner from its frame and handed it to him out of the drawing-room window, having first smashed a pane so as to make it look like an outside job. The question was, which of them?

Speaking offhand, the ones he didn't cotton to were James Cresswell and Norah Margesson. And Norah Margesson had certainly taken the pearls. He looked at Terry Clive, and thought she might be counted out. The snapshot had caught her with rather a jolly smile. She looked cheerful, honest, and—rather as an afterthought—pretty. He found it comic to remember how she had scolded him in the moonlight, with a coat flapping open over her nightgown and a bare foot stamping on the bare, damp stone. A nice kid and a plucky one. He thought he would like to see her again, and thought he'd be lucky if they didn't meet when he was in the dock and she in the witness-box.

Well, it was all very amusing—or at least it would be amusing if his criminal associates would get a move on. He was beginning to be bored by his own society.

He thought it was about time something happened.

CHAPTER XX

THERE was a knock on the door. Alfred, the page, put his head round it without waiting for an answer. A sharp-faced boy who looked ten and was actually nearly seventeen.

"Please, sir, Miss Louisa Spedding to see you—your sister, sir—leastways your half-sister, she says."

Peter had never received such a facer in all his life before. Anyone to see him would have been bad enough—any Miss Spedding worse. But a Miss Spedding who was obviously the Louie of the letter and Spike Reilly's half-sister was purely horrific. He had at the most a few seconds in which to make up his mind what to do. He might bribe Alfred to say that he was out—one doesn't always want to see one's female relations. It was worth trying. He produced half a crown, pressed it into a willing palm, and said,

"I'm out. You've just seen me go, and what's more, you don't know when I'm going to be back."

"Yes, sir—thank you very much, sir." He pocketed the half-crown and glanced over his shoulder. "It's not go, sir—she's a'coming along the passage now." He ducked beneath an arm in a bottle-green sleeve trimmed with fur, backed, and disappeared.

Peter had just time to reach the window and was looking

out of it before the owner of the arm completed her entrance and shut the door behind her. A bright, firm voice said,

"Well, Jimmy, aren't you going to say how-do-you-do? I hope you're glad to see me."

There was no help for it. Pewter turned round. He only hope she wouldn't scream.

Miss Spedding, in appearance, was not the screaming sort. She was a plump woman with firm red cheeks, rather prominent brown eyes, and a solid chin. She had on a bottle-green hat as well as a bottle-green coat. The coat fitted her as if she had been moulded into it. She wore black kid gloves stitched with white, and black laced shoes, and she carried a new black bag with a chromium-plated clasp. She stood just where she was, a yard inside the door, and said,

"Who are you? Where's Jimmy?"

"Well, I think perhaps you've made a mistake—" He got as far as that, and she interrupted him.

"Oh, no, I haven't. That's Jimmy's suit-case all right. Do you suppose I don't know it? And I want to know who you are, and I want to know where Jimmy is."

The game was up. If only the suit-case had been under the bed instead of right under her nose on the nearest chair—

He came forward and said in a lowered voice,

"Miss Spedding—I'm very sorry indeed—but I'm afraid I've got bad news for you."

She didn't move, but her eyes were on his face.

"What is it?"

He said, "Won't you sit down?"

"No. What is your news?"

He said, "I'm very sorry about it. Your brother—he was your brother, wasn't he?"

"My step-brother. Why do you say he *was?*"

"Because he was very ill when I came across him. I sent for a doctor, but he didn't get there in time."

She looked him straight in the face and said,

"Jimmy's dead?"

"I'm afraid so," said Peter.

Miss Spedding walked over to the bed and sat down. She opened her bag and took out a clean folded pocket-handkerchief, but having thus prepared for grief, she did not weep. She said "Oh dear!" once or twice, and then,

"I always said it would come to that, but he wouldn't listen—nobody ever does. Oh dear me—he was ever such a nice little boy, but he got into bad company."

She sat there, her firm rosy face distressed, her black gloved hands clasping the folded handkerchief.

Peter told her about coming to the Brussels hotel and finding Spike Reilly there.

"I did what I could for him—I really did."

Miss Spedding kept her eyes on his face. When he had finished she said,

"I've often thought he'd come to a bad end—prison, or something like that, you know. I daresay it's all for the best. Once you get into bad company it's not so easy to get out again."

Peter said, "No, it isn't." And then, "There was a letter from you among his things."

"Are you going to tell me you read it?"

"Well, I'm afraid I did. You see—"

"No, I don't, but I'm going to. And to start off with, I'd like to know who you are. You're passing under Jimmy's name, and that's his suit-case, so if you don't want me to send for the police you'd better make a clean breast of it all. And don't think you can take me in either, because I didn't bring up Jimmy Reilly without getting to know when anyone was telling lies. Now you tell me straight who you are and what you're up to! Are you a crook?"

"No, I'm not."

"Jimmy was. I suppose you know that?"

"Yes, I know that."

She nodded.

"You're a gentleman. Jimmy wasn't, though he fancied himself and looked down on me because I worked for my living. If you're not a crook, I suppose you're a detective or something like that."

Peter said, "Something like that."

He looked at her solid, distressed respectability and told her how he had changed passports with Spike Reilly and taken on his job. She listened, sitting there on the edge of the hotel bed, and as she listened, Peter became aware that she was believing what he said. When he had finished, she said "Oh dear me!" again. And then,

"You're doing a very dangerous thing, sir. I suppose you know that."

"I suppose I do," said Peter soberly.

"Jimmy worked with a lot of very dangerous people. He got into trouble when he was only nineteen and ran away to America, and he was in trouble there, and in prison too. And I never thought I'd be glad our mother was dead, but I was then. It wasn't from her side he got it, I'm sure. She and my father were cousins, so she married into her own name. And there's no one can say Speddings weren't respectable right as far back as you could go, but my father died when I was ten years old, and she married Cornelius Reilly within the year. And left a widow again six months later with Jimmy on the way. Oh, dear me—he was a beautiful baby. And she died before he went wrong."

"Miss Spedding," said Peter slowly, "do you know who they are—the people your brother worked for?"

"I know they're dangerous."

"I think you know more than that. You wrote a letter to your brother—I think it was about one of these people."

She said, "Oh, no, no!"

"I think it was. It was about a Mrs. Simpson whom you used to know, and you had met her again."

She got up. Her colour had faded a little.

"I haven't got anything to say about Mrs. Simpson. If you read my letter to Jimmy, you know that. I told him straight it wasn't any good his asking—and if I wouldn't tell him, do you suppose I'd tell you?"

"Well, I hope you will. You see, I know a good deal already. I know she was a Miss Deane—Miss Maud Millicent Deane. And she married Simpson, and that's when you knew her."

"There's no harm in knowing anyone," said Louisa

Spedding. "She was all right when I knew her." She stopped, looked at him uncertainly, and said in an altered voice, "What do you want me to say? Mr. Simpson died very sudden—people do die suddenly, don't they? People said things, but if there'd been anything wrong, there'd have been an inquest. I don't know what you're trying to make me say."

Peter knew. He said,

"Did you know her well? How well did you know her?"

She stared at him.

"I was cook in the house—they kept three. And I was there two years. There isn't much you don't know about someone you've lived with for two years. I won't say she wasn't always very pleasant."

"And you recognized her again at once?"

"Oh, I'd know her again anywhere."

"I don't know how you could be sure after so long."

"Well then, I could," said Miss Spedding. "There's something I'd always know her by."

"And that is?"

She shook her head with decision.

"Least said, soonest mended. I've kept out of a lot of trouble in my time by not talking, and I'm not going to do different now. And if you'll take my advice you'll go back to your right name and your right place, and not stir up a lot of trouble for yourself when there's no need." She turned towards the door.

"Miss Spedding," said Peter, "you say there's no need to stir up trouble. It's these people who are stirring it up, you know—theft, blackmail, murder. There was that poor chap of a butler at Mr. Oppenstein's—you must have seen about it in the papers—what harm had he done? Seen someone he might have recognized, and so they killed him. And so perhaps they'll kill someone else if they're allowed to go on. Do you think you've got a right to hold your tongue?"

She said, "Mrs. Simpson hasn't got anything to do with that." But she looked away and didn't meet his eye.

"Your brother thought she had."

Louisa Spedding turned again, and spoke sharply.

"What right have you got to say that?"

"I've got a right to say it because it's true. I told you he talked when he was dying."

"What did he say?"

"He said he could find out who it was he was working for. He wasn't talking to me, you must understand, but to this employer of his. He said, 'Maud Millicent Simpson—what do you say to that? If I can find out about her, I can find out about you,' and a lot more of that sort of thing. And he'd been asking you about her. I read your letter, you know. You can't really look me in the face and say you don't believe Maud Millicent Simpson is mixed up with this business."

Miss Spedding stood where she was. She made no attempt to look him in the face. After a minute she said in an unwilling voice,

"You're a gentleman—you haven't any call to meddle with all this. There are the police, aren't there? It's their work, and they're paid for it. What has it got to do with you?"

Peter put his hands in his pockets, jingled a coin or two, and smiled affably.

"My dear Miss Spedding, I don't like blackmail, and I hate murder."

She frowned suddenly and distressfully.

"Jimmy hadn't anything to do with murder," she said in a shaken tone.

"No, I don't think he had. But I think they meant to try and fix it on him."

"If I thought that—" said Louisa slowly. She came a step nearer. "What makes you say a thing like that?"

"Well, your brother was over here that week-end. Do you know why?"

"He was sent for."

"Do you know why he was sent for?"

She looked away.

"He didn't know himself. They made him come over, and they sent him back again. He didn't know why."

Peter jingled the money in his pocket.

"That's why. If the Oppenstein affair had gone right, they'd have sent him back—with the picture perhaps. If it went wrong, they could put the blame on him."

Miss Spedding's colour rose high.

"It's a good thing he's dead and out of it—and it would be a good thing if you were out of it too."

"I'm going to get them out of it first," said Peter in a cheerful and determined voice.

CHAPTER XXI

LOUISA Spedding stood there flushed and irresolute. She was afraid, but she was angry. She had not shed a tear for Jimmy Reilly, but there was a heavy weight on her heart. If it wasn't for *them*, he'd be alive and respectable—they might be keeping a little shop together the way she'd often planned it. And then murder—that wasn't right. They ought to be stopped. Perhaps this young man was the one to stop them. She said,

"What do you want to know?"

Peter laughed.

"More than you can tell me. But I expect you can tell me some of it. Look here, how did your brother come in contact with these people? Can you tell me that?"

"I'll tell you what I can. He met a man called Grey when he was in America. It wasn't his name of course. Jimmy never knew his real name." She stopped, looked at him very straight, and said, "If I tell you what I know, you've got to leave me out of it. I don't want any trouble. And it's no use the police coming round—they won't get a word out of me."

Peter nodded.

"They shan't worry you. I shan't say who told me."

He felt a strong excitement. Why didn't she get on with it—why didn't she speak?

She said, "All right, I'll tell you."

She went back to the bed and sat down. Her knees were shaking. There was a lot of wickedness in the world. Jimmy was dead. She had always tried to do her duty and live respectable. People who did murder had got to be stopped. Perhaps this young man would stop them—a real gentleman, and nice teeth when he smiled.

She got out her handkerchief again and wiped her forehead.

“This is gospel truth I'm telling you. Jimmy picked up with this man Grey. He wanted to get away from America because of something he'd done—”

“Do you know what it was?” said Peter.

An old-fashioned and unbecoming blush suffused Miss Spedding's face.

“It was one of those kidnapping cases. I don't know what I felt like when I heard about it. But there—it was the company he'd got into, and this Grey told nim there was easy money to be earned over here if he'd do as he was told and not ask questions, so Jimmy took it on. He was to go on the Continent and travel about, and he'd be told what he had to do, a bit at a time, in a cipher they had. Mostly it was posting letters. He didn't tell me what they were, but it was something to do with insurance companies.”

“Blackmail about the pictures—yes, that would be it. Go on,” said Peter.

“There were other things too, but they kept him pretty much in the dark. Sometimes he saw this Grey, but he didn't see anyone else.”

“Did anyone else see him?” said Peter. “That's what I want to know.”

“I don't think so,” said Louisa Spedding. “This Grey, he was the go-between. The ones who were behind it all, they kept themselves to themselves. They wouldn't want for anyone to be in the way of seeing them—only this Grey that they had to trust. And from what Jimmy said, they'd got such a hold over him that they *could* trust him.”

“Then it was only Grey who knew Spike—your brother—by sight?”

“That's right,” said Louisa Spedding. “And I'll tell you how I know about that in a minute. Well, this Grey got into a motor accident over in Austria, and he was so badly hurt that he died, and when he was sure he wasn't going to live he told Jimmy some things."

"What did he tell him?"

Louisa Spedding had her last moment of hesitation. Afterwards, when she had come out of the room and was walking down the stairs, she couldn't think what had come over her. She supposed it was Jimmy being dead that made her feel as if it didn't matter what she said, but she wished that she had held her tongue. Now, with Peter watching her, she let it run.

"He told Jimmy it was a woman who was running the whole thing, and there was a man in it too. He said the woman used to work for a very big crook called the Vulture, but he was dead now. He said he had worked for him too, and when this picture business began this woman sent for him to work under her. They didn't want more people in it than they could help, and Grey had to find them what they wanted."

"*They?*" said Peter sharply.

Louisa Spedding nodded.

"This woman, and the man who was working with her—"

Peter broke in.

"Who is he?"

"Jimmy didn't know. That was the great secret, because he was somebody high up that nobody would suspect. Grey told Jimmy that, and he said to watch out for him, because he'd tear anyone up as if they were a bit of old paper if he thought they were getting dangerous. But he said the woman was worse. He said she could get away with anything, and no one ever crossed her and came out of it alive. That's what he said."

Peter leaned forward. He could hardly hold his impatience.

"And he told your brother her name, Miss Spedding—he told him her name?"

"He said she'd got a dozen names, and she could look like a dozen people. And he said her own real given name was Maud Millicent, and he said that away back when he first knew her, her name was Simpson. And that's why Jimmy told me about her, because he remembered when I was in service with Mrs. Simpson, and he'd an idea he'd heard the whole of that name before—Maud Millicent Simpson. And I don't mind saying it gave me what you might call a fright, meeting her again on the top of all that. And if I'm to tell you what I think, it's this—you've got to be careful, because she's watching you. Why do you suppose I'm here this morning?"

"I've no idea," said Peter.

"Or how did I know where to find you?"

He laughed.

"Still no idea."

"Then I'll tell you. I was rung up on the telephone. I'm housekeeper at Sir John Morleigh's, and there's a telephone in the pantry. The butler said it was for me. And there was someone saying 'Miss Spedding' in a voice I could have sworn I'd never heard before—a kind of a silly giggling voice like a girl's. And it said, 'Your brother Jimmy's over again. I expect you'd like to see him.' So I said yes, I would, and she said, 'Hurry along and go this morning then, or you'll miss your chance, because he's going away again.' She gave me this address and rang off. So I left the kitchen-maid to do the lunch and came along."

Peter was leaning over the end of the bed. He straightened up now with a jerk and walked over to the window. The morning was turning to fog, but the misty street and the yellow-grey sky were somewhere away outside his consciousness—he looked at them, and he did not see them. His thoughts raced.

Someone had sent Louisa Spedding to see him. Why?

Someone had given her this address. Who knew it?

The last question answered itself first. Garrett knew it. But he didn't know where to find Louisa Spedding. At least he hadn't known between twelve and one o'clock last night.

His employers knew it. And there was the answer to his first question.

Garrett would have no motive for sending Spike Reilly's sister to see him, but his employers might have a very strong motive indeed, if they had the least, faintest shade of suspicion that he was not Spike Reilly.

He thought he had just been had up for an identification

parade, and he hoped with a good deal of fervour that Louisa could be trusted to identify him in no uncertain manner.

He turned about and went back to her.

"I think this means they wanted you to take a look at me."

"I've been thinking that."

"Well, what are you going to say to them, Miss Spedding?"

She said irrelevantly, "There isn't any voice Mrs. Simpson couldn't do. Man, woman, or child, she could take anyone off."

"You think it was Maud Millicent Simpson who rang you up?"

"If it was, she didn't mean me to know." She got up from the bed. "I'd best be going."

"And when you've got home I expect there'll be another telephone call, and the girlish voice will want to know how you found your brother, and whether you had a nice time with him."

"I wouldn't wonder," said Louisa Spedding. She moved towards the door.

Peter moved with her.

"Well, what are you going to say?"

She took hold of the door to open it, and then stood with her hand on the knob.

"If I say you're not Jimmy, they'll do you in. And if I say you are, and they find out you're not, then they'll do me in as likely as not."

"Look here," said Peter, "go to the police—go straight from here and tell them all about Mrs. Simpson. Ask the police to protect you, and they'll see you're safe."

"No," she said—"I won't do that. Things would come out about Jimmy—I can't do that. But I won't give you away."

She pulled the door open quickly and went. And shut it behind her.

CHAPTER XXII

LOUISA Spedding came out upon the foggy street. She was vexed with herself, because she was beginning to wish that she had held her tongue. She couldn't think what had come over her up in that room with the young man who wasn't Jimmy because Jimmy was dead. A way with him, that's what he had, and it would have been better if she hadn't given in. She could remember how Cornelius Reilly had got round her mother, and it ought to have been a warning to her. Why, if anyone had told her that she would blab out all that about Jimmy and that Grey, and about Mrs. Simpson too,—well, she just wouldn't have believed it. She was downright vexed with herself, and more than a little bit scared.

Ever since it had first come to her what sort of things and what sort of people Jimmy had got himself mixed up with she had made up her mind that the safe way was for her to know nothing. Anything that Jimmy said or anything he hinted had better go in at one ear and out of the other, as the saying was. Once you began to talk, there was no knowing where it was going to stop, and before you knew where you were you might find yourself in a police-court or worse. And the police were all very well in their way, but you didn't want them mixed up in your own affairs, or in your family's affairs. So she wished she had held her tongue.

She turned the corner of the street and walked in the direction of the main road, where she would get her bus. A woman came out of the first side turning, brushed against her, and said, "I beg your pardon."

Louisa Spedding turned her head and began to say "Granted." But the word broke off, because the woman was Mrs. Simpson. She was dressed different from when they had met in the bus, and she was speaking different too—that sort of a lisp was gone. But whatever she did or didn't do to herself, there was a thing Louisa would always know her by—a thing that very likely she never noticed she'd got herself, because your own eyelids aren't things you notice or see. But there, on the right one, at the inside corner, was a little round brown mole. She might look in the glass a hundred times a day and not see it, because you didn't see it till the lid came down a bit. But Louisa had always noticed it, right from the very first day. She noticed it now behind the tortoiseshell-rimmed spectacles which were one of the things that made Mrs. Simpson look different. She had had on tinted pince-nez before. Come to think of it, she had on the same dress and hat, but the dress was mostly covered by an old raincoat, and she'd got a thick black chiffon scarf tied on over the hat. A regular figure of fun it made her look, and a real old maid into the bargain. No one would ever believe she'd been right down dressy sixteen years ago. But smart or dressy, old maid or widow, nothing was going to stop Louisa Spedding from recognizing Maud Millicent Simpson.

She had all this in her mind as she stood on the damp pavement and took a good look at the woman who had brushed against her. Then she said,

"Well, to be sure, Mrs. Simpson! Fancy meeting you!"

"And fancy you knowing me, Louie," said Mrs. Simpson. Her voice was the voice of sixteen years ago, a pretty, cultured voice.

Louisa Spedding's tongue got the better of her discretion.

"And why shouldn't I know you now? If I knew you on the bus the other day after not seeing you for a matter of sixteen years, if isn't just covering up your clothes and putting on a different pair of glasses that will stop me knowing you today. I should always know you."

Mrs. Simpson nodded.

"Very clever of you. I'm sure I don't know how you recognized me in the bus. Sixteen years is a long time, and I am afraid I have changed a great deal."

Louisa said, "Oh, well—" And then, in a hurry, "I'm sure I'm very glad to have seen you, but I ought to be catching my bus, for goodness knows what the kitchen-maid will be making of the *hollandaise* sauce, and Sir John—well, he's particular."

Mrs. Simpson consulted a wrist-watch.

"Well, Louise, you're too late for your sauce and too late for your lunch, for it's past one o'clock now. You'd better come along and have something with me, and we'll have a talk about old times. And if Sir John gives you notice, you can always come back to me. Come—wouldn't you like to do that? It's not such a big house, but I'd give you whatever he does. Now what do you say to that?"

The way she said it and the way she looked when she said it took Louisa Spedding a long way back. In the old days you never could tell whether Mrs. Simpson meant what she said or not. Louisa didn't know now, but she thought she'd be on the safe side. She said quickly,

"I'm not thinking of making a change—and I couldn't go without a kitchen-maid either."

"And what makes you think you wouldn't have a kitchen-maid, Louie?"

Louisa Spedding stared.

"Why, you wouldn't have room for one, would you?" she said.

They had turned into the side street and were walking along it—a little dark, narrow street without shops, and every window curtained with net, or muslin, or Nottingham lace. Mrs. Simpson gave her a swift sideways glance.

"The house is bigger than it looks."

"It doesn't look big," said Louisa. And then she could have bitten her tongue out, because Mrs. Simpson turned round and smiled, and said in her sweetest voice,

"How do you know how big it is, Louie?"

Well there—she had put her foot in it. And it wouldn't matter how she tried now, Mrs. Simpson would have it out of her. She might have changed in her looks, but she hadn't changed about things like that. Louisa coloured up and tried to pass it off with a laugh.

"Of course I don't know where you live."

"Don't you? I think you do." Mrs. Simpson was still smiling. "It isn't a crime, Louie. But I'd dearly like to know how you found out. Did you engage a detective?" Her tone was light and amused, with an undercurrent of irony. Louisa remembered that too, and how she had hated it sixteen years ago. She was on the defensive as she said,

"Why, it was easy enough, Mrs. Simpson, and no reason against it that I can see. I take that bus every week going down to see a friend of mine, and next time I went I got talking to the conductor. He's been on that route all this year, and if the bus is empty we have a bit of a talk. Well then, he'd noticed when I spoke to you, so I got telling him I'd known you sixteen years ago, and he said, 'That's funny.' and he told me you were a regular passenger. So I asked him if he knew where you lived, and he said you always got down at the corner of Sunderland Place, and he said he'd seen you go in at the third or fourth house in Sunderland Terrace. It all came out quite natural, just in the way of talk."

"I see—" said Mrs. Simpson gently. "But, Louisa, how did you speak of me? Because, you know, I married again, and if you called me Mrs. Simpson—"

Louisa shook her head with decision.

"There weren't any names mentioned, neither by him nor by me. I just said it was a lady I'd lived with a long time back. And we talked about how you came across people years after you'd stopped thinking about them."

"So we do," said Mrs. Simpson. "You're quite sure you didn't mention my name?"

"Oh, yes, Mrs. Simpson, I'm sure I didn't."

Mrs. Simpson manner changed. Her voice became brisker.

"That's all right, Louisa. And now—how stupid I am—I

haven't asked you how you found your brother. Did you have a nice time with him?''

Louisa Spedding felt a sort of shock. She had said to Peter that it wouldn't surprise her if it had been Mrs. Simpson who had telephoned and told her to go round and see Jimmy at the Edenbridge Hotel. She had said that, and she had meant it, but when it came to finding out that she was right she got a shock. Somehow, meeting Mrs. Simpson and talking to her had taken her right back into the safe comfortable days before Jimmy went wrong, when she didn't have to suspect anyone or think before she spoke. But now, with this sense of shock upon her, it came to her that she ought to have been thinking what she said, and not letting her tongue run on. She said,

''Oh, yes, I saw him. We had a good talk.'' And then she fetched a heavy sigh and said, ''I wish we could all go back and be the way we used to be.''

Mrs. Simpson took no notice of this. She looked sharply at Louisa Spedding.

''You did see your brother?''

''Oh, yes, I saw him.''

''Then what's the matter—isn't he well?''

''So far as I know. He didn't say. Oh dear me—why couldn't he settle down respectably?''

Mrs. Simpson made no answer to that. She was smiling again.

''And now we will have our lunch. There's a nice little place just round this corner, but I must telephone to my house first to let them know that I shall not be back.''

They were nearing the end of the narrow street. A telephone-box was visible at the corner. The broad and noisy thoroughfare lay beyond. Mrs. Simpson opened the door of the box and beckoned Louisa inside.

''There's just one other call I ought to make, and I wonder if you would look up the number for me. I'm afraid I can't see well enough with these glasses, and you always had such good sight. The name is Hirstman—H-I-R-S-T. I can be getting my coppers ready.''

It was a close fit for the two of them inside the box. Mrs.

Simpson stood behind Louisa and pulled the door to. The noise of the traffic receded miraculously. Louisa bent over the directory and drew a gloved forefinger slowly down the HIRs.

Mrs. Simpson opened her bag. She looked up the street and down the street. There was a lot of heavy traffic in the road. There were not many pedestrians, because it was lunch-time. And old man went by with a dog on a lead—a man and a girl—three girls talking nineteen to the dozen—and then for thirty yards or so nobody at all. Mrs. Simpson's hand came up from her bag with something muffled in a woolen scarf. She pressed this something against Louisa's neck just under the right ear and pulled a trigger.

Louisa Spedding did not cry out at all. She did not know what had happened. Her body slumped down upon the floor of the box. Mrs. Simpson helped it down. Then she put the pistol away in her bag and walked out of the kiosk.

She went back by the way they had come. There was no one in the narrow street. The fog had thickened and the air was dark. She stepped into an opening about half way down and removed the large black veil which poor Louisa had thought so old-fashioned. It rolled up tight and went into her bag. She changed the tortoise-shell rimmed spectacles for a pair of tinted pince-nez, and she took off her raincoat and hung it over her arm.

When she stepped back into the street she was quite a different woman from the one who had accompanied Louisa Spedding—different in appearance, in dress, and in her walk. There was bright colour in her hat and in the scarf about her throat. Her coat and dress were black. The drab raincoat was tucked out of sight over her arm. The tinted pince-nez made an extraordinary difference in her appearance. She walked mincingly, but at a considerable speed, to the end of the street and turned the corner.

CHAPTER XXIII

TERRY Clive was having lunch with Fabian Roxley. And she was beginning to wish that she hadn't come, because it wasn't being at all a comfortable sort of meal. When a young man sits beside you wrapped in gloom and takes no interest in his food, it generally means that you are in for a scene. And Terry was hungry. She wanted her lunch, and she wanted it to an accompaniment of pleasant friendly talk. It was just like a man to propose to you before you had finished your soup. And what happened then—if you refused him? How could you decently take any interest in a mushroom omelette or a brown-bread ice? And what did you talk about—or didn't you talk at all?

Terry had never yet been proposed to at lunch, so she did not know, but she had a horrid suspicion that she was going to find out. She thought she would make sure of the soup anyhow, because it was mulligatawny, for which she had a passion. She looked at Fabian's gloomy face and said,

"Uncle Basil says it's frightful of me, but I do love mulligatawny."

Mr. Roxley roused himself. He took a spoonful of soup and said,

"Why?"

"Why do I love it—or why does Uncle Basil say it's frightful?"

"Uncle Basil," said Fabian.

Terry laughed.

"Too hot, too strong, too everything. No palate left—all the finer shades destroyed. He says the only excuse for it is being a retired colonel who hasn't got a palate anyhow."

She was just beginning to feel she was doing rather well, because here they were, talking about colonels and palates and mulligatawny—and could anything be safer than that? —when the situation suddenly slipped. Fabian put down his spoon, and said in one of those purposeful voices,

"Look here, Terry. I want to talk to you."

Terry clung to her spoon and continued to take soup. She had very nearly finished it, and a most pleasant warm glow made her feel much better able to confront a proposal than when she had come in all cold out of the fog. She finished the last spoonful, gave a thankful sigh, and said,

"I thought we were talking rather nicely."

Fabian Roxley looked at her.

"I want to talk to you seriously—very seriously."

"Must you—at lunch? I mean, wouldn't afterwards do?"

"No, because I've go to get back and do some work." The waiter came to remove their plates. "Are you sure you won't have anything but omelette?"

"I adore mushroom omelette," said Terry.

"And an ice afterwards?"

"A very large brown-bread ice."

If they could only go on talking about food. But the omelette would take ten minutes, and the moment the waiter was gone Fabian began again.

"Terry, I must ask you—do you really mean to go to the police tomorrow?"

Terry put her elbow on the table and her chin in her hand. You are not allowed to do this at school, so you naturally take every opportunity of doing it afterwards.

She looked very directly at Fabian and said,

"What's all this about? Why don't you want me to?"

He had an elbow on the table too. They were so close that cheek came near to touching cheek and words had hardly to be spoken. He said,

"I'm going to tell you. I hate doing it, but I can't let you go to the police. There'll be too much mud stirred up."

"Go on," said Terry.

"Look here, I've got to know what you saw. I can't go on until I do."

"Nothing doing," said Terry—"absolutely and utterly nothing doing. I'm not telling anyone except the police. And I want to know what all this is about, because I don't like it. You ought to want me to go to the police—not try to keep me back."

Fabian commanded himself.

"I think you ought to have spoken at once, but since you didn't—well, isn't there something rather cold-blooded about it?"

"I don't mind if there is. I want Mr. Cresswell to get his picture back. You know it's not the money—he really loves it. And I don't want Emily to get hurt. If that's being cold-blooded, then I am."

"You know what I think about you. But, Terry, don't you see, if it was one of the guests—if it was—Norah Margesson—" He watched her face.

She took her chin out of her hand and sat up. He was too near. His eyes were too near. Her own dazzled. She leaned back.

"Why Norah Margesson?"

"Because I happen to know she is desperately hard up."

"She always is. So are lots of people. What about you?"

She was smiling, and her eyes sparkled. But Fabian Roxley turned rather white.

"What do you mean by that?"

Terry laughed.

"You said Norah Margesson was hard up, and I said what about you. Aren't you hard up? I know I am."

His hand had been pressing into his cheek. The pressure relaxed. He said,

"Most people are these days, my sweet. Do you know, I thought you were going to accuse me of pinching the picture. It was a bit of a jar, and I was just wondering what one could say. A little hard on one's lunch, don't you think?''

Terry's eyes continued to sparkle.

"Oh, darling, I've been much too nicely brought up to fling bombs at my host in the middle of lunch—I really have. I should certainly have waited until we had had our coffee.''

Fabian laughed. He had really had a shock. Terry touched his emotions. It was a relief to laugh.

"Why should you be hard up, my child? Don't they give you any of your own money to play with until you're twenty-one?''

"Some. But of course it's not enough—money never is.''

"I've noticed that.''

"And Uncle Basil says it doesn't amount to much anyway, because of things going down, and exchanges—what would the exchanges be doing?''

He laughed again, without strain this time.

"Well, they might be down, or they might be up.''

Terry said, "Something like that,'' and the waiter arrived with the mushroom omelette.

Whilst he was serving them, Fabian looked at Terry and thought her fresh and pretty in her blue suit and odd little tilted hat. Fresh and pretty, but no fresher than dozens of girls whom he knew, and not as pretty as half a dozen he could name. But she stirred him as he had not meant to be stirred. The last thing on earth he had ever intended was to fall in love with Terry Clive. A banal expression, a most banal experience. And just when he needed all his wits about him to reach another rung on the difficult ladder he had set himself to climb.

When the waiter had gone away he came back to Norah Margesson.

"You see, my dear, it would make an absolutely crashing scandal. Emily Cresswell wouldn't bless you for that.''

Terry was ruffled. Why was he trying to bounce her? Why couldn't he take a hint? And why wasn't she being allowed to eat her mushrooms in peace? She said with a little warmth,

"You know, darling, this isn't the sort of scandal I really like talking about at lunch. It's not spicy enough."

"You may not like it, but—"

Terry lost her temper.

"Look here, I just won't go on talking about that horrid picture all through lunch! And I never said it was Norah Margesson, so I don't know why you're going on about her."

"All right, all right—we'll talk about anything else you like. What shall it be? Ants—bric-à-brac—Cochin China—delicatessen—eels—or the latest factory act? The life-story of the eel is enthralling, but I expect I've forgotten some of the best bits."

They talked amiably about a great many things for the rest of the meal. Fabian could make himself very agreeable when he chose. Terry's annoyance subsided, but over the coffee she began to feel a little nervous again.

Their table was set in a recess. A small orchestra was playing dance music, syncopated song-hits, and movie melodies. The Sahara could have offered them no greater privacy, and whether it was the singing, swinging rhythms or something more compelling, Fabian had begun to look at her in a quite horribly tendentious manner. It was like suddenly finding the fire too hot and not being able to move away from it. She didn't like it, and she couldn't run away, because there was the coffee, and when you've been properly brought up you can't just leave your coffee and go.

She said quick and light, "And now you can tell me all about ants and bric-à-brac."

But Fabian shook his head.

"I'm afraid not, Terry, I'm afraid I want to talk about you." After a pause he added, "And me."

Nothing is more annoying than to blush when you most particularly want to be cool, calm, and sophisticated. She said,

"I'd much rather you didn't."

"I'm afraid I've got to. I—I can't just go on like this. I expect you know how I feel about you."

"I do wish you wouldn't," said Terry.

"Well, I've got to—I can't help myself. Terry, don't you think—"

Terry hadn't really known what she would think. Fabian was in love with her, and Fabian would propose to her if she let him. She hadn't really got farther than that. She certainly didn't want him to propose to her now, but he seemed to be doing it. And right there Terry knew why she didn't want him to do it. She admired him and she liked him, and they had had a lot of good times together. But marry him—Never, never, never in the world! She felt the most frightful embarrassment, because she ought not to be listening to his voice with that tone in it. And the things he was saying—they were for someone who loved him, and not for Terry Clive who wanted to put her fingers in her ears and run away.

She did actually push her chair back a little way as she said, "Oh, *please*, Fabian—I don't want you to—I told you I didn't."

"What's the use of saying that? I love you. I've got to tell you that."

"No, you haven't—not if I don't want you to. And I *don't*."

Fabian Roxley looked at her. All his lazy calm had fallen away. His feature seemed to have sharpened. The muscles of neck and jaw were taut, and his eyes were fever-bright. He looked at Terry who was out of his reach, and saw some other things withdrawing and withdrawn. Things that make a life—things expected, carelessly welcomed, prized without thought, prized despairingly as they withdrew.

He said, "Terry!" and something in his voice hurt her at the very quick of her heart. It was the first time she had ever heard that note of desperate, utter need. And Terry, who flowed out in comfort to any hurt thing, had no comfort to give. Tears stung her eyes. She said,

"Please, Fabian, *please*. I can't—I really can't."

There was a brief silence.

Fabian Roxley pulled himself together.

"If you change your mind—" he said. And then, "I can't change mine."

Terry pushed her chair right back and got up. It was no good trying to be cool and sophisticated. It was the horridest thing in the world to have to hurt someone like this, and the only thing she could do was to go away as quickly as possible.

And of course because they were civilized people Fabian had to get up too, and come downstairs with her, and put her into a taxi. Neither of them spoke. Terry's cheeks were burning and her eyes stung. This was going to be goodbye, and they *had* had good times together.

She got into the taxi and said her thought aloud.

"We *have* had good times—haven't we?"

He said, "Marvellous," and stood back, lifting his hat. In the cold, foggy light he looked suddenly ten years older.

He gave the address to the driver, and she saw him turn away.

CHAPTER XXIV

TERRY felt what a great many other people have felt in their time, a passionate desire to skip the next two days and arrive at Wednesday morning, when either James Cresswell would have got his picture back or she would have been to the police and told them what she had seen. You can always turn over the pages of a book and avoid what is tedious or painful, but the dull and ugly days have to be lived through, one slow minute at a time.

A quarter of an hour after she got home Norah Margesson rang up.

"Is that Terry Clive?"

Terry said it was, and wondered what Norah had got to say to her.

"I wanted to speak to you." Miss Margesson's voice had an aggressive note.

"Well, I'm here," said Terry.

"I suppose you didn't really mean what you said yesterday—all that about going to the police?"

"Of course I meant it."

Norah gave a hard, angry laugh.

"My dear girl, you can't do a thing like that."

Terry's temper got the better of her. She said,

"Watch me!"

There was a brief pause. Then a changed voice said,

"You can't do a thing like that—you really can't."

"I'm afraid I'm going to."

There was another and a longer pause. And then,

"Terry, you're not going to tell them I went out on the terrace! Because it's got nothing—nothing to do—" The voice stopped on a sort of gasp.

Terry thought for a minute.

"I shan't say anything about it unless I have to."

"What do you mean by that?"

"It might come out."

She heard Norah draw in her breath sharply. Then, with another change of manner,

"My dear, there's nothing to come out. I'm sure I don't know what you thought you saw, but the whole thing is really very simple. A friend of mine wanted to see me rather specially on his way back to town, and I promised to slip out for a moment. And as I had broken the string of my pearls, I thought I would let him take them up to town and get them restrung for me. And when I got to the bottom of the steps, there was a perfectly strange man, and I was so frightened I ran away. And I do wish I hadn't, because of course he must have been waiting there to steal the picture."

Terry's anger died down and a cold feeling of shame took its place. She said,

"It's no good, Norah—they were Emily's pearls. You came out of her room and went down the stairs. I saw you. And I saw the pearls under the hall light. It's no use saying they were yours. I saw the clasp."

There was another of those gasps.

"What are you going to do?"

"I told you. I shan't say anything unless I have to—Emily would hate it. It's no use our going on talking about it—is it? Goodbye."

Well, that was that. She wondered if anyone else would ring her up—Pearla Yorke, or Mr. Applegarth. She put the wireless on rather loud and hoped she wouldn't hear the telephone bell.

Basil Ridgefield got back for tea. He had been to a stamp auction, and for once in her life Terry was glad to talk about stamps. He was very much pleased at having acquired a fifteen-cent American stamp with the Stars and Stripes inverted for £120, which, he told her, was less than half the catalogue price. He had also secured for £50 an unused horizontal pair of twenty-four-cent stamps of a dull purple colour. Terry looked at them, and tried not to show how much the prices shocked her. All that money for three little bits of dirty paper! But Uncle Basil was pleased, and it was a nice change to be with someone who was pleased, after that harrowing lunch—and Norah.

Mr. Ridgefield went on talking about stamps with considerable enthusiasm whilst he partook of three cups of tea and a muffin-dish full of hot buttered toast. But when the muffin-dish was empty and he had replaced his cup on the tray he fell suddenly silent, and then said with a complete change of manner,

"Terry, my dear, I've been thinking over what you said about going to the police, and I don't think it will do."

Terry said nothing. Her mouth set firmly, and an obstinate gleam came into her eyes. She had told everyone what she was going to do, and she meant to do it. They could badger her till they were black in the face, but she meant to do it.

A fatigued expression passed over Basil Ridgefield's features. He had not been Terry's guardian since she was ten years old without being able to recognize these danger signals. His ward had some extremely charming qualities, but she could be as determined as a mule. He said in his gentlest voice,

"You see, my dear, you are still very young. You do not think about the social repercussions, but I am bound to think about them for you. I don't want to press you to tell me what you saw, but don't you think it would be better if you could bring yourself to talk the whole thing over in a friendly manner before you risk the scandal and publicity which may result from going to the police? Let us suppose that one of our fellow guests was involved—though I find it impossible to believe such a thing. What is likely to result? Consider pain and embarrassment not only to the Cresswells, who are my very old friends, but to all the innocent members of the house-party, and—though perhaps this will not weigh with you—a considerable measure of social discredit for yourself. Odium of that sort is not to be incurred lightly. You will probably think I am being old-fashioned, but it doesn't do a young girl any good to be mixed up in a social scandal, still less in a police-court case. It doesn't look well for her to put herself forward as an accuser. You mustn't mind if I say that it takes a good deal of the bloom off."

Terry listened. Her expression became less stubborn. Distress came into it. She felt the impact and the pressure of age, authority, and experience. He was much older than she. He had always been kind to her. He knew his world. He was trying to be kind to her now—she felt quite sure about that. And he would think her stupid and ungrateful. A bright colour came into her cheeks. She tried to explain.

"It isn't what you think—it really isn't. I don't want to accuse anyone. You see, if they give the picture back, I won't say anything—I won't feel I've got to. Whoever took it has got the chance of sending it back. I've thought about it a lot, and if they sent it back, I think it would mean that they wouldn't take any more pictures, because they would know that I knew something, and they would be afraid to go on, because of course if they did, I should *have* to go to the police."

Basil Ridgefield adjusted his monocle and looked at her with rather an odd expression.

"And hasn't it struck you that you may be putting yourself in a very difficult not to say dangerous position, my dear? I don't know what you saw, and you don't seem inclined to tell me, but I should strongly advise you to forget the whole thing. Shall we say you had a bad dream—quite a vivid dream, but one which can now be forgotten? I think it would be much safer to look at it that way."

Terry leaned forward. Her eyes were very bright.

"Who wants to be safe?" she cried.

A faintly sarcastic smile just touched Mr. Ridgefield's lips.

"Oh, I do for one." He got up from his chair. "I must go

round and tell Horace Wimpole about the auction. He hated missing it, and I promised I'd look in."

When he had gone Terry ran after him to the door. Her soft heart smote her, because he really had been very sweet. He might have stamped, and said his foot was down, and things like that. And he hadn't.

She looked over the stairs and saw him, half way down. He looked back at her. She blew him a kiss.

CHAPTER XXV

IT was about six o'clock when the telephone bell rang again. This time the voice that said "Miss Clive?" was an entirely strange one. Terry said, "Yes," and the voice said, "Miss Terry Clive?", and Terry said "Yes" again. It was a woman's voice. At least she thought it was a woman's voice; she wasn't quite sure. There was a curious whispery sound about it. It said,

"This is rather a delicate matter. Are you alone? You don't mind my asking, do you?"

Terry wondered what was coming next. She said,

"No—I'm alone."

"Well then—I think some friends of yours are anxious to recover a piece of lost property."

It was exactly like getting an electric shock. She felt it run tingling all over her as she said,

"What do you mean?"

"I think you know very well what I mean. You offered certain terms. Well, now we want to know whether we can rely on your keeping your part of the bargain."

Terry said, "Of course you can."

"If the property is recovered, no further steps will be taken?"

"Not by me."

"You undertake to hold your tongue?"

"Yes."

"But have you held your tongue? That's the question."

"Yes, I have."

"You haven't told anyone what you saw?"

"I haven't told anyone."

"Nobody at all?"

"Nobody at all."

The voice became brisker.

"Very well then, it only remains to hand the property over to you."

"To me?" Terry heard how surprised her own voice sounded.

"Certainly to you. We are not in a position to approach your friends."

"You could send it by post, or carrier, or something." She wasn't really sure how you did send pictures.

There was a laugh, instantly suppressed.

"My dear Miss Clive! A valuable piece of lost property like this? Your friends wouldn't thank you. Suppose it got damaged or—stolen. One has heard of such things."

Terry's cheeks burned. She was being laughed at, and she didn't like it. She said in a stiff young voice,

"What do you propose?"

"Well, since we are being so obliging, we thought you might care to come half way to meet us. We can't very well come to you, and we're not quite in a position to give you our address, so the idea was that the transfer should take place upon what one might call neutral ground. If you will take a taxi to the corner of Massingbourne Crescent, someone will meet you there and hand the property over."

Terry put her hand over the receiver and thought. It sounded all right. She could ring up the garage they always dealt with and have a taxi from there. And she wouldn't get out. Whoever it was who was going to meet her would just have to come and talk to her where she was. She didn't see how anything could possibly go wrong.

There was a crackling against the palm of her hand. She thought, "You can laugh at me, but you can't make me listen unless I want to.'' Then she put the thing to her mouth and said,

''All right, I'll do it.'' She rang off, and rang up the Rockingham Garage.

Miss Lamb, the young lady who sat in a glass cage and answered the telephone, said, ''Oh, certainly.'' And then, ''Yes, it's a nasty fog, Miss Clive, but I'm sure it will be all right.''

Miss Lamb hung up the receiver and continued in her own mind the highly dramatic rehearsal of what she intended to say to Ted Williams when he came round at half past six to walk home with her—''It's all very well you thinking you can go on as if you were one of those sheikhs, but if you think I'm the sort of girl that's going to put up with being one of a crowd, well, you've just to begin and think all over again—that's all. And if you think you can take Mabel Hill out Saturday, and Ruby Pope Sunday, and then come along on the Monday and expect me to walk home with you as if nothing had happened, well, I'm not having any, and you can go back to your Mabel and your Ruby if they'll have you, which I shouldn't think they would, not if they've got any proper pride in themselves—but that's their look-out and not mine, thank goodness.'' Well, then, of course he'd be angry—bound to be, and there'd be a bit of a flare-up, and after that he'd come round and want her to make it up with him. And perhaps she would, and perhaps she wouldn't. It didn't do for a girl to make herself too cheap—

She was still undecided when the telephone bell rang again. A woman's voice said,

''The Rockingham Garage?''

''Speaking.''

''Miss Clive has just ordered a taxi—''

''Yes—it'll be round directly.''

The voice said, ''Will you please countermand it. Miss Clive has decided that it is too foggy to go out.''

Miss Lamb put back the receiver.

Terry powdered her nose, touched up her lips, put on her hat and coat, and ran down the stairs. The taxi arrived on one side of the hall door as she arrived on the other. She thought how quick they had been. Jenkins was opening the door as she got to it. She told him to say that she wouldn't be long, and ran out to the car.

The fog was much worse than it had been in the middle of the day. She did not much like being out in it, but it fascinated her too. Everything had such a queer under-water look, and the street lamps were like milky moons, each in a halo of its own but not really giving any light.

She wasn't quite sure where Massingbourne Crescent was, but the taxi driver seemed to know. They were getting along at a good speed. She lost her landmarks almost at once, and wondered how he was able to make his way with so much certainty.

Then she began to think about other things—about who was going to meet her at the corner of Massingbourne Crescent, and whether it would be the young man to whom Norah had given the pearls, and from whom she herself had recovered them. Because of course he must have been waiting there to take the picture, and if he had taken it he might be the one to bring it back. Terry hoped he would. She had got the better of him once, and that naturally put her in good heart.

When they had been driving for about twenty minutes the car stopped. The man got down and opened the door.

"You didn't say what number, miss."

"No. I'm expecting someone to meet me."

They both peered into the fog. It was thickish here. You could just see the houses on this side of the road, but not on the other. With the door open and the fog seeping in, Terry had a drowning feeling. It was bitterly cold, and a quick shudder shook her. Just as it passed, she heard steps on the pavement—slow, hesitating steps, coming on and stopping, coming nearer. They came right up to the car. There was the sound of a cough. A woman said,

"Miss Clive?"

Terry leaned out and looked. She couldn't see very much, but what she saw was reassuring. The voice was an elderly voice, and the woman who stood on the kerb was an old woman with a stooped figure, decent elderly garments, and a tremulous gentility of speech. She coughed feebly with her hand at her mouth, and half whispered,

"So stupid—such a bad cold—and this fog. May I get in and talk to you?"

Terry moved to make room and put out a hand to help her in. The driver shut the door and remained close by on the pavement. It did not enter Terry's head to be nervous. She would not have found it possible to believe that she was in any danger.

The woman coughed for some time. In the semi-darkness Terry could see her dimly, one hand pressed down upon the straining chest. The paroxysm passed. She leaned back with a heavy sigh.

Terry said, "You oughtn't to be out. Let's be as quick as we can, so that you can get home. Have you come about the picture?"

"Oh, yes—about the picture."

"Have you got it?"

"Not here. We must drive a little way. Oh dear!"

"They oughtn't to have sent you—you're not fit to be out." Terry's voice was indignant. She opened the door and called to the driver, "We'll have to go on." Then, to the woman in the corner, "Which way?"

"Along the Crescent. Oh dear!" She coughed again.

The car began to move. Looking to right and left, Terry could see nothing. She guessed at houses on one side and trees on the other behind a wall of fog. She felt blind, and didn't like it. The woman had opened her bag and was fumbling in it. She still coughed.

Then, with the extreme of suddenness, a hand took Terry by the elbow. Not a large hand but a very strong one. It held her rigid and startled. And on that the other hand came up with a stabbing motion. Needle-sharp and deep, something stabbed right into her arm. She cried out and tried to wrench away, but the grip on her elbow held. The needle that had prickled her was withdrawn. The hand which had held it came round her neck and pressed a pad of something down upon her nose and mouth. She tried to drag herself free, but she was in a clasp of steel. She tried to scream, but the small sound which came was muffled and died against her lips. No second scream would come. She could no longer feel that hard and cruel grip. She could no longer remember why she ought to scream. An unconsciousness as deadening as the fog closed down upon her senses.

After a minute or two the woman released her, pushing her over into the corner of the car. She picked up the hypodermic syringe from the seat where she had let it fall and put it carefully away in her bag. Then she leaned forward and rapped on the glass. The car stopped.

The driver got down and came round to the window. He stood looking in and said,

"O.K.?"

The woman laughed and said,

"Perfectly. Did you hear anything?"

"Not enough to swear by. What next?"

"Drive to the house. Don't be afraid—she won't come round."

He got back into his seat. The car moved on.

CHAPTER XXVI

ABOUT twenty minutes later Alfred, the page at the Edenbridge, knocked at Peter Talbot's door and told him he was wanted on the telephone. Peter's eyebrows went up. He whistled softly, dropped the book he was reading, and strode off down the passage to the telephone-box which the management had recently installed there. He remembered that in Vincent's time you had a choice between making a call in the lounge hall with everyone listening, and in the office where the audience consisted only of the clerk.

He felt a consuming curiosity about this call, because only his employers and Garrett knew where he was, and if one of them was calling him up, it certainly wasn't just to pass the time of day. He lifted the receiver, and heard what Terry Clive had heard, the sound of someone coughing, and then a woman's voice, frail and elderly, with the cough still jarring it.

"Is that Mr. Reilly?"

Peter said, "Speaking," because he thought that that was what Spike Reilly would be likely to say.

"Oh dear," said the voice—"that's not enough—I must be sure. Give me your full name please."

It was a gentlewoman's voice. It sounded like the voice of a pretty sick woman too. Peter's desire to know more about it flared into a ravening curiosity. Thanks to the passport system, he was able to give the desired information.

"James Peter Reilly."

"But you're not called all that. What are you called?"

"Spike."

"Oh dear," said the voice—"but your sister doesn't call you Spike, does she?"

Afterwards it was this question that really made Peter see red. Not very rational perhaps, but human enough, because poor Louie Spedding who had never harmed anyone was lying dead, and the woman who had murdered her used her name to trap him with. But at the time he did not know that Louisa was dead.

He said, "No, she calls me Jimmy," and heard the voice broken by a fit of coughing. It emerged in a fragile condition.

"Well then, you are to go at once to the corner of Massingbourne Crescent. Take a suit-case and anything you want for the next few days. That is all. Goodbye." The receiver clicked at the other end of the line.

Peter went back into his room and packed. His mind was seething with conjectures. Was this a flitting consequent on the Turner having become a bit too hot to hold on to, or was it a further plunge into crime?

He had a look at a tape-map, and located Massingbourne Crescent. Without going more than fifty yards out of his way he could pass the telephone-box at the end of Sitfield Row. He thought it very unlikely that he would be followed. He thought he could make sure about that, and he thought it would be just as well to give Frank Garrett a ring before he went trekking off into the unknown.

He paid his bill and walked out of the Edenbridge, carrying his suit-case. The fog came up against him like a wall. At the corner of the street he stood for a while, accustoming his eyes to the dazzle of it. Well, at any rate he could not very well be followed in a fog like this. And then half way up the next street it thinned. He found Sitfield Row quite easily, and walked along it to the telephone-box at the corner without any idea that Louisa Spedding had walked this way to her death not so many hours before. He stood on the very spot where she had been shot and dialled Frank Garrett's number. The receiver clicked. A man's voice with a strong Cockney accent said,

"'Ullo?"

Peter assumed a much higher register than his own.

"Can I speak to Colonel Garrett?" (This was Hopkins, and Hopkins might know his voice.)

"Colonel Garrett is h'out," said Hopkins, dealing firmly with an extra H.

"Do you know where he is? I want to catch him."

"No h'idea." Then, after a pause, "What abaht a message?"

Peter considered. He failed to think of one that would be any good, said "No, thank you," and rang off.

He tried Frank's office, drew a blank, and gave it up.

It took him a considerable time to reach Massingbourne Crescent. The fog was bad in patches, as London fogs are apt to be. He lost his way once or twice, and found that other people had lost theirs.

In the end he arrived at one of those crescents set back from a thoroughfare with a belt of trees in front, the whole drowned in fog and apparently dead. Not a light showed anywhere. Peter thought it just the place for a nice secluded crime. It occurred to him to wonder whether his employers had conceived the idea of putting him on the spot. His right hand went down into his overcoat pocket and took hold of the neat little pistol which he had bought for a hike through Anatolia last year. He had never had to use it there, and he derived a certain macabre amusement from the thought that he might be about to loose it off in defence of his life in the very heart of London.

A taxi was standing by the farther kerb. Its lights made misty orange pools. Someone got out of it and moved towards him. The misty lights showed him that it was a woman. She stood between him and the taxi and coughed, a hand at her chest, her body bowed and shaken. On the last of the paroxysms he caught the words "Oh dear!" and moved towards her. This was certainly the woman who had talked to him on the telephone, and as certainly he could have nothing to fear from her. He put a flavour of Irish-American into his accent as he said,

"I think we've just been talking on the phone. The name's Reilly."

"Spike Reilly?"

"Yes, that's right."

"You're late, but I suppose it was the fog. Oh dear! You'd better come along and get in."

She weighed heavy on his arm as he helped her into the taxi. As the door slammed, the car started up and they were moving along the dark crescent as they had done an hour before with Terry Clive. But Peter was not to know that—not yet at any rate.

The woman sat back in her corner coughing and shaking. He thought she was old, and that she had no business to be out with a cough like that, but he sat in his own corner and held his tongue. If anyone had got anything to say, let them say it. Mr. Peter Talbot would be all attention.

When they had gone a little way the woman's cough stopped, and she said in a thin voice with an odd tang to it,

"You're to take your orders from me, Spike Reilly."

"Yes."

"I am taking you to a house. You will be on guard there. You were in a kidnapping case in the States, weren't you?"

"Sure I was."

"So I heard. What happened?"

Was this a trap? He didn't know. Neither did he know what had happened when Spike Reilly was in America, except that he had had to leave in a hurry, from which one might deduce. . . . He put a growl in his voice and said,

"There was an accident—I had to clear out."

The woman coughed.

"This is a kidnapping case. And there are to be no accidents. Do you understand? It's a girl who was at Heathacres—a little fool who looked out of her window and saw what she wasn't meant to see. She'll have to go of course, but it's got to look like suicide, so I'm choosing the time and the place. Meanwhile there'll be three of you there—two always on guard, and you're to be one of the two."

"All the time?"

She repeated the words, and accentuated them.

"All the time. I don't trust the other two not to play tricks. They're useful, but they're rough. And she's not to be mauled about. There mustn't be any marks on her when she's found. I had to bruise her arm just now, and we've got to wait for the mark to go, and the mark of the hypodermic too. You'll get five hundred down when it's over, and a share of whatever we get out of the insurance company for the picture. Does that suit you?"

While she was speaking Peter's thoughts raced. Here—here beside him, moving smoothly through the fog, was the woman whom he had come into this job to find. The woman Spike Reilly had named when he was dying, the woman Frank Garrett had been after for years, the woman he had talked about to Louisa Spedding—Maud Millicent Simpson. He knew her only as a shadow in the fog, a tenuous voice and a skillfully acted cough. If he let her go now, what had he to identify her by? Nothing, and less than nothing. If he could make something to identify her by—He had had an idea about that before he came to keep this appointment. It mightn't be any use—but it might. . . . Where there was nothing to go on at all anything might help. Anyhow, no harm could come of it unless he was clumsy. He mustn't be clumsy.

His hand went into his pocket, and came out with the nail-scissors which he had slipped in there just before he started. They were new scissors and very sharp. Maud Millicent talked. He answered. And as he answered, his hand went out with the scissors in it and snipped five nicks in the rather full old-fashioned skirt she wore—five tiny nicks about knee level where the black stuff lay spread out on the seat between them. Something to identify her by? The best he could do anyway. . . .

If he jammed his pistol into her ribs here and now and told her the game was up—what then? The driver was in it of course, and he couldn't really shoot her. That was the snag.

And then there was the girl. She had looked out of her window and seen what she wasn't meant to see. Why, of course he had seen her looking out when he was waiting in the bushes outside Heathacres. And she must have done it again and seen—well, he wondered just what she had seen. He thought how she had come running along the terrace and down the steps to get the pearls away from him. A plucky kid. What was her name? Garrett had given it to him with all the other names. . . . Terry—yes, Terry Clive—Aunt Fanny's little friend. He thought about Terry Clive. If he didn't let them take him to the house where they'd got her, what would happen—with the guards who were too rough to be trusted?

As he hung in the balance of decision, they passed through a patch where the fog was thin. The light of a street-lamp flickered across them from knee to crown. He was looking at where the woman sat in her corner. The unexpected light passed over her and was gone again. He saw a black dress and a feather boa twisted high about the throat. He saw a black hat tilted forward. He got no impression of any features—only pallor, and the light flashing back from large round glasses which covered her eyes. He might have seen more if he had not seen right away in the first flash of the light her right hand bare upon her knee, and in it, not much longer than the hand itself, an automatic pistol.

He thought that settled it. They were two to one, and the advantage lay with them, because they would have no reluctance at all about shooting him out of hand. He reflected that being a decent member of society could be quite a handicap. He could not, for instance, have brought himself to shoot Maud Millicent Simpson in cold blood, yet in no other way could he hope to come alive out of a scrap with the two of them. And even if he had their ruthlessness at his command, how would he explain two corpses to the police? And what meanwhile would be happening to Terry Clive?

The woman's voice cut through his thoughts. It had a taut, impatient sound.

"Well, what about it? Not very responsive—are you?"

Peter made up his mind.

"Oh, I was just thinking about what you said. I didn't know you wanted me to talk."

"I don't— I want you to listen. And I want to be sure you're clear about your instructions. Will you repeat them to me."

He sat right back in his corner, facing round towards her.

"I'm in charge with two men under me—that's what you said, isn't it?"

She gave a short laugh.

"That is what it amounts to."

"Who are the other two?"

"Jake, and the Bruiser. You'll have to watch your step with them—they're tough. But they won't be there together. They'll take shifts."

"And I'm on all the time?"

"Yes. It's only for a few days."

"All right."

She leaned forward.

"Now listen to me! This is the way you'll play it. It'll take three or four days for the marks to disappear, and we can't get her off till then. There mustn't be any marks when she's found. So no one's to lay a finger on her. You're there to see that no one does. Grey said you put the come hither on the girls. Well, you get along with it and put it on this one. The rougher the others are, the better she'll like you—do you see? That's your part. Play it for all it's worth. Let her think you're standing up for her—that you've fallen for her—that you'll try and get her out of the mess. Then when we're ready she'll go with you and be glad of the chance. We can't use a drug, or there'd be traces afterwards, and it's much safer to take her alive than dead. So she's got to go willingly, and you're the one to get her to do it."

"And where do I take her?"

"You'll be told later. Now listen! She's in the basement

of a house I use sometimes, and she's to stay in the basement. There are doors at the top and bottom of the stairs leading up to the ground floor. They are locked, and I have the keys. The girl is to have no opportunity of approaching the windows which look into the area. She's not to be alone in any room with a window from which she might signal. The room she is in has shutters. They are locked, and they are to stay locked. Do you understand all this?"

Peter laughed, and was astonished at the sound of his own voice.

"Sure—that's easy! No need to tell me things like that."

"You'll listen all the same!" she said with a sharp note of authority. "She's to be well fed, well treated, and kept happy. You've got to make her trust you. And there's another thing. She's not to see a newspaper—not on any account. I won't have one brought into the place. You didn't buy one as you came along just now?"

"No, I didn't."

"Well, it's up to you to see that Jake and the Bruiser don't bring one in. I've told them, but you'll have to keep them up to it. No one's to bring a paper into the place at all."

Peter wondered why. And as if she had heard his thought, she said,

"I don't want her upset. Every rag will be splashing her case all over the front page. They'll put ideas into her head."

He wondered still. The thing stayed like a question in his mind. When he knew the answer, he thought it was a tidy stroke of business to have got Louisa Spedding's brother out of the way and out of the reach of the Press before the story of Louisa's murder broke.

But at the moment, for all he knew, Louisa was cooking Sir John Morleigh's dinner and wondering whether she had said too much about Mrs. Simpson to Peter Talbot.

The car moved on, and stopped presently in a quiet, foggy street.

CHAPTER XXVII

PETER stood in a basement kitchen and heard the car recede.

They had come to a dark street where tall old houses rose like cliffs and were lost in the fog. And then down area steps, the driver going ahead and ringing a bell which could be heard giving a prolonged tinkle from somewhere inside the house. After an interval footsteps, and the door opening an inch or two upon the chain. A mutter from the driver, and he turned on his heel and was off up the steps to his taxi. The door swung wide, and Peter came in upon a dark, stuffy passage. There was a slam behind him, and the turning of a key in the lock. The man who had let him in went past him without a word, and through a half open door on the right.

Peter followed him into the lighted kitchen. He took stock of it now. A good-sized room lying to the front of the house below the street level. Two windows furnished with strong wooden shutters looked into the area. The shutters were closed. They had been painted, but the paint was scaling off. There was an old rusty range, a deal table, some wooden chairs, and two more of basketwork very down at heel, with padded backs and seats covered in a chintz whose pattern had long been lost beneath successive layers of dirt. A fire burned in the range, and the room was hot.

There were two men at the table, with a pack of cards between them and an unshaded electric light bulb overhead. The man who had let him in had his back to the door and was dropping into his chair again. A gentleman whom Peter had no difficulty in recognizing as the Bruiser stared at him out of small piggy eyes—a powerfully built hulk of a man with a pale, heavy face and a blank, bald forehead. Peter thought it must be a long time since he had been in the ring, and that he would be put to it to last a couple of rounds today, but he still had a fist like a ham and a formidable reach.

Then it was Jake who had let him in and who now turned to look at him out of a pair of bright, shifty eyes. Not a very likeable person Jake. Quick on his feet, quick with his hands, and quite possibly quick with a knife. Black eyes in a sallow, dirty face. Black hair, with a lock falling forward. Long, delicate fingers, and nails well rimmed with black.

Both men stared, and Peter gave them an indifferent nod.

"Spike Reilly," he said, and went over to the fire. "One of you can go off now. Which is it going to be?"

Jake threw down his cards and got up.

"We tossed for it, and he lost," he said. "Twelve hours on and twelve hours off—what a life!"

Peter stopped him.

"Just a minute. You've had your orders the same as I've had mine. No papers to be brought in—that's very particular."

"That's all right."

"What about food?" Peter threw back his head and laughed. "We're to be well fed—that's orders too."

"O.K. There's enough in the larder. But we'll be dead if we eat our own cooking." He took the door key out of his pocket and tossed it to the Bruiser.

"Come along and lock up after me," he said.

The two men went out together. There was a whispering in the passage. The outer door banged. The sharp click of the lock came to Peter in the silence, and the rattle of the chain.

The Bruiser came back, sat down again at the table, and

began to deal the cards. Presently he jerked his head in Peter's direction and said in a hoarse voice,

"Play?"

Peter said, "Presently. I'll take a look at the girl first. What's the lay-out?"

The big head jerked in the direction of the door.

Peter went out into the passage and along it. There was a locked door facing him. He had two keys tied together with a bit of string—the key of the girl's room and the key that locked her shutters. Neither of them fitted this door. The passage went on, and brought him to two more doors. The first was ajar—a lavatory with a dirty basin, a cracked piece of soap, and a grimy roller towel.

One of his keys fitted the last door. It opened, and he felt for and found the switch. The light poured down from the ceiling and showed him a small room with linoleum on the floor and a narrow iron bedstead against the farther wall. There was some bedding. Blankets and a couple of pillows. And Terry Clive, lying on her left side facing the door. She was still in her blue dress, but the hat had been thrown on to a chair, and they had taken off her coat and put it over her. It covered her to the waist. Her right arm lay outside it, the hand hanging downwards quite open and relaxed. Her bright curls were rumpled, her lips parted, her eyelids not quite closed. There was a glimmer of grey between the lashes. She had the pallor of very deep sleep, and the innocent, unguarded expression.

A cold, still anger came up in Peter as he looked at her. He put up his hand to the switch, but before he could pull it down Terry Clive had opened her eyes and was looking at him. He remembered her eyes—lovely eyes, wide and clear and candid. They stared at him without a trace of fear, but with the utmost surprise. Then she got up on her elbow.

"Who are you? What's this place? How did I get here? I was in a taxi talking to an old lady with a cough. I told her she oughtn't to be out. What happened? Where is she?"

"I don't know," said Peter in his natural voice.

Terry sat up, pushed away her coat, and swung her feet down on to the floor. One hand went up to her tumbled hair.

"Will you please tell me what happened. I didn't faint—I've never fainted in my life."

"No, you didn't faint."

"How did I get here? Can't you tell me what happened?"

"You were brought here. Does your arm hurt you? She bruised it, didn't she?"

She looked at him. She was neither dazed nor confused. The look was steady and clear. She put her hand to her left elbow and felt it. Then she said,

"She caught hold of me. Why?"

"To run a hypodermic syringe into your arm."

The colour came into Terry's face. Her chin lifted.

"Why?"

"To bring you here, Miss Clive."

Something flickered in her eyes. She sprang up.

"Who are you? I've seen you before. You were in the garden at Heathacres. You had the pearls. I knew I'd heard your voice."

"Well, that makes it all quite easy—doesn't it?" said Peter.

She opened her lips to speak, and was suddenly giddy. The floor tilted and sent her stumbling against Peter—stumbling, and catching at him for safety. His arm held her, and she heard him say from a long way off, "You'd better sit down. It's all right, you know—nothing to worry about."

She found herself on the bed again, sitting with the pillows propping her, and an arm behind the pillows. The voice of the young man who had tried to steal Emily's pearls assured her again that there was nothing to worry about. Anger dispelled the last remnants of her dizziness. She sat right up and said in an indignant voice,

"I'm not in the least worried, thank you. I was just giddy. Anyone might be giddy if they'd been hypodermicked and—and kidnapped."

Peter withdrew his arm and got up. Behind the sparkle in her eyes he thought he could discern a faint expectation. He thought, "She hopes I'll say she hasn't been kidnapped." And what was the use? If he was to get her clear and run

Maud Millicent Simpson down, he must play the gaoler and the bravo. He said,

"Well, that's reasonable enough."

Terry looked at him. She couldn't believe her eyes, and yet she had to believe them. He didn't look like the sort of person who would drug you and kidnap you, but he did look like the man at Heathacres—the man who had had Emily's pearls. She wouldn't have been sure if it wasn't for his voice. And it was quite a nice voice too. What business had a drugging kidnapper to have a voice like that?

She rose to her feet, picked up her hat, and pulled it on. There was a cheap looking-glass on the rather battered chest of drawers beneath the shuttered window. Terry went over to it and stood there patting her hair into place and adjusting the brim of the hat. Her bag was lying in front of the glass. She opened it, took out powder-puff and compact, and tidied up her face, all with her back to Peter, and with the greatest appearance of unconcern. She might have been any girl who was getting ready to go out.

Peter watched her, and wondered what next. He thought he would hold his fire. But in the end she turned round, swooped up her coat from the bed, and said,

"And now I think I'll go home."

He admired the assurance with which she said it, but he did not stand away from the door.

"I'm ready to go home," said Terry Clive.

"Well, I'm afraid—"

"Please stand away from that door."

Peter remained where he was, his hands in his pockets, a shoulder against the jamb. He saw her colour flame into brilliance.

"Did you hear what I said?"

He nodded.

"I'm afraid you don't understand the situation, Miss Clive. You were brought here for a purpose. I'm afraid you will have to stay here until my employers consider it safe to let you go."

Terry went back a step, and said,

"What purpose?"

"Well, I rather gather you were thinking of having a heart-to-heart talk with the police. The idea is to prevent you having it. It's a pity you looked out of your window, and it's a pity you didn't hold your tongue about it. As it is—well, there you have it."

Terry went back as far as the bed and let her coat fall.

"You mean to keep me here?"

He could admire the way she took it, head up and colour bright. He nodded and said,

"You'd better get this straight. It's no use your thinking you can get round me, because you can't. And it's no use your thinking you can get away, because you can't do that either. If I wanted to let you out I couldn't. There's another man on guard with me, and he has the key of the outer door. He's a very rough customer, and you'd better keep clear of him. I've got the key of your room, and I'll see that he doesn't bother you. You'll be well treated. I don't want to lock you in except at night. There's a wash-place next door you can use. I'll go along now and get you something to eat."

CHAPTER XXVIII

PETER Talbot was not given to having sleepless nights, but that night he lay awake and watched the dying glow from the range and wondered whether a bigger fool than he had ever walked into a more obvious trap, and wondered how he was going to get out of it, and how he was going to get Terry Clive out of it. Here he was, bedded down for the night on a mattress against the kitchen wall, his feet half across the door which gave upon the passage. This was Terry Clive's security. The Bruiser couldn't open that door without waking him—he could bank on that. But the door was locked, and the key was in the Bruiser's pocket together with the key of the outside door and the key that locked the shutters front and back.

The keys were in the Bruiser's pocket, and the Bruiser was sleeping noisily on a twin mattress to Peter's on the farther side of the kitchen. His snores mingled with those of a fine bull-terrier which he had brought in from the yard before he went to bed. This and the removal of his boots were the only preparations he made. Now the blankets covered him and the bull-terrier snuffled at his feet. But whereas the man might not have waked to the touch of a very careful hand feeling for his keys, the dog certainly would. Every time Peter turned, the snuffle dropped to a whisper. When a coal fell in the fire the white head came up, an eye gleamed from the pink skin which surrounded it. When Peter rose and crossed the floor the lips drew back to show white teeth and firm pink gums, and a warning thrum came from the muscular throat. If he was any judge of dogs, he had about as much chance of getting those keys as he had of mounting the kitchen poker and flying up the chimney. Whoever had organized this show—and he supposed it was Maud Millicent Simpson—deserved full marks for ingenuity. He was a check on the Bruiser, and the Bruiser was a check on him. The unpleasant word check-mate peeped from the shadows of his mind and was sworn at for an intruder. Maud Millicent undoubtedly knew her job. She wouldn't have lasted all these years at it if she hadn't.

Peter went over the whole lay-out, and found it discouraging. There was the kitchen with its two windows on to the area, shuttered now and barred behind the shutters. Beyond the kitchen a large scullery, a coal-cellar, the larder, and a door leading into the yard. The scullery had a window over the sink, the larder had a small square window high in the wall, and the coal-cellar had nothing but a grating about eight inches square. The scullery window was barred and had a shutter which locked. The back door, like the area door, had a heavy lock, and was further secured by a chain and padlock. All the bars were sound and good, and all the locks were strong. He judged it quite impossible to open them by force, to pick the locks or file the bars, without rousing the bull terrier. His name was Alf, and Peter would have liked him a good deal if they had met in less difficult circumstances. But for the moment they were in opposite camps.

Not for the first time, Peter felt the handicap of not being a criminal. He had a pistol in his pocket. He could shoot Alf and the Bruiser as they slept and get away at his leisure. As far as possibilities go he could, but when it came to actualities, he couldn't. It needs practice and a considerable induration of the heart and mind to be able to kill in cold blood. Peter lacked these qualifications. It would have given him a good deal of pleasure to knock the Bruiser out—his conversation, though sparse, had been disgusting. He would have liked to make friends with Alf. But, friend or enemy, he didn't see his way to doing murder.

He thought how much more comfortable things would be if Frank Garrett knew where he was, or even if he had any idea of his own whereabouts. He might be almost anywhere on the tape-map. They had driven for the best part of half an hour. You can get a long way in half an hour, or you can drive round and round and come back to very much where you started.

He turned on his mattress and faced the wall. On the other side of that wall, on the other side of the locked door by his feet, was the passage with the area door at one end of it and Terry Clive's door at the other. But halfway along there was another door which, he felt sure, concealed the stairs. Maud Millicent had spoken of these stairs. She had said that they had a door at the top as well as at the bottom, and that the doors were locked, and that she herself had the keys. Peter's fancy played about those doors and the stair which led to the upper part of the house. No interior door would have so strong a lock as an outside door, and no upstairs window would have bars. Give him ten minutes alone in the house and he would back himself to smash those locks, and, once upstairs, he could take Terry Clive out through the nearest window into that safest of all safe places, a street commanded by a thousand other windows. Daylight and the King's highway—he asked no more.

He fell asleep on that, and plunged into a vivid dream. He was on safari in a taxi driven by the Bruiser. Jake and he were shooting bull-terriers with machine-guns at about eighty miles an hour. The bull-terriers ran like the wind, and presently they put up Terry Clive out of a patch of spiny cactus, and she ran like the wind too. She was barefoot and in her nightgown, just as he had seen her at Heathacres, but she had dropped her coat and left it lying on the yellow sand. One of the bull-terriers was Alf, and he ran with her step for step. And just as he was beginning to gain on them Peter suddenly felt that he couldn't bear it. He tumbled his machine-gun out of the taxi and jumped after it. Then he and Terry and the dog were all running together, whilst Jake sprayed them with bullets. They ran all across the Sahara and down the Nile. And then he caught an aeroplane by the wings and pulled it down and they flew away, with Jake and the Bruiser coming after them in another plane. It was a very exciting flight. Peter sang at the top of his voice, and the wind sang in his ears, and Alf twined himself affectionately about Terry's feet and was sick. And Terry said, "I want the pearls. Give them back to me at once," and the bullets began to fall all round them again, so they jumped for it, he and Terry and Alf, and came down by the Marble Arch. They had to run for their lives, because Jake and the Bruiser were after them on motor-bicycles. And all at once they had turned a corner and were sprinting down Sunderland Terrace where his Aunt Fanny lived, and, quite without any intermission, they were in her drawing-room, where she sat drinking tea with her friend Miss Hollinger. The odd thing was that neither Aunt Fanny nor Miss Hollinger seemed to know that they were there. Alf snuffed at the furniture, and Peter and Terry stood there holding hands like ghosts come back to visit the glimpses of the past. But Terry's hand was warm in his—Aunt Fanny said, "O dear—I never thought he would be taken first." And she put her handkerchief to her eyes and said, "I haven't bought my mourning yet. I wouldn't like not to wear mourning for Peter." But Miss Hollinger passed up her cup for some more tea and said primly, "We must look on the bright side, dear Miss Talbot. It's an ill wind that blows nobody any good."

He woke up. The kitchen was dark, the fire dead in the range. Alf and the Bruiser snored. The dream was gone.

Peter turned over and went to sleep again.

CHAPTER XXIX

TERRY Clive ate her breakfast—a boiled egg, bread and butter, and a hot, strong cup of tea. Then she looked in the glass, thought how pale she was, and took steps to remedy this. No one was going to think she was afraid, or that she hadn't slept, or anything of that sort. Especially not the young man who had boiled her egg and who had tried to steal Emily's pearls.

He knocked presently on the door, and stood just inside it when she said, "Come in."

"I hope the egg was all right."

"Yes, thank you."

Peter looked pleased.

"I hope you like eggs, because I can see that cooking is going to be the difficulty. Jake has just got back, and the Bruiser is going off. I left them arguing about how to cook a steak. None of it sounded right to me."

"There are always eggs," said Terry. "But, actually, I thought about going home."

"To the fatted calf? I'm afraid you're expected to stay to lunch."

"Look here," she said, "I want to go home. What are you going to get out of keeping me here? Whatever it is, I'll double it. If you're afraid I'll talk, I won't. You're not like those other two men—you don't want to hurt me. Let me go."

Peter gazed at her with as much sarcasm as he could muster and said,

"There's nothing doing. Here you are, and here you stay, with Jake and Alf and me to see that you do. And Alf's about the only one of the three you might be able to bribe."

"And who is Alf?" There was a hopeful note in Terry's voice.

As if he had heard the repetition of his name, the bull-terrier came padding down the passage, ears at half-cock, nose wrinkled, and hackles ready to rise. He came snuffing into the room, and straight into Terry's heart. Peter saw how she could look when she was friendly.

She said, "Angel!" and went down on her knees to put her arms round Alf's neck. There was a moment of suspense. Most dogs like you or they don't. Bull-terriers are very quick off the mark. They love you—or they hate you, and Terry's face and her unguarded throat were horribly near those very sharp, strong teeth. Peter's heart gave a jerk, but before he had time to move he saw Alf's expression change. The hackles lay down, the eyes goggled, the lips stretched with an idiotic grin, a large pink tongue came flopping out in an attempt to lick as much of Terry's face as possible. She fended him off, laughing, and with joyous woofs he launched a playful attack which nearly bowled her over.

A growl from the Bruiser and a piercing whistle from Jake restored order. With a final lick and a regretful eye, Alf slunk back to the kitchen. Terry, still laughing, said,

"Oh, what a *lamb!*"

"Eminently bribable. But you'd better be careful. He belongs to Jake, and Jake—"

A little cold shiver ran down Terry's spine. She said, "What about Jake?" and did not know that she had stopped laughing.

"The less the better, I should say."

Terry looked at him.

"What do you mean by that?"

Peter did not answer her directly. He frowned, came nearer, and suddenly said in a quite, non-carrying voice,

"You've got a bruise on your arm."

Terry's hand went to her elbow. She said,

"Why—yes. It isn't anything. It'll be gone in a day or two."

Peter shook his head.

"I don't think so—not if you've any gumption."

She felt the shiver again.

"What do you mean?"

Peter dropped his voice lower still.

"Your arm is very badly hurt. You are all black and blue. Say so in front of the others if you get the chance. Make the most of it."

He turned and went away past the door which led to the stairs and on into the kitchen. The shutters had been opened. A grey light came in through the upper part of the windows. The Bruiser was making preparations to depart.

"You've got a lot to say to that girl," said Jake suspiciously.

Peter put on a swaggering air.

"You've got your orders, and I've got mine. I'm to soft-sawder her, jolly her along, keep her from worrying—or trying to get away. She got bruised bringing her here. My orders are to keep her quiet till the bruises are gone. You get on with your job, and I'll get on with mine."

"Oh, you're doing fine," said Jake with a sneer, and went out to lock up after the Bruiser.

Terry slipped into the kitchen as soon as he was out of it. He found her there looking at the rusty range with disfavour. He opened his mouth to speak, but Peter got in first.

"She says she can cook."

Jake stared.

"Who does?"

"She does. Why not let her?"

"I cook very well," said Terry. "I got a diploma. You might as well let me do something. It's frightfully cold in my room. After all, I'd be earning my keep."

Jake looked from her to the windows as if he were measuring the distance.

"You can't see in," said Peter. "And if you could, what would you see? A girl cooking—the most ordinary, natural, every-day thing in the world."

Jake lit a cigarette. Then he went over to the Bruiser's mattress and lay down. All his movements were quick and jerky. He called Alf to him and made the dog lie down at his feet. Then he said,

"Cook away if you want to—I've no orders against it. But no nearer the windows than what you are now, or I'll set the dog on you."

"On me?" said Peter.

Jake used language.

"No, on her." He used more language.

Terry stuck her chin in the air and asked where the larder was. It was heaven to have something to put her hand to. If she had had to stay in that cold room with nothing to do but sit on the edge of her bed and think, she might have found horrible things to think about. But you can't think about horrible things when you are cooking, especially when every solitary thing you've got to use has been put away dirty and has to be scraped and boiled and scrubbed before you can do anything with it.

Terry scraped, cleaned, boiled, and scrubbed. There was a bar of yellow soap, and you can do wonders with soap and boiling water. She washed dish-cloths, dusters, and the roller towel from the lavatory. She set Peter to scrub, first the kitchen table, and then the kitchen floor. She would have liked to put Jake to black-leading the range, but that would have to be done when the fire was out, and she wanted the oven for her beefsteak pie. There was plenty of food in the larder—a large piece of steak; eggs; onions; apples; bread; milk brought in by Jake; a six-pound bag of flour; a hunk of cheese; and a dozen bananas.

Beefsteak pie and banana fritters for lunch, and something with eggs and cheese for supper. There was sugar, so she could make a cake.

When everything was clean she began her pie. Peter found himself admiring. He thought a good many girls would have gone limp in the spine and pink about the eyes.

He watched Terry rolling out dough, and putting little dabs of butter all over it, and rolling it out again. She had firm, pretty, capable little hands.

On the other side of the kitchen Jake lay on the mattress smoking, with his eyes half shut.

Terry sprinkled more butter and rolled out her dough again. She said without looking up,

"Why do you do this sort of thing?"

"Kidnapping?"

"Yes."

Peter laughed.

"One must do something for a living."

She said viciously, "You might scrub floors. I expect you'd learn in time."

"Women have no sense of justice. This floor is beautifully scrubbed."

She folded the dough over and rolled it out again.

"What is your name? I suppose you've got one."

Peter said,"Spike," and then, "Pretty—isn't it?"

"Frightful! And I don't believe it either. Nobody could possibly be called Spike."

"Lots of people are—in America."

"But you're not American."

"I'm afraid not. As a matter of fact they threw me out."

"What for?"

"Kidnapping," said Peter pleasantly.

She looked up quickly, and their eyes met. He saw hers wide and startled—yes, definitely startled—before they brightened into anger. She changed colour—a sudden pallor, a sudden flaming blush. She bit her lip like a child that doesn't want to cry, and brought the rolling-pin down hard upon her folded dough.

Peter had sensations—anger because she could take him so easily at his word, and something softer than anger because her youth and courage plucked at his heart and she was in danger. And for the matter of that so was he. He looked past her at Jake, and saw him with his eyes shut and a cigarette hanging crooked from the corner of his mouth. He might be asleep, or he might not. Probably not.

Peter laughed just under his breath and said, "Let us tell each other the story of our lives."

"Thank you, it doesn't interest me," said Terry. She set the dough aside and began to cut up the steak.

Peter sat on the corner of the table and watched her. He had no idea that cooking was such a complicated business. It seemed only fair to provide entertainment by the way.

"Shall I tell you about my first crime?"

"No, thank you."

"A pity about that. *Tout comprendre, c'est tout pardonner*—to understand is to forgive. You're a little inclined to misjudge me, you know. In the matter of Mrs. Cresswell's pearls now—you simply jumped to the conclusion that I was going off with them."

"Weren't you going off with them?"

Peter laughed.

"Miss Margesson would have been very much surprised if I had."

"But she gave them to you."

"Not to me, but to someone she was expecting by the name of Jimmy. As an alternative to Spike, I have been called Jimmy too, so when she said Jimmy and pushed the pearls into my hands I didn't know what to think, and before I could get going she ran away, and you came along and told me off."

"You expect me to believe that?"

"I don't know. You're young and innocent—you might."

She flushed again, more vividly than before.

Peter leaned sideways and wrote with his finger on the spilled flour beyond the pastry-board: "Say your arm hurts."

Terry said, "Why?"

He rubbed the flour smooth with the flat of his hand and wrote again: "Don't be a fool."

Terry swept the words away with an indignant hand and went over to the range. She brought back a frying-pan with some melted fat, tipped the cut-up steak into it, and went back to the fire.

"I hope you're grateful to me, cooking for you like this. I

feel a lot more like having my arm in a sling, I can tell you.''

''What's the matter with it?''

She pushed the bits of meat about in the sizzling fat.

''You know perfectly well I've got a bruise the size of a house.''

''There are worse things than bruises,'' said Peter grimly.

There was a gleam between Jake's lashes. So he wasn't asleep. Well, he was welcome to what he could hear. When he went out tonight and made his report—Peter had an idea that Jake would make a report—he could make the most of that bruise. But if ever Peter wished for anything in his life, he wished he could follow Jake and identify the person to whom he reported.

A very savoury smell began to come from the steak. Alf's ears went up like twin points of exclamation. As plainly as if the words had been spoken, they said,''Oh, boy!'' With a furtive sideways glance at his master the bull-terrier rose to his feet, stretched, and began to edge noiselessly towards the smell. His pink nose snuffed the delicious fragrance. He made googoo eyes at Terry, who threw a glance at the mattress and, stepping back to the table, found a long delicious strip of fat and meaty gristle. It went down Alf's throat with a golloping sound. Jake swore, called him back, and clouted him.

Terry went on making her pie.

CHAPTER XXX

HUMAN beings are very adaptable. By the end of the day Terry was housekeeping. She had a grocery list written out for Jake to take away with him when he went off duty, and she sent the Bruiser back to wipe his feet when he came in wet and muddy.

The extraordinary thing was that he went. Peter caught his breath, but the Bruiser went back meekly enough. They heard him scuffing his feet on the mat by the area door. He came, after all, of generations of women who had told their men they wouldn't have boots like that on a clean scrubbed kitchen floor. Breeding tells.

But it was Peter who black-leaded the stove when Jake came back in the morning—black lead was one of the items on Terry's list. He also lit the fire and carried coals. The Bruiser was only interested in getting away for his day off, but Jake came and leaned against the kitchen table and watched with jeering eyes.

They had haddock for breakfast. It came wrapped up in newspaper, which Terry said was revolting. Whilst she was washing the fish Peter picked up the sheet and went to burn it. He had it in his outstretched hand, when his eye was caught by a headline and a name—of all names in the world Louisa Spedding's name. Something went hard and cold in him as he flattened the paper out.

TELEPHONE-BOX MURDER.
WHO SHOT LOUISA SPEDDING?

Between him and the paper came the picture he had seen in the taxi by the flash of a street-lamp—Maud Millicent Simpson's hand resting quietly on her knee, and a little pistol not so much longer than the hand.

He stood over the range and read what was there to read. Miss Roberta Jones of Cardiff, up in London on a visit to her uncle, Mr. Robert Jones of Tooting, had entered the telephone-box at the corner of Sitfield Row at 1.45 p.m. precisely. A second later she had rushed screaming into the traffic of North Street. Commotion. Hubbub. The discovery of Louisa's body. Police whistles. The collection of an interested and horrified crowd. No one had seen Louisa enter the box. No one had seen anyone come out of it. No one could suggest any motive for the murder of a respectable middle-aged woman who had neither husband nor lover. The police were exploring every avenue. They would be glad to interview the deceased woman's half-brother, Mr. James Peter Reilly, who had walked out of the Edenbridge Hotel, Minden Avenue, without leaving an address some time in the late afternoon of Monday, the day of the murder. He is stated to have had an interview with his sister there between twelve and one o'clock, and with the exception of the murderer he was probably the last person to see her alive.

Peter crumpled up the paper and pushed it down among the kindling coals. There was a great anger on him for the death of this harmless, innocent woman. She had come to see him—no, she had been sent to see him. There was design in that. She had gone out from him in trouble at the death of her brother, and she had been most brutally murdered. He watched the paper burn and go away into a handful of black shaking ash rimmed and shot through with fire. It was the most damnable and deliberate murder. She had been sent to make sure that he was Spike Reilly, and she had come away from him and met Maud Millicent Simpson, and Maud Millicent Simpson had shot her in cold blood. He was as sure of this as if he had witnessed the crime. Who else could have done it? Who else had any interest in doing it? Maud Millicent had been recognized, and that meant death to Louisa Spedding. But Maud Millicent would use her first—send her to see her brother, meet her afterwards, and talk in friendly fashion. . . .

His anger mounted. Terry saw his face as he turned round from the range, and was startled. Just for a moment she knew what it was to be afraid.

The day lagged and dragged. Jake lay on his bed and smoked and slept, or appeared to sleep. Alf was put out into the yard, where he whined, and snuffed, and butted the back door with his nose until Jake went out and hammered him, after which he went and sat down on a pile of damp straw and made miserable slobbering noises to himself.

Terry cooked, washed up, polished all the spoons and forks until they shone, and baked a super sponge-cake for tea. Jake, finishing his third slice, laughed suddenly and said,

"Almost a pity to waste a cook like you, miss."

Whereupon Terry laughed too, and said, "But I don't think I'm wasted. You are all very complimentary about my cooking."

Jake winked at Peter.

"Ah, but you won't be able to keep it up."

She looked at him in surprise.

"Why not?"

"Our cooks don't stay," said Jake, and laughed consumedly.

For a second time in the day Terry saw Peter look like murder.

"What did he mean?" she said when Jake had gone out to the yard. "And why did you look like that? You frightened me."

Peter said, "Are you frightened?" and Terry said, 'Sometimes."

She waited for Peter to tell her that there was nothing to be frightened of, but he had a hard look and frowning brows. She said quickly,

"How long is this going on? I want to go home. What do they want? Is it money?"

She said "What do they want?", not "What do you want?" It pleased him, but he thought it dangerous. He said,

"Not money—at least I don't think so. It's what you saw—they're afraid of what you saw. And, by the way, what did you see?"

Terry shut her lips in a firm red curve. Her eyes met his. She shook her head and did not speak.

"Shall I tell you?" said Peter. "I will if you like. You see, I know, because I was in the bushes, and I saw what you did. Shall I tell you what you saw? That's one thing about this place, there's plenty of time for conversation. Well, you looked out of your window, and you saw someone come from the glass door on to the terrace—the same door that Norah Margesson came out of when she gave me the pearls. The moon had gone in, and it was too dark to see much more than a shadow. There were three windows on the left of the door as I looked at it. The shadow went along to the nearest of those windows and took out a pane of glass. All professional, with treacle and brown paper. I could just hear the glass tinkling, and I got some of the treacle on my thumb later on—but that's my affair and nothing to do with what you saw. When the shadow had finished its job it went back into the house and locked the door. I don't know whether it was a male shadow or a female shadow, but perhaps you do."

"I'm not telling anyone what I saw."

"You were supposed to be telling the police yesterday, weren't you? Shall I tell you what I think? I think you were bluffing. If you'd recognized the person who came out of that door, you'd have put the screw on that person good and hard. You wouldn't have gone all round the house-party saying you'd seen something and you were going to the police if the picture didn't come back by Tuesday morning."

"How do you know what I did?" said Terry in a whisper.

They could hear Jake in the scullery calling to Alf.

Peter laughed.

"I know quite a lot of things, Terry. I know you were bluffing."

"You *can't* know what I saw—nobody can!"

He struck the table lightly with the edge of his hand.

"I can't, can't I? Well, I tell you I can. And it's not guessing either. What's the good of pulling your bluff on me? I was there, wasn't I? The only thing about it is that you were a bit nearer than I was. It's just possible you could make a good guess at whether it was a man or a woman who came through that door. Could you?"

Jake had gone out into the yard again. He left the back door open, and the wind blew in. It smelled of rain.

"Well?" said Peter. "Could you tell whether it was a man or a woman?"

"What difference does it make—now?" Her breath caught on the last word.

Peter thought he had shaken her. He said in a rough whisper,

"It makes all the difference. You've got to tell me what you saw. Don't you see, you little fool, that you've got into this mess because you talked too much—and not enough. If you had kept your mouth shut, nobody would have known. You'd have been safe at home. If you'd told the police then and there—"

Terry's eyes blazed. She said on a furious breath,

"How could I tell the police? If it was one of the people in the house—they were all people I knew—how could I tell?"

"You did the most dangerous thing you could have done."

She said, "Dangerous?" and then, "They want money, don't they? But they haven't said so."

"What's the good of money? You've shilly-shallied till they don't know what you know. Don't you realize the mess you're in? There's somebody's neck at stake now."

"What do you mean?"

"The person who did this job is liable to swing for the Oppenstein murder—that's what I mean."

They sat with the tea-things between them, and the

cake Terry had made. A neat, tidy kitchen—a most domestic meal—and quick, angry talk of murder past and perhaps to come. Peter had not meant it to go so far, but his temper had struck a spark from her resistance. He saw the colour die out of her face.

The back door banged. Jake was coming in. Peter said quickly,

"Don't look like that. But you'll have to do what I tell you."

CHAPTER XXXI

MURDER past and murder yet to come. That was the burden of Peter's thoughts through the long evening and late into the night. As he saw it, Maud Millicent had laid a very pretty trap for him, and if he had really been Spike Reilly, he did not see how he would have escaped it. There was the murder of Solly Oppenstein's butler, Francis Bird. He thought Spike Reilly had been cast for the part of First Murderer. The Turner might at any moment be found tucked away in his car. He thought it would be found there, and it would, of course, have his finger-prints all over it. But the Turner was a small matter. All day it had been borne in upon him that he was intended to make a really sensational appearance as the murderer of Louisa Spedding. Spike Reilly was Louisa's only relative. She had probably saved money, and what she had saved she would have left to her brother. And he was the last person to have seen her alive. The ingenuity of Maud Millicent's plan chilled him to the marrow. Louisa had been sent to see him and then murdered. He had been tricked into disappearing. Where would suspicion rest but upon James Peter Reilly? The trap was neatly set. If it hadn't been for the breakfast haddock, he wouldn't even have known that Louisa was dead. No newspapers were to be brought into the house, lest Terry Clive should see what she wasn't meant to see. And he had actually swallowed that. Terry Clive my foot! It was Spike Reilly who wasn't to see a paper and find out that poor Louie had been murdered.

He thought the game had gone on long enough. He had hoped for a visit from Maud Millicent. He had met her, talked to her, and had not a single clue as to her identity. He had seen an old woman, and he had listened to a shaky voice and a made-up cough. He had seen a hand just for a moment in the flicker of a street-lamp—a small hand with a pistol in it. London was full of women whose hands would fit that picture. There was only one Maud Millicent, and he wanted desperately to find her.

Once he left this house, he left the chance that she might come there. He thought that she would have to come there. There was the matter of the bruise on Terry's arm. Nothing was to be done until the bruise was gone. Well, Maud Millicent would have to be sure that the bruise was gone. Would she take his word for it? He wondered. If she did, she would have to see him. But he thought she would come herself. He banked on that. Jake and the Bruiser didn't come into it at all, because without using force neither would get a chance of seeing Terry's arm, and force was not to be used. No, it lay between Maud Millicent and himself. Whether she trusted him, or whether she trusted no one but herself, there would have to be a meeting between them. He must hang on for that, and Terry must hang on too. If the worst came to the worst, he thought he could hold Jake up.

Jake wouldn't shoot if he could help it—he could reckon on that. He had an automatic in his pocket, and he would be quick on the draw—probably quicker than Peter. The Bruiser didn't worry him much. A slow fellow, and only there at night. The sound of his snoring filled the room. Peter took out his pistol and handled it. There was a little light from the fire. He sat up, turning himself so as to screen the pistol, and opened the breach. The magazine was full, but he would just make sure—

The magazine was empty.

He scrambled up and felt in his pockets for the space clip. He knew where he had put it. He could see himself standing at the dressing-table in his room at the Edenbridge, putting the pistol here, an extra clip of cartridges there—

But they weren't anywhere.

Jake, of course—the real pick-pocket type. It enraged him to think of Jake's hand in his pocket, slipping in, slipping out, palming the clip, getting away with the pistol, putting it back empty. . . . The anger burned itself out. No use being angry.

What did it mean? That was the thing. It meant something—but what? Had Jake acted under orders, or was it a private flutter of his own? He could think of reasons why Maud Millicent should wish to have him disarmed. If he was to figure as the villain of the piece, the murderer of Francis Bird, of Louisa Spedding, and perhaps of Terry Clive, it would be just as well to make sure that he was not in a position to break out of the trap which had been so carefully set. He might give trouble. With a pistol and two clips of ammunition he might give a quite considerable amount of trouble.

On the other hand, Jake might have acted without orders. He might be up to some game of his own. Or he might be suspicious, and afraid of being taken at a disadvantage. Possession of the only firearm would naturally impart a comfortable sense of security. Peter would have liked to accept this theory, but the more he thought about it, the less he believed in it.

No, Jake was acting under orders, which meant that Spike Reilly was in for it. He looked back over the whole astonishing ten days,and saw quite plainly that Spike Reilly had been brought over from Brussels for this one purpose. He was the tool who had outlived his usefulness, the fool who had begun to ask for more, to brag, to hint at blackmail. He had become a liability, and Maud Millicent saw her way to converting him into an asset. The real Spike Reilly would probably have walked blindfold into her trap.

The question was what Peter Talbot, with his eyes open, was going to do about it.

CHAPTER XXXII

MAUD Millicent came in the dark of the Thursday evening.

Louisa Spedding had been dead three days. Terry Clive had been missing three days. The papers clamoured. Scotland Yard hummed. Mr. Basil Ridgefield wore out its corridors with his pacings, and the patience of its officials with his continuous insistence that something should be done. The inevitable reply that the police were doing everything in their power pacified him not at all. He returned to his house to snatch a hasty meal, to ring up members of parliament, and to write indignant letters to the press. After which, refreshed in pertinacity, he once more returned to haunt police headquarters.

In those two or three days Fabian Roxley went haggard and yellow. He was punctual and efficient at his work, but he had the eyes of a man who has forgotten how to sleep, and who does not remember when he last tasted food. Garrett snapped and swore, kept his promise of secrecy, and told himself fifty times a day that he was a fool for doing so—and, quite possibly, an accessory to murder. For all he could see, Maud Millicent had scored again. Francis Bird was dead, Louisa Spedding was dead, and Terry Clive and Peter Talbot were off the map, and because he had promised Peter Talbot to hold his tongue he was holding it. When two more bodies were fished up out of the river he could tell himself how clever he had been. He had a more vicious snarl for himself than any which his subordinates had to endure. But one thing he promised himself—if Maud Millicent got away with this, she wouldn't get away for ever. He would get her, if it took him from here to Timbuctoo and from now to Doomsday.

The odd house-keeping in the basement went on. The Bruiser was there at night, Jake in the day, Peter Talbot all the time. The Bruiser slept by night, and for the most part Jake pretended to sleep by day. Sometimes he went out into the yard, but when he did this he left the back door open and took the key with him. Sometimes he would be away as much as ten minutes, throwing a lump of coal for Alf to fetch. Terry tried to make friends with him over Alf. She had never met anyone she couldn't make friends with before, but the expression in Jake's eyes stopped her dead—a knowing, leering glitter which made her feel rather sick. She failed with the Bruiser too. He was not so offensive as Jake. He had more the look of a sullen brute. He would come in, eat his supper without a word, and then fling himself down on the mattress in the corner.

These two rebuffs drove her closer to Peter. She came inevitably to regard him as an ally. He was on guard, but she began to think of him as on guard against Jake's insolence and the Bruiser's brutality. They had shown no more than a hint of these things, but she was aware of them, and aware that Peter stood between her and any more open manifestation.

Peter, for his part, was pulled in two directions. At their first meeting Terry had walked into his mind. She had stirred him to amusement. He had admired her courage, the way she looked, the way she spoke, the way she had told him off and made him give her back the pearls. Now she began to walk into his heart. He was with her all day. He saw that her courage never flagged, and that even in imprisonment she could set about making a home. He liked that, but there were a dozen quite irrational things which made him like her more—the way she laughed, the way she caught her lip between her teeth, the way she looked at him, the way she looked at Alf, the way she spoke, the way she walked, the way she beat up eggs in a china bowl. Peter, in fact, was falling in love, and falling rapidly. He spent hours of those three nights wondering whether to try and knock the Bruiser out and get Terry away. If he failed, if for instance the Bruiser were to knock him out, Terry would have no protection, and he would lose the chance of identifying Maud Millicent Simpson. If there had been any certainty of getting Terry away, or even a good chance, he must have taken it. But the risk was a horrible one. He decided to wait on the event.

Maud Millicent arrived in the deep dusk when one car looks like another and all the cats are grey. The man who had driven her came down the steps and rang the area bell. When the door opened he stood aside and she passed him and went in. Peter, in the kitchen with Terry, saw her standing on the threshold looking at them. He received an extraordinary shock. It was the Bruiser whom he had expected to see, but here in the doorway was Maud Millicent. It could be no one else. Maud Millicent in the guise of a young woman smartly dressed in black, the latest extravagant hat tilted to show the latest extravagant hair, so pale as to look primrose under the light. She was slimly belted under a square-shouldered black coat swinging open. There was a bunch of greenish orchids at the bosom of her black dress. There were pearl studs in her ears. Her lips were vivid with paint. But from the lips upwards there was something so horrid, so unnatural about her aspect, that Terry drew in her breath with a gasp and Peter had a moment of nausea. All the upper part of her face was covered by some kind of a mask shaped to the contours of nose, cheek and brow, and tinted as the face of a doll is tinted. The eyebrows were arched and painted in a flat, shallow brown, but where the eyes should have been the mask was cut away. The effect of the living eyes looking out of this coloured mask was horrible. They raked the kitchen at a glance, took in the tidy floor, the shining range, the young man and the girl at the table, the whole orderly, peaceful scene.

Peter pushed back his chair and got up, but Terry sat where she was. It was she who had been facing the door. She went on facing it now. She had one hand on the table. With an effort of will she kept it from closing. The other hand was in her lap. It clenched hard and drove the nails against the palm.

The eyes which looked through the eye-slits of that unnatural mask came coldly to rest upon her. Without turning her head Maud Millicent lifted her voice to say,

"You two men can stay where you are. I'll call if I want you."

This lifted voice was hard and sweet. It was the voice which belonged to the mask. The sweetness was a metallic, mechanical sweetness. It had no human quality.

She came towards them, her hands in a small black muff. Peter wondered whether the little pistol was there too. She came to the corner of the table and looked for the first time directly at him.

"You seem to have carried out your instructions," she said.

He said, "I've done my best."

A faint mockery crept into the metallic voice.

"You've made her comfortable."

"She has made us comfortable," said Peter.

"Domesticated? That was more than you could have bargained for. Well, you won't have to play gaoler much longer. What about the bruise? It's had time to come out. Is she marked at all?"

Peter said, "I've no idea."

Maud Millicent laughed.

"What wasted opportunities!" She turned to Terry Clive. "It was the left arm. Roll up your sleeve and let me have a look at it."

Terry sat where she was, the one hand clenched in her lap and the nails driving home, the other lying open and steady on the table. She lifted her eyes to the eyeholes of the mask and said,

"Why?"

Maud Millicent did not move. She did not raise her voice. Something came from her—a terrifying sense of power. Terry had never felt anything like it before. It shook her. Maud Millicent said,

"Do you want me to call the men in to strip you? Do what you are told!"

Terry's hand went to her sleeve. She pushed it up a little way, and felt her fingers shake. That made her so angry that it did her good. Her blood ran hot. She stood up and held out her arm. The hand was brown to the wrist, but the arm milky white. Only three or four inches of this whiteness showed, then the blue sleeve began.

"That is no good. Push it right up above the elbow!"

Terry shook her head.

"It won't go any farther."

"Then take your dress off! I've got to see the arm. If you're modest"—the voice sneered—"Spike can look out of the window. Hurry up or I'll have Jake in to help you!"

Terry undid the buttons of her dress and pulled it over her head. She stood up in her short peach-coloured petticoat and held out her left arm. Maud Millicent drew an ungloved hand from her muff and took her lightly by the wrist. The arm was turned this way and that. The metallic voice said,

"There's no bruise. I couldn't have held her so hard after all. There's just the faintest mark where the hypodermic needle went in, but that's easy to fake." She was talking about Terry, but she wasn't talking to her. She dropped the wrist she was holding, put her hand to the breast of her coat, and said, "Turn your arm. Come right under the light." And then, before Terry knew what was going to happen, the muff was under her elbow and Maud Millicent's hand with a pin in it had traced a straggling scratch which crossed the mark of the hypodermic.

Between pain and surprise Terry cried out.

Peter turned round, to see the blood running down her arm. The eyes behind the mask met his with a glitter in them. The hand that had held the pin went back into the black muff.

He commanded himself. He wondered how much of his fury had shown in his face. Not much, he thought. Maud Millicent was certainly armed. If she shot him down, Terry was as good as dead. Jake and the driver were just on the other side of the open door.

Maud Millicent Simpson laughed.

Terry said, "How dare you?" And in the same breath, "It's nothing." She put out her hand to Peter. "It's nothing really. But why did she do it? Is she mad?"

"What a comfortable thought!" said Maud Millicent. "Make the most of it. You're just about finished with, you know."

"What will you take to let me go?" said Terry with stiff lips.

Maud Millicent laughed again.

"What do you think?"

Terry said, "I don't know."

"Nor do I. And I haven't any more time to waste on you. Put on your dress! Spike, you'll come with me."

She walked out of the door and down the passage to Terry's room. Peter followed her. If she shut the door, could he rush her, get the pistol, or stop her getting it? The temptation shook him. If he tried and failed—finish for Terry. But there was no safe way—no way which didn't hazard both their lives. He thought he would hear what she had to say.

She didn't close the door. She left it wide open and went over to the window on the far side of the room. Standing there, she could look right down the long passage to the area door where Jake and the driver waited. They were in sight, but not in hearing. The setting was perfect for an interview with a gang member whom you had ceased to trust, or perhaps had never trusted. He wondered whether she trusted anyone at all.

She stood with her back to the window and said low and hard,

"You've done very well. You seem to have made friends with her. Nothing could be better. The whole thing can be cleared up now. That little scratch on her arm is the sort of thing anyone might have—an unfastened brooch would account for it. The mark left by the hypodermic needle goes out. Terry Clive goes out too—" She paused, and added, "tonight."

Peter said, "How?" He hoped his voice was quite ordinary.

She stood there with her hands in her muff, an elegant, ultra-smart young woman. The unshaded light in the ceiling dazzled on the pale hair, on the pearl in her ear, on the painted lips and the hard texture of the mask. She said,

"This is how."

Peter moved a step and turned to shut the door. Her voice came at him like a pistol shot, just the one word,

"No!"

He made his face stupid and turned back again. She had him covered. The hand in the muff held a pistol—he was quite sure of that. He looked enquiry, and she said,

"Leave that door alone! Stand away from it! I want to keep my eye on the others. What are you afraid of? They can't hear us."

Peter said, "Oh, no."

He saw her smile. Would he recognize that smile? He wished he knew some way of recognizing her. Louisa Spedding had said, "No matter what she did or how she changed, I should always know her." Why hadn't he made Louisa speak? He could have made her speak. If he got free of this place he might meet Maud Millicent in the street and never know her again. She could be any woman, play any part. He thought with contempt of his feeble efforts to identify her by snicking her dress in the taxi. The old woman's dress belonged to the old woman's part—she might never wear it again. Neither of the two women he had met was the real woman. Nobody knew what the real woman looked like.

He stood respectfully before her and listened to his orders.

"I want this business closed down. We can finish it tonight. I shall go into the upper part of the house. Presently I shall call for Jake, and he will come up to me. The area door will be unlocked. You will pretend to discover this, and you will make the girl believe that you are going to get her away. She's got to leave this house of her own free will and without a finger laid on her. If any busybody happens to be looking out of a window, they will see a girl getting into a car with her young man, and they'll never give it another thought. You understand, that's what it's got to look like—a young man going out with his girl. I'll give you a quarter of an hour for talking, and then if the street is clear, Bert will whistle *Tea for Two*. You'll wait long enough for him to pass, and then you'll bring her along. I suppose you can drive a Morris?"

"Oh, yes."

"Very well—you will drive out of London by the Great West Road."

Peter's heart leapt. Let him get Terry away in a car, and he would back himself to win the game. But was it possible that they would let him get away with the car and Terry? If he was unsuspected, why not? Or was there a trap? On this road he had taken there was no step which might not send him crashing into some hidden pit. Yet the step must be taken. He repeated her last words,

"The Great West Road. And then?"

"We shall catch you up. You wouldn't be able to manage alone. We shall be in a Packard saloon, and we shall toot three times as we pass you. After that all you have to do is to follow us. Do you think you can get the girl to go?"

"Oh, yes—we're quite friendly—she'll jump at the chance. It's as easy as kissing your hand."

She smiled. It did actually make Peter feel physically sick to see the slow, painted smile beneath the painted mask.

"Kiss as much as you like," she said, "and make the most of your time. She won't be so pretty to kiss after tonight."

She turned round to straighten her hat at the glass and to smile at her reflection there. Peter could almost have shot her then if his pistol hadn't been dead. For the first time in his life he wanted to kill. He stood aside as she came past him to the door, pausing there a moment to say,

"You understand? A quarter of an hour for talk—Bert

whistling *Tea for Two* when the street is clear—a minute to let him get away—and then you take her out to the Great West Road and drive on until we pass you. You've got all that?"

"Oh, yes—it ought to be easy enough."

"Five hundred pounds if you bring it off," she said, and walked away down the passage to the door which gave upon the stair.

He heard the jingle of a key-ring. He saw the door he had wanted so badly to open swing back against the wall. Maud Millicent went up the stairs. Bert opened the area door and went out. Jake remained where he was.

Peter set his teeth and went into the kitchen.

CHAPTER XXXIII

TERRY was standing by the table. She had put on her dress again. Her face had no colour. Her eyes were bright and strained. She had a flinching look as he came in, but she controlled it. It hurt him so much that he could hardly control himself. He shut the door and came to the other side of the table.

Terry said, "What are you going to do with me?"

He put his hands on the table and leaned across it.

"Terry—don't look like that."

Her eyes dwelt on him. They were burning bright.

"What are they going to do with me? What is that woman going to do? You won't tell me, but I know. They're going to kill me—you know that. She's given you your orders, hasn't she?"

"Terry!"

Her look changed to a puzzled one.

"Why are you doing it? Is it for money?"

"No, it isn't for money."

She leaned on the table.

"Then why? You don't hate me, do you? I haven't done anything to make you hate me. You're not like Jake. You don't *want* to hurt me, do you? I can't see why you should."

"Don't, my dear! Terry, please don't!" He took her

hands across the table and held them. They were very cold indeed. "Terry—don't! I won't let them hurt you. I'll get you away."

Her hands stirred in his.

"Get me away?"

"If you'll do exactly what I tell you. She's gone upstairs. Listen—she's calling to Jake."

They stood there hand in hand, and heard Jake come along the passage and go clattering up the stairs a couple of steps at a time. Terry said in a whisper,

"He's gone upstairs."

They waited. Her hands clung to Peter's. Warmth was coming into them.

"Yes, he's gone upstairs," said Peter. "They've both gone up. And Bert went out—he's the driver—so that means there's no one on guard. Wait a minute till I go and see if there's anyone at the door."

He went to the area door and opened it. A cold, heavy air flowed sluggishly into the house. There was no fog but a pitch-dark night heavily clouded and without star or moon. He went half-way up the area steps, and saw the car, and the driver leaning against it.

Bert came over and whispered, "Are you ready?" And when Peter nodded he began at once to whistle stridently and rather out of tune:

"Tea for two, and two for tea,
Me for you, and you for me—"

He walked away. The sound of his feet on the pavement and the sound of the whistling receded.

Peter went back into the kitchen. He said quickly,

"Get your coat. The car's there. We've got a chance of getting away with it."

He saw her face change. Colour came into it. She went past him quick and light—so light that he could hear no sound of her feet as she ran down the passage. Then she was back, the coat flying loose and a hand on his arm. But at the area door she checked. There was a whisper close at his ear.

"Why it is open? Why have they left it open?"

He whispered back, "I'm supposed to be on guard. It's all right."

And then up the steps and across the pavement to the car.

He had a moment's indecision as they emerged from the area. Suppose they linked arms and ran for it to the corner. Suppose they were to ring the next-door bell. He took a quick look up and down. The road fairly bristled with "To let" boards. They stretched misshapen hands in the dim light of a street-lamp which seemed a long way off. A deserted road, a dead road, a road of derelict houses leading to a dark square. He could just distinguish a blur of trees.

No, better take the car, steer for some frequented road, and stop the first policeman.

The whole thing passed like a flash. Then they were in the car. The first tremor of movement, the gathering speed, the wheel between his hands, gave him an intoxicating sense of power, so easily, so lightly, so quickly they were away.

Terry's shoulder was tense against his. As they turned the corner and began to skirt the square, he said, "We're off!" and felt her relax. He could have shouted.

And then from behind him came the voice of Maud Millicent Simpson.

"Very neatly done, Spike. I'll give you a bonus for that."

Peter held the wheel steady. He felt as he had felt when a brickbat had dropped on his head when he was ten years old and he had gone in too close to watch the fascinating business of demolishing a rickety old house. There was the same horrid shock, the same angry surprise. But, whereas the brickbat had plunged him into unconsciousness, this shock intensified consciousness to an almost unbearable degree. With every sense heightened, he realized how cleverly, how fatally he had been tricked. What a fool he had been to dream that they would let him get away with Terry and a car. Before she had finished promising him a bonus it was all there in his mind—the complete picture of the dupe he had been and the danger they were in. The bonus he was likely to get was death, and he knew it. He spoke without undue delay in a rather grumbling voice,

"What's all this? I thought you were following us."

He heard Jake laugh. So the two of them were there in the back of the car. He hadn't thought to look, and there hadn't been time. They must have come out of the front door as soon as she had called Jake up to her and just got in there at the back and ducked down. It was the simplest, the easiest trick in the world.

Maud Millicent said in her hard, sweet voice, "I thought we'd give you a surprise. No use taking out two cars when one will do, and you might have had trouble with her—later on in the lighted streets. She might have wanted to stop a policeman and have one. I thought we'd really do better all together."

"It looks to me as if you didn't trust me," said Peter, still in that grumbling voice.

He mustn't take it too smoothly. If they had a chance at all, it lay in letting them think that he had no real suspicions. A man who thinks he's going to be murdered doesn't grumble.

Maud Millicent laughed quite musically.

"What a thing to say—and when I've just promised you a bonus! Don't be foolish, Spike—you've done very well. Here she is without a mark on her, and if anyone saw her get into the car, they would swear she came of her own free will, which is just what you were told to contrive. I'm sure she believed every word you said about getting her away. Almost any girl will fall for a repentant crook. It's so flattering to feel you've converted someone—isn't it, Miss Terry Clive? Quick, Jake!"

Terry had snatched at the handle, throwing her weight against the door, but even as she did it, Peter's hand left the wheel and caught her arm. There was a moment of horror, a moment of breaking strain, and then Jake had her wrists, pulling her back. She had no chance. He held her, not tightly, but in a clasp she could not shift. Peter's hand went back to the wheel.

Maud Millicent said, "Turn her!" and Terry was pushed into the corner of the seat against the door she had tried to open. She saw the outline of a hand. The light of a street-lamp passed across the hand. She saw that it held a pistol.

What sort of nightmare was this? She looked at the pistol with wide, straining eyes. Why hadn't she been quicker? If she had got the door open—She hadn't got it open. He had stopped her. He had tricked her, lied to her, betrayed her. It was not fear that drained the blood from her lips and the courage from her heart, but the agonizing pain of betrayal. It hurt so much that she had not cared what would happen to her after her desperate thrust at the door. It was not a bid for freedom, it was the blind panic instinct of escape from a proximity which had become unendurable. To sit beside him with her shoulder touching his, to hear him speak—it was more than she could bear. She thrust wildly at the door, and his hand came out and stayed her.

Now she stared at the pistol, and wondered whether they were going to shoot her, and whether it would hurt very much. She wasn't afraid. She leaned back against the side of the car where Jake had pushed her, and heard Maud Millicent say with an edge on the sweetness of her voice,

"You really are a fool, Terry Clive. We've got a fairly long drive before us, and you wouldn't enjoy it much with a broken arm or a broken leg. Hasn't anyone ever told you it's dangerous to jump out of a moving car? We were doing about twenty-five, I should think. You wouldn't have been killed, you know—no such luck. But you might have broken most of your bones, or you might have been dragged and got your face messed up, and that really would have been a pity—wouldn't it, Spike?"

Peter hunched his shoulders and put a growl into his voice.

"Oh, come off it! What's the good of this sort of thing? How do you expect me to drive in traffic with a girl trying to throw herself out of the car? Why couldn't you leave her to me like you said you were going to? She was as pleased as Punch until you butted in. First you say how well I've done, and then you go and spoil it. Why can't you leave the girl alone?"

Maud Millicent laughed a little.

"Very cock-a-hoop all of a sudden, aren't you, Spike? Now, Terry Clive, will you listen to me. We're taking you down into the country. If you do what you're told you'll be all right. If you give any trouble you won't. And if you try to call out or put your hand on that handle again, I shall shoot you. Don't buoy yourself up by thinking that this is a bit of bluff—it isn't. Or that I wouldn't dare, because I would. I could have shot you a dozen times in the last five minutes, and no one would have turned his head. Everyone's taken up with the noise they're making themselves. Now—are you going to be sensible?"

"What do you call sensible?"

"You'll go quietly and not give us any trouble."

"Where are you taking me?"

"That is our affair. You do what you're told and I'll tell Jake to let go of you."

"Tell him to let go," said Terry.

"Do you hear, Jake? She doesn't really care about having you so close. Not very flattering, but one just has to take the rough with the smooth. I expect she'd be kinder to Spike. What a pity we didn't think of it before. I could have driven the car, and we could have let Spike sit behind with her. She wouldn't have minded his arm round her."

Terry was quite rigid with anger. She didn't feel hurt and vulnerable any more. She felt hard enough to break anyone who touched her. She could have smashed that door open now, she could have jumped out of the car without hurting herself. She said in a small, clear voice,

"Tell him to take his hands away."

"Well, Jake, there you are. Go on—take them away. Now, Terry Clive, let's see how nicely you can behave. You lift a hand or open your mouth, and it's the last thing you'll ever do in this world. Jake's going to change places with me, and I'm going to keep this pistol resting on the seat where you'll feel it against the back of your neck. You needn't work up a faint or anything like that. It won't go off so long as you behave yourself."

"I don't know how I'm supposed to drive with all this sort of thing going on," said Peter gloomily. "What happens if we have a smash?'' He was wondering if it wouldn't be a good thing to stage one. A nice mild smash—nothing like it for collecting a crowd and a policeman. "Ten to one I'll run into something, with all this going on and a car I've never driven before. What happens then?''

Maud Millicent addressed him with sweetness.

"A bullet for you, and another for her. So you'd better give your mind to your driving,'' she said.

CHAPTER XXXIV

THEY had been driving for the best part of an hour. Peter had become to all appearance an automaton. When Maud Millicent said "Faster," he accelerated. When she said "Slow down here," he slowed down. When she said "Next turning to the left"—or right, as the case might be—he took it. They had cleared London long ago. He was no longer quite sure where they were, but presently they came out upon what he thought was the Guildford by-pass. Then the directions began again.

She had a map spread out upon her knees. He could hear it crackle, and he caught the flicker of a torch as she moved it to and fro. No, perhaps not she. Perhaps it was Jake who held the torch, because whether they were in traffic or in dark lanes, whether they dropped to twenty or raced along the straight at fifty-five, Maud Millicent's hand with the pistol in it stayed just there at Terry's ear. She was thorough, she was careful, and she was utterly ruthless. She would shoot Terry Clive with as little compunction as she had shot Louisa Spedding. She had explained that in her most mellifluous voice—any trouble of any sort, and she would shoot them both. The car would be found stranded by the side of the road. One of those murder-suicide cases so dear to the sensational press—SOCIETY GIRL AND GANGSTER—FATAL ROMANCE. It sounded horribly plausible. If she didn't choose this way out, it was because she had some better plan up her sleeve. Peter kept wondering what it was, and whether it would offer him a chance of getting away with his life and Terry's. Because he was under no illusion. They were in one danger, he and Terry Clive. They had seen too much, they knew too much, they were inconvenient. And they were about to be eliminated.

Peter had no intention of being eliminated if he could help it. Maud Millicent had said something about Sussex, and Sussex suggested the sea. A good way of eliminating them would be to have the car driven over a cliff. He had certainly gathered that an accident was to be staged. Well, if there was to be an accident, Jake and Maud Millicent must avoid the actual crash. They would find some excuse to leave the car, some means to ensure that he remained in it. He wondered how they were going to manage that. Spike Reilly, even if not a highly intelligent person, might be supposed to possess the elementary instincts of self-preservation. How did Maud Millicent expect or hope to induce him to drive himself and Terry Clive over a cliff? No, it would have to be something not quite so crude as that. He would very much have liked to know what. One thing was certain, if Jake and Maud Millicent left the car, his number and Terry's were up. And yet it was only there that he could see the faintest chance of escape. As long as that pistol was trained on Terry the slightest move on his part would touch it off. But if he could lull their suspicions, play the stupid grumbling dupe, and blunt even in a small degree the keen razor edge of Maud Millicent's watchfulness, there might be a moment, just one, in which he could make a desperate bid for safety.

All the chances were against a chance for him and Terry. He was already distrusted, already condemned. He couldn't speak to her or warn her. The critical moment might find her drowsy, dulled with misery, half fainting—and he needed to have her every sense alert, responsive.

Why should she respond? She had despised him, liked him in spite of herself, trusted him greatly, and dropped from that to a shattering sense of betrayal. Would she trust him again in some perilous instant of which she knew nothing, and could know nothing until it broke upon them both? How could she? How could he have the faintest hope of it? She sat there, drawn away from him, pressed against the side of the car, quite silent, quite motionless. He had not looked at her once, and he was sure that she had not looked at him. Yet he knew just how she sat, just how she held her head, just how her hands gripped one another. He knew that she was wounded past belief. He did not think she was afraid. He felt as if he had stabbed her and was leaving her to bleed to death. He felt the conflict of her thoughts, the conflict of his own.

Silence—a dark car—dark by-ways—a dark windy night. . . . His thoughts were strange to him. He contemplated them with surprise, with quickening interest, with excitement. Terry and himself. He had the feeling that they were isolated from everyone else in the world, two creatures alone in a creation so new that it had all to be discovered. The first man and the first woman—Adam and Eve—Peter Talbot and Terry Clive. . . . He thrust with a savage jab of humour amongst these thoughts. What a garden of Eden! At any rate the serpent was not far to seek.

The jab fell harmless. He couldn't speak to Terry, but he was aware of her as he had never been aware of anyone before. It was just as if he could think her thoughts as well as his own. They filled him with compunction and with tenderness—a flood of pity and of love. All at once he was exalted, confident, secure. He felt invulnerable. It was his hour. And when a man comes to his hour he comes to mastery. Apprehension, doubt, uncertainty dropped away. He had no idea how he was going to save Terry, but he was quite sure he would save her. He continued to drive with the mechanical precision of a robot.

Terry sat quite still in her corner. At first the stillness was rigidity, paralysis. There had been shock, pain, anger, very sharp anger, and then—nothing at all. No thought, no feeling, no fear. Her eyes were open. They saw a continuous line of hedgerows slipping past. Sometimes there was a tree, sometimes there was a break where a side road came in. Sometimes, but not very often, another car went by, coming towards them with headlights dipped, or coming up from behind them in a glare of light. The trees and the tops of the hedgerows were blowing in a very high wind. When they slowed down she could hear the sound of it, blowing high up in the empty arch of the sky, tearing across the open fields, battering against the roof of the car. She did not think about the wind. She heard it, and she saw the trees bend. It blew across the surface of her mind. She did not think about anything.

Time passed, but she did not know how much. She began to feel again. First physical things. Her shoulder was stiff. Her left arm hurt where it was pressed against the side of the car. She moved it, shifting on the seat, and at once felt something else—the muzzle of the pistol against the back of her neck, and a wild, sudden stab of fear. She said in a small, piteous voice like a child's,

"Please, may I move? I'm so stiff."

Maud Millicent said, "Anything in reason," and Terry straightened herself so that she could lean into the back of the seat.

Now she could look straight down the road they were travelling on. It was a great relief. That sliding hedgerow had begun to make her feel giddy. The rigidity passed from her body. She relaxed. She began to think again. All her thoughts were slow and weak. Something had hurt her very much, and she didn't want to be hurt again.

She began to think about Peter. She didn't call him Peter of course, because she only knew him as Spike Reilly, but she didn't call him Spike. She had never called him Spike. She had no name for him. He had called her Terry, but she had no name for him. She thought about him. The thoughts got stronger. They didn't hurt any more.

She hadn't trusted him. She hadn't trusted what she knew about him. She had panicked, and hurt herself. Now she wasn't going to panic any more. He had said he would get her away if she did just what he told her. She thought they were in a very tight place. She thought, "I must be ready to do anything at any moment. Perhaps there isn't any chance—but perhaps there's just one chance in a thousand. If there is, I've got to be ready for it—I've *got* to be ready for it."

Something strange had been happening. She had been cold through and through—rigid and paralysed—blind, deaf and idiotic with cold. And then very gradually she had become aware of a warmth that was melting the cold away. It was like coming out of icy weather into a warm, cheerful room. A comforting sense of safety was seeping into her, and she had the feeling that this warmth and this comfort were coming to her from Peter for whom she had no name. She began to feel very sure that she could trust him. No one who made you feel safe like that could possibly let you down. All she had to do was to make sure that she didn't let him down.

The car slid on into the dark, and the wind blew.

CHAPTER XXXV

THE map on Maud Millicent's knee rustled. Her voice took a more definite tone. She said,

"Turn to the right, and in about a quarter of a mile right again to the top of the hill. There's a gate half way, but it will be open."

So they were arriving. Peter took the right-hand turn, and found the hill a steep one. They were running over open down, no hedgerows now and no trees, and he thought they were running towards the sea. He had his window open, and the wind was salt against his lips.

Well, they were still in the car, Maud Millicent and Jake, and as long as that was the case he and Terry were safe. Unless she had planned a bullet for them both, and a convenient grave in the sea. But the sea had a way of giving up its dead, and a bullet would set Scotland Yard upon their track. No, they wouldn't shoot unless there was no other way. Suicide or death by misadventure—that was what it had got to look like.

They passed between crumbling gateposts with a rickety gate slanted back to leave the road open for them. It ran uphill all the way to where dark tossing trees opened fanwise about the tall shape of a house. The house stood up gaunt against the sky. A dark sky heavy with clouds. A black house just visible against it. No light anywhere—no faintest glow at any window, no brightness from the fanlight over the massive door.

He slowed down, and was about to stop, when Maud Millicent spoke.

"Not here. There's a side door. Go on round the house. The garage is there too."

The house was large and square. The trees splayed out in front of it on either side.

Maud Millicent said, "Shut off your headlights now," and he obeyed.

They skirted the house, and she said, "Stop! I'm getting out here. The garage is right in front of you. Drive in. I'll get this door open and meet you there. There's a way through from the house."

As he drew up, she jumped out. Jake followed her. The door slammed. Maud Millicent called, "Straight on into the garage," and turned to fit a key. Peter and Terry were alone in the car, and on the instant he said her name in a whisper desperately controlled.

"Terry—"

She said, "Yes—" in the same low, urgent tone.

The car was moving, because he dared not let it stand. He had a sense that they were watched, that Maud Millicent had turned from the door, and that she was watching them—watching the car, watching what was going to happen to the car.

Peter said, "Quick, Terry—unlatch your door! Be ready to jump—in an instant—"

She said, "What is it?" and he said, "I don't know."

He took his right hand from the wheel and unlatched the door on his side.

The garage faced them. The door was wide open. It was quite empty, quite bare. As they moved slowly towards it, Peter could see how bare and empty it was. As a rule there is all sorts of truck in a garage. But not in this one. It was bare as the back of his hand.

They were double the car's length from the side door, and from Maud Millicent and Jake. They were a car's length from the garage. They moved slowly. The bonnet and the front wheels entered the garage.

Peter switched off the sidelights and said, "Jump, Terry!"

He saw her swing the door out and slip through the gap. He took his hands off the wheel and went out on the other side. The car went on at its slow, purring pace. Peter ran round the back of it, ran into Terry, clutched her, and ran back out of the garage, slanting away from the house—back, with a deafening sound in his ears, in his brain. There was a cracking and a breaking, a tremor beneath their feet as they ran, a grinding crash, and a great buffet of wind blowing in from the sea.

Peter looked back. He could see nothing. They went on running. He looked back again. There was the flash of a torch. He turned left-handed for the trees and then checked, because they had almost blundered in among them. He let go of Terry to feel his way. There were trees, but they stood apart from one another and gave no cover. He caught Terry's arm again and ran with her across the front of the house and round to the other side. It was all dark. The wind shouted overhead.

They felt their way along the wall of the house and came upon two or three steps leading up to a garden door. It stood recessed and made a shelter from the wind and from their own desperate confusion and hurry—a small space no more than a yard square, but a refuge. They stood there, shoulder pressed to shoulder, hearts beating, breath coming fast. It might have been a dozen years ago and a game of blindman's-buff or devil-in-the-dark—Terry eight years old in a party dress, and Peter rising seventeen. They would have been farther apart then. Twenty-eight is not so far from twenty. They were very close now, for safety, and for the need they had of one another. Peter's arm went round her. She said,

"What happened?"

"Everything went."

"What happened?"

"I don't know. I think we're on the edge of a cliff—this house—everything. I think that's why they brought us here.

I think the house is derelict because the sea has eaten the cliff away. The garage—'' He stopped.

Terry said,''It fell—''

''I think it fell. I think they knew it was ready to fall. It stood farther back than the house, nearer the sea, nearer the edge of the cliff. It must have been left like that, with the cliff fallen away underneath it. It would hang on for a bit, but it wouldn't bear the weight of a car. They knew that.''

Terry drew away a little.

''Did you know it?''

Why did she say that? She didn't know why. It said itself.

Peter stepped back against the wall.

''No, I didn't know. I don't know now—I'm guessing.''

She said in a passionate voice through the wind, ''Who are you—who are you—who *are* you?''

''I'm Peter Talbot.''

Terry's heart sang, and stopped singing.

''But he's dead—Peter Talbot is dead.''

''Not yet,'' said Peter, and laughed a little grimly. He took her by her two shoulders and shook her. ''Look here, Terry Clive, you've got to make up your mind about me. It mayn't be easy, but you've got to do it. If you keep shilly-shallying, we shall probably both be dead quite soon. Maud Millicent is an accomplished murderess, and she's out to get us. I hope she's under the impression that she has got us, but I'm not as sure as I'd like to be. She may have seen us get out of the car—it depends on how good she is in the dark. And Jake—if he had cat's eyes he might have seen us. But I don't think they did see us, or we shouldn't have got away.'' He laughed and added—''as far as this. We haven't got away yet. When that garage went I didn't hear any splash. There was every other sort of noise in the world—there was too much noise. If the garage had gone down into the sea it wouldn't have made so much row—at least I don't think it would. So I'm pretty sure it crashed on a dry beach. If we'd gone into the sea, they wouldn't have had to worry about us any more, but if the car is high and dry at the foot of the cliffs, I think they'll want to make sure we're safely dead. I don't know how much of a drop there is, or whether there's any way down. If there is, I should think she'd send Jake to have a look-see, and wait for him to come back."

Terry caught at his arm.

"There's a car! I heard it!"

There was a sudden lull in the wind. It dropped between two gusts, and in the silence Peter heard what Terry had heard, the sound of a car coming nearer. He left the recess, and saw headlights—coming on—quite near. He sprang back just in time. The car swung round in front of the house.

What a damnable complication. It had been in his mind to give Terry time to take breath, and then make off by way of the trees on this side of the house. But they gave no real cover. They ceased a hundred yards away, and to wander in the darkness on this crumbling cliff would be a good deal like jumping out of the frying-pan into the fire. He had just decided that to try and make the main road by way of the drive would be the lesser risk, when that confounded car came butting in. It was one thing to chance pursuit on foot, and quite another to risk being run down by a car. There was no cover of any sort once you got away from the house. They had not passed a farm or a dwelling for at least three miles. The downs—well, it might come to that, but he hoped not. He knew this sort of country, with the chalk crumbling away, undercut, hollowed by water, breaking into clefts, dropping in sudden deep holes. And the night as dark as storm could make it.

He said quickly, "Don't move. I'll reconnoitre," and slipped out of the shelter into the wind again.

The car was at the front door, lights on and engine running. He tried to think what this would mean. He had rejected at once any idea that the car might belong to the owner of the house upon his lawful occasions. Two things determined this—certainly that Maud Millicent would never have risked staging her "accident" in the neighborhood of an inhabited house, and an overwhelming conviction that the house was not inhabited. It was a shell, a dead thing, the corpse of a house abandoned to decay.

Then why was the car left here at the front door with

lights on and engine running? The answer was that someone was in a hurry. He thought if he were Maud Millicent Simpson he would be in a hurry to leave the place where he had just sent two people crashing to their death. He deduced Bert and a second car—Bert with orders to follow at a safe distance and be ready to pick her up as soon as the job was done. He had wondered a little at Bert walking off into the night whistling *Tea for Two*. He felt quite sure now that he had merely walked off to de-park this other car.

Peter got near enough to be sure that the car was empty. This meant that Bert had joined the other two. Presently they would get into the car and drive away. Would they—would they, by gum? Or would they find nothing but the smell of the exhaust, and a tail-light well away down the drive?

He pelted back to Terry.

No.

He pelted back. But Terry wasn't there. There were the three steps up. There was the recess and the door. But no Terry. He felt along the wall outside towards the back of the house. The wind blew in from the sea. He reached the corner, looked round it, saw a dazzle of light, the beam of a powerful electric lamp, and sprang back. He thought he was in luck. If the beam had been swinging his way it must have caught him full in the face. But it was swinging back again—over the cliff—and down. In the flash of it he had seen how near the house stood to a raw, broken edge—how very near to its fall. Half a dozen yards away, no more, the cliff fell sheer.

Terry wasn't here.

He turned and went back again, and just as he came level with the recess where he and Terry had stood, someone came round from the front of the house swinging a small bright torch.

CHAPTER XXXVI

PETER didn't wait to see who it was. At the first flash he jumped for the little porch. He flattened himself against the door, pressing back against it, and saw the torch cut across his line of vision with its narrow ray. If they came as far as the porch they couldn't miss him. They were bound to come as far as the porch.

His hand went behind him almost mechanically and felt for the handle. The door gave suddenly as he leaned against it and nearly brought him down. He staggered, and saved himself, blessing the wind which would cover the noise of his feet on a bare boarded floor. He got the door shut and stood leaning against it. Why was it unlocked? Where was the key? And was this where Terry had gone?

He ran his left hand down the inside of the door. The key was sticking in the lock. He turned it, and felt an illusory sense of safety. In point of fact the house might very easily prove a trap. But it seemed likely enough that Terry was here, and if she was here, he had to find her. He groped his way along a passage, and came to doors that faced each other across the narrow space.

The right-hand door was ajar. He opened it wide and went in. The room felt small. It was darker than it had been outside. There was a smell of rotting wood. After a moment he made out the window—just one on the right, looking to the side of the house from which he had just come. And then, startling and sudden, the beam of the torch stabbed in through the uncurtained pane. It missed him. He drew back in a hurry and sheltered behind the door. The momentary flash showed him a small, square, empty room with broken floor-boards.

He tried the room on the other side of the passage—warily, lest the beam should follow him there. He found a dilapidated cloakroom with a lavatory beyond, horribly damp, horribly mouldy, quite empty.

Along the passage again, and happier for getting away from that prowling torch. His outstretched hands touched something rough and clammy—a baize door closing the passage. It swung as he pushed it, and he came through into what he supposed to be the hall of the house. There was a feeling of space in front of him, on either side, and overhead. The place mouldered where it stood. It fairly reeked of decay.

He put his hand in his pocket and got out his own torch. It wasn't safe to use it, but he might have to use it. Actually, nothing was safe. He might have to weigh a danger against a danger and grasp the lesser evil. It would be madness to show a light in any of the rooms, since it appeared that the windows were all unscreened, but here in the hall it might be possible for a single guarded moment. Anyhow it must be risked, because he must find Terry, and find her quickly whilst the car was there for them to take.

He moved out into what he thought would be the middle of the hall, switched on the torch, and turned the light upon his own face. That was the safest way. If Terry was here she would see him, and if she saw him she would surely come to him—

That would depend on whether she really trusted him or not. He didn't know whether she trusted him. If she didn't, if she was running away from him, they might just go on playing devil-in-the-dark around this crazy house until it fell in on them or Maud Millicent came along and shot them down.

He kept the light on his face for something like a minute.

Nothing happened. He switched it off and called Terry's name softly between the gusts of the wind. There was no answer. A quick, shattering anger ripped through him. If she had done what she was told and stayed where she was put, they would be away by now, getting out of this cracked murder-game, getting back to sanity and civilization. Why on earth couldn't she do what she was told? The uncivilized man in Peter could have taken a savage pleasure in knocking Terry's head against one of these dripping walls.

He went on across the hall, and found a door half open. Drawing-room or dining-room this would be, and it should have windows on two sides of it, to the front and to the side where Maud Millicent and Jake had got out. He saw the front windows at once—two of them, very high, very wide, very bare. The lights of the car outside showed them up and made a faint yellowish dusk at that end of the room. Right opposite him as he came in, three more windows looked out upon the way by which he had driven to the garage, and to what had been meant to be his death and Terry's. He could only just make them out. Terry wasn't here. She would not have taken refuge so near that waiting car.

He returned to the hall and felt his way towards the back of the house. He came upon a passage leading to the right. He thought it served the door by which he had set Maud Millicent down. He had barely passed it, and was feeling his way by the wall, when he heard a sound which turned him cold. The door at the end of the passage had been opened. The wind threw it back against the wall with a crash and rushed past it into the hall behind him. A man swore, the door was violently slammed. Light came from the passage, and for a moment he saw the place he was in as you see a place in a dream—the big empty hall, stairs going up wide and shallow to a landing where they branched right and left, a broken baluster, dark gaps where a tread had fallen in. All this in front of him and to the left. On his right, a yard away, a closing door. In that moment of half sight he could swear he had seen it move, and a hand moving it—just the fingers—holding the edge of the door and then withdrawn.

They must have turned their light away. Perhaps they had

gone into some room that opened off the passage. The hall was dark again. It seemed darker than before. He reached the door with a stride, pushed it, was held by something that pushed from the other side, and lost his temper. The door jerked in. He followed it, and heard Terry catch her breath in the dark.

He said, "Terry—" and she ran to him, catching at his arm, holding on to him as if she would never let him go.

He swept her behind the door and pulled it back to cover them. If they came past and saw a door wide open on an empty room, they might let it go at that. What a hope. What a damned nightmare. If they were being seriously looked for, he thought they were as good as dead. Three to two, and the three armed and desperate.

They stood flattened against the wall, heard a trampling of feet, and saw the darkness in the room go grey. Terry pressed hard against him—hard. He dropped a hand on her shoulder and kept it there. He had no more anger. He knew it now for what it was, his fear for Terry—his fear—

The men stopped outside the open door—shone the torch into the room. A hole in the middle of the floor, a pile of dust and debris on the crumbling hearth, plaster fallen between the windows, the shape of a chandelier, stark and stripped of its dancing crystals—these things were there to be seen. Peter and Terry behind the door saw nothing—only the light flashing in and out again.

Jake said, "What's her game? How did they get in anyway? I want to get back out of this. Aren't they dead? Didn't I see them go down with my own eyes?"

"Perhaps you did—if you can see in the dark." Bert's tone was contemptuous.

"Where else could they have gone?"

"Perhaps in here. That's why we're looking."

Jake swore.

"I tell you they went over the cliff. What makes her think they didn't?"

"You heard what she said the same as I did—he shut off the lights too soon, and the girl didn't scream. She says the girl would have screamed."

Terry made a fierce little movement. She felt Peter's hand heavy on her shoulder.

Jake said, "If a hundred perishing girls had all screamed together, you wouldn't have heard them. You couldn't hear nothing in that perishing wind."

"You asked me what she said. I've told you, haven't I? She says the girl ought to have screamed. I'll say she knows what she's talking about. But if you don't think so, well, you just go and tell her."

"Well, I say they're goners, the two of them. You can see the car down there on the rocks, and I say they're under it. It's turned over, isn't it? And that's where they'd be—under the car and all smashed to blazes. We ought to be half way back to town by now instead of searching a mouldy old house that's due to fall into the sea any perishing minute."

"It'll last the night, I shouldn't wonder!" Bert's tone was sarcastic. "But you won't if you don't get on with the job. If you want her coming in to see what we're doing, I don't."

They went on to the back of the hall. A door banged. The light was gone. The voices died away.

CHAPTER XXXVII

THE hand on Terry's shoulder pushed her. Peter said,

"Quick—before they come back!"

They came out into the hall and light-footed down it to the room on the right, the room he had let alone before. He thought it would be the dining-room. A big room anyway, with two great glimmering windows looking to the front of the house. To the front of the house, but to the back of the car which was standing there. Sash windows nine foot high and as heavy as a cartload of bricks. As like as not the cords would have perished. Was it going to be possible to get one of the blighted things open without making noise enough to bring the hunt down upon them? Most sounds would be drowned by this wind. But suppose he had to smash the glass. Breaking glass had a sound of its own. He thought it would be heard if there were anyone there to hear it.

He took the farther window, and had his work cut out to move the catch. The cords seemed to be there all right. If they would take the weight of the pane for five minutes, it was all he asked of them. But he would have to move the frame first, and it was stuck like glue. No, much worse than that—like wood that has grown together into a solid piece. He shook, heaved, shook again, heaved with all his might, and felt something give—it might have been one of his own muscles. He strained at the sash again and felt it move. After that it ran up a couple of feet and stuck. He stood back panting. The blood was drumming in his ears.

"How much noise did that make?"

"Not much. It wouldn't be heard above the wind."

He leaned out through the two-foot gap. The first thing he saw was the tail-light of the car, a red eye watching them. After the black inside of the house the outdoor darkness seemed no more than a dusk. The car stood up black against the gravel of the drive and the reflection of its own side-lights. The head-lights were off. He couldn't hear the engine running because of the noise of the wind, but he could smell the exhaust. Well, here was their get-away. But it was too easy. No one but a congenital idiot would give them an opportunity like this, and whatever else Maud Millicent was, her bitterest enemy could never have judged her deficient in brains. He thought, "If I'd just tried to kill two people and wasn't sure whether I'd brought it off or if they were somewhere about the place looking for a chance to escape, what would I do? Well, if I'd thought of it—and I might have thought of it, or I might not—I don't know that I could have done better than set a trap like this—car all ready, lights on, engine running, and when the poor boobs make a dash for it a neat, quick bullet in the brain." Yes, that was it. This wasn't a get-away, it was a trap.

All the same—all the same—if he could outwit her—turn the tables—

He whispered quick to Terry, "Will you do just what I tell you?"

"Yes."

"Stand here by the window and watch that car—the car and the steps. I'm going to bang on the front door from the inside. I think Maud Millicent is in the car. She's either there or in the porch. If she's in the car, I think she'll get out when I bang—bound to. If she's in the porch, she'll turn towards the noise. You've got to slip out of the window and run round to the far side of the car. Can you drive?"

"Of course I can!"

"It looks like a Vauxhall—"

"That's all right."

"You've got to be ready to slip into the driver's seat and let her go. See if you can get the car door open, but don't get in till I say go. She'll shoot at sight—she mustn't see you. Have you got all that?"

Terry said, "Yes."

"Then here goes!" He gave a low laugh, flung an arm about her, kissed her, and was gone.

The kiss was very unexpected, a sudden hit or miss affair which landed on one side of her mouth and left her gasping. She knew very well what lay behind that snatched, crooked kiss. It meant, "I'll have this, because perhaps it's all I'll ever have, and perhaps it's good-bye, and perhaps—"

She leaned out of the window and watched the car. The drop was no distance, a couple of feet, no more. And the back of the car—how far away? Say ten feet. She tried to see through the rear window if there was anyone in the driver's seat. She thought there was, but she couldn't be sure. Something dangled and bobbed there, something that took the faint light and turned it green—one of those air-balloon dolls bobbing in the wind.

She was still peering at it, when Peter's first loud bang set her blood racing. It was followed by a crash and a fierce, insistent drumming from the inner side of the front door. Even though she had known it was coming she wanted to look that way. She resisted, and kept her eyes upon the car.

There *was* someone in the driver's seat. A shadow passed between the green balloon and the light which made it transparent. For an instant the colour and the glow were cut off. The left-hand door opened. Someone leaned out, leaned back.

There was another burst of banging. The head-lights of the car came on with a very startling effect. Such a bright light after all this groping in the dark—every pebble casting a small black shadow—a bush of holly with its leaves sharply etched and burning green.

Maud Millicent Simpson looked out of the left-hand door, looked before and behind, slipped out like a shadow, and ran up the steps.

Terry swung herself over the window sill, dropped to hard

gravel, and reached the far side of the car. She heard Maud Millicent's voice above the wind.

"Who's there? Jake—Bert—is it you?"

What was Peter's plan? Would he open the door and come charging out? But Maud Millicent would shoot him—he wouldn't have a chance. She mustn't think about what Peter was going to do. She must get on with what he had told her to do.

She opened the door by the driver's seat and got in, crouching down so as not to be seen. Peter had said not to get in, but it might make all the difference in the world. She didn't believe that they were going to be shot, she thought they were going to get away. She took off the hand-brake. She felt adventurous and confident.

It had all passed in a bare half minute—Peter banging—Maud Millicent to the door—Terry to the car—Terry's thoughts—something singing in her. And then, out of nowhere at all, Peter slipping into the near seat—her foot on the clutch pedal, her hand on the gear level—

They were off. The light slid from the holly-bush, picked up a patterned tree trunk grey with lichen, orange with fungus, slid from that, and showed the bright, straight path to safety. There was a shot. Something crashed and splintered. Another shot, and a bang behind them. There was an odd gassy smell. Terry was flashed back to being seven years old—a pink balloon and, when it broke, tears and that queer smell. She was shaken with laughter. She cried in a laughing, shaking voice,

"She's murdered her mascot! There was a green balloon doll. It must have been blown up awfully tight to go pop like that."

"Oh lord—I thought it was a tyre!" said Peter.

A third shot sounded faintly behind them. He began to sing at the top of his voice in a loud, rough baritone to the tune of John Brown's body:

"Glory, glory, hallelujah!
Glory, glory, hallelujah!
Glory, glory, hallelujah!
And we go marching on."

He stopped abruptly when they got to the gate, and said,

"Turn left, and then left again. Oh lord—I wish we'd got that map! But we'll have to do the best we can. Just keep on driving whilst I get my shoes on."

"Your shoes?"

"My child—you didn't really think I'd produced all that row with the naked hand, did you? The shoes were a very bright thought. They made the most infernal clatter, and as soon as I heard Maud Millicent on the side of the door, and Jake and Bert coming up swearing hard from the back premises, I was able to fade away silently on my stocking feet, and no one a penny the wiser till the car got going. But I wish—lord, how I do wish!—that I could have seen her face when she realized that we'd scored her off."

Terry took the second left-hand turn, and said, "What do we do next?"

"You stop the car and we change over. I'm going to drive."

"Why?"

"I just think I will."

Terry wouldn't have admitted it for the world, but her hands were shaking. That is to say, they would have shaken if she had let them. She was having to make a conscious effort all the time to hold them steady on the wheel. She changed over without a murmur. The car leapt on.

Peter said, "There ought to be an A.A. telephone-box hereabouts. There was a big cross-roads and a telephone-box—I remember thinking it might be handy at the time."

"What are you going to do?"

"Ring up a man called Garrett."

"Colonel Garrett?" Terry's voice was eager.

"And how do you come to know anything about Colonel Garrett, Miss Clive?"

Terry said, "Thank you! Why shouldn't I know about Colonel Garrett, when Fabian Roxley is his secretary and he's a cousin of Miss Talbot's?"

Peter laughed out loud.

"And if I was really Peter Talbot, and not Spike Reilly, I'd know that—wouldn't I!"

"Yes, you would," said Terry.

She was remembering that he had kissed her, and she was remembering that he had saved her life.

He was still laughing. He said,

"That was a bad break, wasn't it? What do you really think, Terry?"

She sat back in her corner.

"You called me Miss Clive just now—"

"Make the most of it. I shall never do it again. Well, what about it? You haven't answered my question. Am I Spike Reilly, or am I Peter Talbot?"

Terry said what she had said before.

"Peter Talbot is dead—he died in Brussels. Miss Talbot cried a lot. She sent a wreath."

"I know. I'm awfully sorry about it. But I really am Peter Talbot. You can ask Frank Garrett when we get to town. But suppose I wasn't—suppose I was Spike Reilly, with a perfectly hideous past—wouldn't you feel a nice womanly urge to reform me?"

"No,I wouldn't!" said Terry.

"You pain me. I thought a nice girl always wanted to do that sort of thing."

"Well, I don't!" Terry spoke with decision. "I've had all I want to do with crooks, and I haven't got any urge to reform them. The police can do that."

"The original Hard-hearted Hannah! And are you going to hand me over to the police to be reformed along with Bert, and Jake, and Maud Millicent?"

"If you're Peter Talbot you wouldn't mind being handed over to the police," said Terry.

"But if I was Spike Reilly—would you hand me over?"

"I expect you know I wouldn't," said Terry in a small, disconsolate voice.

"Thank you for those kind words, my sweet. And here is our cross-roads. I think you'd better stay in the car. I won't be any longer than I can help."

CHAPTER XXXVIII

PETER was ten minutes.

Garrett was in, and never had he been hailed with more enthusiasm. The voice in which Peter delivered himself of a "*cher maître*" was positively impassioned.

"Where have you cropped up from now?" barked Garrett.

"Sussex," said Peter succinctly. "Listen, Frank—"

"I was beginning to think you were dead again. You wouldn't have got another wreath either."

"No flowers, by request," murmured Peter. "Look here, Frank, this is urgent. I've got Terry Clive—"

"*What?*"

"Safe and sound. And I'm bringing her straight to you, because I think you'd better chaperon us to Scotland Yard. I don't want to go to the jug just now, and I'm afraid I'm going to want a little explanation. That's where you come in. Meanwhile stir everyone up and get the wires humming. We've just left Maud Millicent Simpson, and a fellow called Bert and another fellow called Jake in an empty house on the edge of the cliffs about six or seven miles from here. Have you got anything to write with? . . . All right, here are descriptions. Maud Millicent—as smart as they make 'em in black—hat like a saucer on one side of her head—platinum blonde hair—black dress with a belt—swagger coat with square shoulders—bunch of green orchids—pearl earrings like studs—very bright lipstick. I can't describe her features, because she was wearing a mask—painted, not black—revolting! She is slight, and, I should say, about five foot seven or eight. . . . Bert—good driver—about five foot nine—square shoulders—thick neck. I've never seen him in the light so I can't do any better than that. . . . Jake—small and quick—about five foot six—very light on his feet—black eyes—black hair, with a bit coming down over his forehead—sallow face—no moustache—long fingers—dirty—shabby blue serge suit—I don't know about a coat or muffler. . . . I don't suppose the police'll get them, but they can always try. We pinched their car and got away. They can be charged with attempted murder. Also Maud Millicent shot Louisa Spedding. I'll just give you my bearings here and the route to the house. They won't be there of course, but they hadn't a car, and perhaps the police could do something with a cordon. . . ."

He came back rather cock-a-hoop, Terry thought. He sang John Brown's body for a bit, and then dropped to conversation, leading off with,

"Think what a chance you've missed."

"I suppose you want me to say 'How?' or 'Why?' or something like that."

"And you're not going to? Quite right—that's the proper spirit! You would only be leading me on, and a nice girl never leads anyone on. But as a matter of fact I only want you to admire my trusting disposition, and as you probably won't say 'Why?' to that either, I won't hold up on you. You admire me with an A because I am Admirable, Altruistic and Adventurous. How did I know you wouldn't run off with the car whilst I was talking to Frank? If I was Spike Reilly, you'd never have a better chance of getting rid of me—you could step on the gas and be gone. *Haven't* I got a trusting disposition?"

Terry faced round. She drew breath to speak. She opened her mouth and shut it again.

"Why didn't you?" said Peter in a casual voice.

"Why should I?" said Terry rather quickly.

"Motive—to get rid of me. For good and all, like I said. Opportunity—one which may never recur. Means—this very competent bus. Why didn't you do it?"

Terry said nothing.

"Why didn't you do it, Terry?"

"What do you think I am—" The words rushed out with the effect of having escaped.

Peter said something under his breath. It sounded like "Rather sweet," but she couldn't be sure of that. The words that had escaped were followed by others.

"If you were fifty Spike Reillys, I wouldn't go off and leave you when you'd just saved my life."

"If I were fifty Spike Reillys, I'm afraid you wouldn't get the chance, my child. Speaking as one Peter Talbot, I'm extremely glad you didn't. I don't feel like footslogging. I'm in a hurry to see Frank Garrett, and—" his voice changed—"I rather like driving with you, Terry."

"I don't know why." She didn't mean her voice to wobble, but it did.

Mr. Peter Talbot remarked, "Liar," in a pleasant conversational manner.

Terry said nothing at all. She drew rather a quick breath, and consoled herself with thinking that the sound could not possibly have been heard above the running of the car.

Peter laughed.

"I did once offer to tell you the story of my first crime, and you weren't taking any interest. Just as well perhaps, because it really wasn't fit for Jake's ears. But I'm going to tell you about it now. If you are too bored you can always say the multiplication table to yourself, or something like that. Well, Peter Talbot—you are quite clear about my being Peter Talbot now, aren't you?"

"I don't know why you should think so," said Terry with some spirit.

"That's all right. And you probably know that I'm a cousin of Frank Garrett's."

"I know Peter Talbot is a cousin of Colonel Garrett's."

"That's what I said. And I write, you know, but that's not the crime I'm telling you about. I merely mention it because it accounts for my wandering round Europe. Frank Garrett asked me to pick up the trail of the original Spike Reilly. There was an idea that he might be mixed up with a picture-stealing-cum-blackmail racket which was fluttering the dovecots over here. It was all quite private and unofficial, but he had a sort of hunch that Maud Millicent might be mixed up in it, and Maud Millicent makes him see red. She's the nice feminine creature we've just got away from by the skin of our teeth. I've also met her as an old lady with a cough. Frank says she can play any part. She's been wandering in and out of international and political crime for years, and he'd give his eyes to get her. There you have the *mise-en-scène*. The affair boiled up this end when an attempt was made to get away with Solly Oppenstein's Gainsborough. You remember? They didn't get the picture, and the butler, Francis Bird, was shot. That was last Saturday week. Spike Reilly was in England that week-end, but I don't think he had anything to do with the murder. His business was to write the blackmailing letters to the insurance companies. I think he'd begun to get a bit too inquisitive about his employers, and I think they had the bright idea of putting the murder on him. I think somebody was getting rattled.

"Well, things being like that, I walked in on Spike Reilly at the Hotel Dupin in Brussels last Tuesday week, and found him getting ready to die. He actually did die whilst I was there—quite natural causes. And this is where the crime begins. I pinched his passport and came over here as him."

Terry said "Oh!" on a soft, excited breath, and then, "Why?"

"Well, I found some papers, and he said some fairly compromising things. He talked about Maud Millicent, and I gathered he had had ideas about blackmailing her and some man, but he didn't know who the man was, and I thought I'd like to find out. You know, it was the sort of thing you do first and think about afterwards—if you thought about it first you'd never do it at all. I did it, and I got away with it. I decoded Spike Reilly's cipher instructions, and did just what they told him to do. Nobody seemed to know him by sight over here, or I'd have been done. This sort of organization can't afford to be matey, and I gather that Spike was picked up for them in America by a man called Grey, now deceased.

"Well, they accepted me up to a point, and sent me along to Heathacres to take over Mr. Cresswell's Turner. Garrett told me to carry on, so I did. He was mad to get Maud Millicent. And then Spike Reilly's sister turned up to see me—a very decent soul called Louisa Spedding. We had a heart-to-heart talk, and when she knew Spike was dead she was all for helping me to put it across the people who had let him in. It was a very interesting talk indeed. She knew Maud Millicent, really knew her—had been in her service when she was plain respectable Mrs. Simpson before she took to crime. She hadn't seen her for donkey's years till just the other day. *And she had recognized her.* Maud Millicent had certainly never reckoned on that. Terry, she's a devil. Do you know what she did? Rang the poor thing up, sent her to see me—said her dear brother was over and gave her the address. I think they must have wanted to check up on me—to make sure I really was Spike Reilly—perhaps—I don't know. Anyhow Louisa came and saw me, and went away again. Half an hour later she was found shot in a telephone-box at the corner of Sitfield Row, and I'm as sure as I've ever been of anything in all my life that it was Maud Millicent who shot her."

Terry said "Oh!" again. A cold shiver ran over her. It had so nearly happened to them—it had so very nearly happened to them. Her hand went out involuntarily towards Peter. He dropped his left hand from the wheel and took it in a firm, warm clasp. It felt like ice in his.

"Cold?" he said.

Terry said, "Yes." Then she pulled her hand away and said in a hurry, "That was a lie. I'm not cold—I'm frightened. She frightens me."

"She's a devil," said Peter. "And when she'd shot Louisa and kidnapped you, she sent for me as calm as you please—that was the time she was an old woman with a cough—and killed two birds with one stone by putting me on guard over you. You had to be looked after till the marks on your arm were gone. She was afraid of Jake and the Bruiser getting rough. And she didn't want me to find out about Louisa for a day or two, until she'd got it all fixed up to bump us both off. You were a nuisance, and Spike was a nuisance—and she has a short way with nuisances. We're very well out of it, my dear."

There was a pause. Then Terry said,

"Are we out of it?"

She heard him laugh.

"We're out of the frying-pan, and with care and a spot of luck we needn't fall into the fire."

He took a sharp turn to the right as he spoke, and Terry called out,

"That's not right—I know it's not. We ought to have kept straight on."

"Oh, I'm just being careful."

"What do you mean?"

"Well, they might get hold of a car. It's not very likely, but suppose they did. I think we'll cut across country a bit and see if we can't strike another main road. I feel we might do better with a road of our own—more haste, worse speed, and all that kind of thing."

CHAPTER XXXIX

TERRY Clive sat in one of Garrett's comfortable old chairs and drank hot soup. It was between one and two in the morning. Garrett had produced soup out of a tin and an aged saucepan to heat it in, tea out of a brown teapot with a cracked spout, an admirable green gorgonzola, a tin of biscuits, and some bar chocolate. With this strangely assorted food she and Peter had refreshed themselves. Terry refused the tea, and got a second cup of soup instead. Garrett, who presumably had dined, partook of everything with zest, finishing up with a breakfast cup of horrifically strong tea well laced with whisky.

"And now," he said, "we make up our minds what we're going to say to Scotland Yard."

"What have you said?" Peter asked.

Garrett gave him a malicious glance.

"Oh, I've thrown you to the wolves good and proper. You've been travelling with a false passport, conspiring to obtain a valuable picture, receiving said picture knowing it to be stolen, and even taking a part in the kidnapping of Miss Terry Clive. It will look very well indeed in the headlines, and your next book will sell like hot cakes."

"I don't think my publishers will care about it," said Peter. "They are very respectable. I don't think Aunt Fanny will like it either. I think you'd better keep me out of the headlines, *cher maître*."

Terry looked rather wan. She said, "Can he?" in a frightened voice, and Peter grinned and said, "He's going to."

"Nepotism," growled Garrett.

"Not a bit of it! You got me in, and you've got to get me out again."

Garrett scowled.

"It's Miss Terry Clive who's got to get you out. What are you going to say, Miss Clive, when I take you round to Scotland Yard tomorrow morning—no, by gum, it's this morning? Are you going to tell the truth, or are you going to keep something up your sleeve?"

Terry said, "What do you mean?"

The scowl was turned on her.

"You've been keeping cards up your sleeve all along, haven't you? Nobody knows what they are except yourself. May be rubbish—may be all the winning trumps. Are you going to put those cards down on the table and let us see what they are?"

Terry said, "Yes."

"All right. We know all about the house-party at Heathacres. We know all about the guests. We know that it must have been one of the guests who came through the glass door on to the terrace at one-fifty a.m. and took a pane out of the drawing-room window from the outside. Half an hour later Cresswell's Turner was handed out through that broken pane to Peter, who had been told off to come and take it over. You were looking out of your window, Miss Clive, and you saw something. What did you see?"

"I saw someone come out of the door and take out the pane," said Terry.

"Who was it?"

She put down her empty cup and leaned forward.

"Colonel Garrett, I don't know. The moon had gone behind a very thick bank of cloud. I just saw a shadow— Oh! How do you know I saw anything?"

"Well, you told Fabian Roxley you did, and he told me. Your window was directly above the glass door, wasn't it?"

"Not directly. It was farther along."

"But you looked down on the person coming out of the door?"

"Yes, I looked down."

"Now, Miss Clive—you say you saw a shadow. You must have got some impression from what you saw—at the time, I mean. I want to know just what impression you got. Did you think you were seeing a man, or a woman?"

"I couldn't say."

Garrett was sitting astride a small chair, his arms across the back and his chin down on his arms.

"Suppose you had to say." He shot the words at her like bullets. "Suppose you had to choose between its being a man or a woman?"

"I don't know. Do you want me to say what I think now, or what I thought then?"

"What you thought then."

Terry took a long breath.

"I think—if I'd had to say then—I should have said it was a man."

Garrett looked hard at her.

"And if you had to say now?"

She put a hand to her cheek.

"It wasn't Emily Cresswell—I know that. I don't think it was Pearla Yorke—oh, no, I'm sure it wasn't. And—no, it wasn't Norah Margesson."

"Why wasn't it Emily Cresswell?"

Terry laughed and shook her head.

"She couldn't—that's why. If she tried to cut a picture out of its frame she'd drop it and bring the house down. She's rather like the White Queen, you know."

Peter laughed and said, "Alice Through the Looking-glass, *cher maître*, in case you've forgotten—vague, and her hair coming down."

Colonel Garrett said "Tcha!" and pursued his interrogation. "Why wasn't it Pearla Yorke?"

"Not her line, and not tall enough."

Garrett pounced.

"Now we're getting something! It was a tall shadow, was it?"

"Taller than Pearla Yorke. She's very slender too."

"And the shadow wasn't? Well, Miss Margesson is tall. Why wasn't it she? You'd just seen her take Mrs. Cresswell's pearls, hadn't you?"

"That's why," said Terry. "She knew I'd seen her, and she was scared stiff—she wouldn't have dared."

Garrett nodded.

"That's a point. That leaves the four men. James Cresswell—by all accounts crazy about this picture, crazy about losing it—financial position secure, no reason in the world to play a trick on an insurance company—"

"Oh, no, it wasn't Mr. Cresswell."

Garrett snapped, "How do you know?"

"He's got a way of walking—it's not exactly a limp. Oh no, it wasn't he."

Garrett grinned suddenly.

"We're getting on! The other three men are all tall, and that fits. Take Applegarth first—no motive at all—very wealthy man—complete alibi for the Oppenstein affair. What are your reactions to Applegarth, Miss Clive—considered as a shadow?"

"He's too broad and stout. He wouldn't fit at all."

"And that brings us down to Fabian Roxley and Mr. Basil Ridgefield." Colonel Garrett's eyes were like points of steel.

Terry felt a sudden terror of what she had said—of what he might be going to make her say. She beat her hands together and cried out in a frightened way,

"But it can't be Fabian or Uncle Basil—it can't be anyone!"

"It was someone," said Garrett with a rasp in his voice.

Terry sat there looking at him. Peter got up out of his chair and came over to the fire. He stood there behind Garrett facing Terry, his back against the mantelshelf and his hands in his pockets. He said,

"Terry, it's no good. You've got to the place where you can't get out of telling us what you know. You do know something—you've known something all along—and it's much too dangerous to go on holding it up. If you hadn't held it up to start with you wouldn't have been kidnapped, and we shouldn't both have come as near being murdered as makes no difference."

Her eyes brightened fiercely.

"Are you going to say it was my fault?"

"If you want me to," said Peter obligingly. "It was, you know, and it will be again if you go on holding things up and there are any more corpses. Speaking from the purely selfish point of view, I don't want to be a corpse. I don't even want you to be one."

"A Daniel come to judgment!" said Garrett, with his barking laugh. "Now, Miss Clive—"

Peter saw the colour leave her face. He said,

"The truth won't hurt any innocent person, Terry."

She said in a low voice, "I know—but it's so difficult. I will tell—I will really. I said I would if the picture didn't come back."

Garrett opened his mouth to speak and then shut it again with a snap. Terry's right hand took hold of her left and held it tightly. She said in a voice that was uneven and distressed,

"I didn't say anything that wasn't true. I looked out of the window and I saw someone—and I couldn't have said who it was—I really couldn't. It was just a shadow. I told everything about that right from the very beginning."

"Then what didn't you tell, Miss Clive?"

Terry looked at him earnestly.

"It was very little—very little indeed. It was just that I wanted to know who had gone out like that, so I opened my door and listened."

"You looked out?"

"No. I got into bed, but I couldn't sleep. I listened. I didn't go to sleep for a long time, and—and—no one ever came past my door at all."

Garrett made an extraordinary grimace and snapped his fingers.

"Now we're getting down to it! And who ought to have come past your door, Miss Terry Clive?"

"No one—no one."

Garrett jerked his chair nearer.

"Come along—out with it! I've seen a plan of the house, you know—stairs coming up in the middle, and a bedroom wing on either side. Which side were you?"

"Left," said Terry.

"And who else was along there?"

"First Mr. and Mrs. Cresswell—they have two rooms. And then me, and Mrs. Yorke beyond, and Mr. Applegarth opposite, and bathrooms and things."

"And the other side, on the right of the stairs?"

"Norah Margesson first, and then two empty rooms, and at the end of the passage Uncle Basil, and Fabian over the way."

"And no one came along your passage at all? You're sure of that?"

"Yes, I'm quite sure."

"That leaves us where we were before. If you count Norah Margesson out—and I agree she's highly improbable. . . . Are you quite sure that she knew you'd seen her with the pearls?"

"Oh, yes. She looked back over her shoulder and saw me coming along the terrace. She ran like the wind."

"Well then, I think we can cut her out. And it's a man we're looking for—a tall man—"

Terry said, "Oh!"

"That's the one thing you were certain about, Miss Clive. Your shadow was too tall to be Mrs. Yorke, you remember."

Her eyes widened piteously.

"Yes, it was tall."

"Fabian Roxley is tall," said Garrett.

"Yes—he's very tall—he's six foot one."

"And Mr. Ridgefield—what is his height?"

"About six feet."

"A good deal slighter than Fabian, eh?"

Terry said, "Yes."

Garrett thrust his head forward over the back of the chair he bestrode.

"Can you put your personal feelings on one side? Women never can. I want you to try. You saw this shadow. It had shape—it had height, breadth, thickness—because you said one person wasn't tall enough and another was too broad. So in your own mind your shadow has a definite shape. Which of these two men best fits into that shape? They are not at all alike in the day-time. Even in a thick dusk there must have been a difference. Come, Miss Clive—who fits?"

Terry's hands fell open on her lap.

"I—don't—know."

"You *must* know!" Garrett's tone was very sharp.

Terry broke.

"I don't—I don't! I don't really! Don't you think I want to be sure as well as you? There was something all over his head—like a cloak. It was Uncle Basil's cloak, because—afterwards—I found—I found a smear of treacle on it—and a splinter of glass. It was his cloak, but that doesn't say it was he. It was hanging downstairs in the cloakroom—anyone could have taken it. Don't you see that anyone could have taken it? You're trying to make me say that Uncle Basil or—or Fabian—Oh, don't you see, if it was one of them, then he knew that I was going to be kidnapped and—and murdered? And they wouldn't—because they love me."

Peter's eyes met hers across Garrett's hunched shoulder.

"Does Fabian love you?"

Everything went out of Terry—anger, defiance, pride. She said in the forlorn voice of a child,

"I thought he did."

CHAPTER XL

"AS a matter of fact, the picture was returned yesterday."

Garrett had got up from his chair and was pouring himself out another cup of well stewed tea. He put in four lumps of sugar and another tot of whiskey. His expression was that of a dog who has stolen a bone and means to keep it.

Terry had been lying back with her eyes closed. Her lashes were wet. She looked exhausted, but at Garrett's words she sat up. A tear ran down her cheek, but she took no notice of it.

"The Turner has come back?"

"Yes," said Colonel Garrett, setting the whisky bottle down with a bang.

Quite a bright colour came into Terry's face.

"I said I would tell if the picture didn't come back. You made me tell, and you never said it had come back!"

"You wouldn't have told if I had."

Peter said in a curious angry voice,

"What does it matter? You said you wouldn't tell if the picture was back before Tuesday. Well, it wasn't back before Tuesday. And you were kidnapped *and* nearly murdered. I don't think there's anything left of their side of the bargain—if you're going to call it a bargain. And anyhow what you had to tell doesn't amount to very much that I can see.'' He went across to Garrett and caught him roughly by the arm. ''Look here, Frank, I've had enough! She's all in—she ought to be in bed. What are we going to do with her?''

Terry's colour faded.

''I can go home,'' she said. ''Please, I'd like to go home.''

Peter said, ''You can't.'' He shook Garrett insistently. ''She can't go back to Ridgefield's house. I won't have it—do you hear? She's not running any more risks.''

Terry said, ''Oh—'' Her voice shrank, her whole body shrank. It came to her that she hadn't anywhere to go, or anyone to turn to. She stared at Peter with a lost look.

There was a dead silence. Into the middle of it came the harsh buzzing of an electric bell. Colonel Garrett cocked his head, looked at the clock, and gave vent to a short ejaculation.

''Two in the morning—and that's the front door bell! Having fun, aren't you?'' He frowned horribly. ''Here, this may be anyone—I don't know. People don't come at this hour unless—anyhow you two had better not be seen. Take her in there with the telephone, Peter, whilst I see who it is. You can light the gas fire, but don't talk too loud. I'm not advertising you.''

The little room off the hall was horribly cold. Terry sat down in the first chair she came to. The gas fire lit with a pop and began to glow. They heard the bell ring again and go on ringing as Garrett came to the door and made a noisy business of shooting back a bolt and turning a key. It stopped suddenly when the door opened, and was flung right back so that it struck against the wall of the room they were in. They could hear every sound. They could hear Garrett stamp back a couple of paces. They heard him say with a rasp in his voice,

''Good lord, Fabian! What brings you here at this time of night?''

Peter was on his knees by the hearth with the matches still in his hand. Terry leaned forward and caught at his arm. They stayed like that whilst Fabian Roxley said heavily,

''I couldn't sleep. I saw your light. Can I come in?''

They heard the door bang and feet crossing the hall. They heard the sitting-room door. And after that voices—a come-and-go murmur of sound without any words.

Terry didn't move. She sat there straining, her hands clenched on Peter's arm, every sense keyed up, every muscle tense. After a little while Peter let the matchbox fall. The small sound made her start. A hard shiver ran over her. He turned and put his arm round her shoulders. He unclasped her hands and put them to his lips, kissing them gently. He went on kissing them. She leaned her head against his shoulder and began to cry. He said,

"It's all right, Terry—it's all right. You've got me—I won't go away. You've got me for keeps."

In the sitting-room Fabian Roxley stood at the window. He had his back to the room, but he was not looking out. The curtains showed a handsbreadth of dark street and darker sky, but he was not aware of these things. At the sound of Garrett's voice offering him a drink he turned heavily round, presenting a grey, drawn face and haggard eyes.

"I can't sleep," he said. "It's no use—you can't go on when you can't sleep. So when I saw your light I thought I'd get it over."

Garrett looked at him.

"Drunk?" he said. "Because if it's that, I won't waste whisky on you. If it isn't, you'd better have some."

Fabian Roxley came forward. He moved slowly, as if his limbs were heavy. He said,

"I'm not drunk, sir. I wish I were."

He tipped whisky into a glass and drank it neat. And fell into Terry's chair and sat there staring at the fire. Garrett pitched a log on to the embers and pushed it with his foot. A shower of sparks went up. A bright jagged flame licked the dry bark.

"And now what?" said Garrett with his back to the fire.

"She had a hold over me," said Fabian Roxley in an odd indifferent voice. "Something I did. I was horribly dipped, and Elsinger—it all seemed quite easy at the time and it didn't hurt anyone, but she found out somehow and threatened me.''

Garrett said sharply, ''You took a bribe and let yourself in for blackmail—is that what you're saying?''

Fabian lifted a hand and let it fall again. His eyes dwelt on Garrett without fear or shame—the eyes of a man who is too tired to care.

''Yes, that's it—a little information in advance, and no harm done. It seemed all right at the time. Then I got dipped again. No luck with cards or horses, but you keep on thinking it's bound to turn—that's how. And she came along and suggested this picture racket.''

Garrett said explosively, ''Maud Millicent Simpson?''

''I suppose so. She called herself Madame X. If I hadn't come in with her, she'd have given me away. She had proof that I had taken the money. And nobody was any the worse—only the insurance companies. It's difficult to feel passionately about defrauding an insurance company.''

Garrett's eyes snapped. He restrained a snort, but not with marked success. Fabian Roxley said,

''I was sorry about Oppenstein's butler, but he recognized me, so there wasn't any way out of it. I told her after that that I couldn't go on. She agreed. She was inclined to blame me about the butler, and she said we'd better get someone to put it on, so that I could go on being useful in other ways. There was a fellow called Reilly who did the correspondence with the insurance companies—she said he was getting dangerous. She said we'd better get him over and put it on him, so we did. We had him out to Heathacres, and I gave him the Turner. It was all arranged to look like an outside job. But Terry Clive saw me. That's what we hadn't reckoned on. She saw me out of her window. I think she wasn't quite sure who it was she had seen, but she would have come to be sure. She went round telling everyone in the house that she had seen something. She said she wouldn't say what she had seen if the picture was put back. I wanted to send it back, but Madame X wouldn't have it. She said I might as well make a signed confession and have done with it. The picture had got to be found in Spike Reilly's car, and she wanted a day or two to complete her plans. I didn't know what they were. I thought Terry was in danger, and I did my best to find out how much she knew, but she wouldn't tell. Then she disappeared. I haven't been able to sleep since. I tried to get hold of Madame X. I've never known where she lived or what she called herself—I've never had anything except an accommodation address."

Garrett stopped him sharply.

"I'll have that address."

"They don't know anything. Do you think I haven't tried?"

Garrett dragged a notebook from his pocket.

"The address!" he barked.

"Fifty-seven Paley Street. It's a tobacconist's shop."

Garrett scribbled.

"All right—go on! How did you and Maud Millicent meet? And where?"

"When she wanted to see me she used to write or telephone, and pick me up after dark in a car. I've never seen her in daylight. I don't know what she looks like—she's always worn a mask. There wasn't any way I could get at her. And I've been going mad."

Garrett struck backwards at the log with his heel. There was a rush of flame. He said violently,

"Mad all along, I should say. Good God, Fabian—do you mean all this—is it true?"

Fabian Roxley said, his voice quite gentle, quite indifferent,

"Hardly the sort of thing one makes up to pass the time, sir. I'd have carried it through if it hadn't been for Terry. A damnable mistake to let one's feelings get involved. I couldn't stand not knowing—about Terry—"

Garrett gave his harsh laugh.

"You must have known damn well what was likely to happen to Terry Clive if she got in Maud Millicent's way! What happened to Louisa Spedding?" He barked the question at Fabian, and saw him wince.

He said, "Don't!" in a shuddering whisper.

"And why not?" said Garrett mercilessly. "You can do the thing, but you can't bear to hear about it! That poor devil of a butler got in your way. He recognized you, and so there wasn't any way out of it—you shot him! Capital punishment for recognizing Mr. Fabian Roxley—a government servant—part of our machinery of civilization—part of our system of law and order! I wonder what he thought about it all before you shot him—but perhaps you didn't give him time to think! Louisa Spedding recognized Maud Millicent. Capital punishment for that—and, I imagine, no time to think! Terry Clive on the edge of recognizing you. You've quite a good brain, Fabian—what did you think was likely to happen to Terry Clive? And you sit there and whine about your feelings, and tell me you haven't been able to sleep! What do you expect me to do—tuck you up in bed?"

The violence with which the last words were spoken appeared to penetrate that dazed indifference. Fabian Roxley got to his feet and stood there staring.

"What are you going to do?" he said. "Arrest me?"

Garrett's face for once was a blank. He looked past the big, unsteady figure as if it was not there. He said coldly,

"I'm not a policeman, thank God. You'd better go."

Fabian went on staring for a minute. Then he turned and went towards the door. Garrett's voice followed him.

"Terry Clive has been found."

Roxley stopped dead, put a hand on either jamb of the door, and stood there with his back to Garrett, swaying. His voice caught in his throat. He tried to speak before he got out the one word,

"How?"

"How do you suppose?" said Garrett in the cold tone which made a stranger of him.

There was a long and dreadful pause. Then Fabian Roxley straightened himself and went out of the room and across the hall. Garrett heard him groan. So did Terry Clive. She lifted her head from Peter's shoulder and pushed him away.

"What was that?"

She got up and opened the door. Fabian turned and saw her. She said his name, very quick and frightened,

"Fabian—" And then louder, "Fabian, what is it?"

The change in his face might have startled anyone—that

grey haggard mask suddenly alive with rage, congested—the eyes glaring. Terry cried out and fell back against Peter. She said, "Fabian!" again, and hardly recognized the voice which answered.

"A trick! All a trick! You've tricked me—the lot of you!"

"Fabian!"

Words poured from him with a kind of maniac fury.

"Dead, were you—dead, and driving me mad! Whilst you laughed at me with your lover—who was dead too! Dead, and mad, and—no, no, not yet—you needn't laugh yet! I'm not dead yet, and I'm not mad—not yet—not yet!"

He wrenched at the door, flung it back upon its hinges, and went in a blind rush across the landing and down the bare stone stairs, taking three steps, four steps, five, in a clattering stride which checked and tripped but never fell. They heard the footsteps become hollow and faint. They heard them die away.

Terry stood shuddering in Peter's arms. Garrett came out of the sitting-room, gave them his familiar scowl, and slammed the door.

CHAPTER XLI

SCOTLAND Yard next day. A brief, exhausted sleep in Garrett's narrow slip of a spare room, where the bed was as hard as Maud Millicent's mercies.

Terry had not thought that she would sleep, but she laid her head on a brickbat of a pillow and knew no more until nine o'clock. Peter appeared to have slept in a chair. He was in very good form, and he and Garrett between them made her eat quite a good breakfast.

Then Uncle Basil, arriving all in a hurry, and shaken quite out of his usual immaculate neatness. His hair was ruffled, and he was badly shaved. It was very comforting. When you have always taken someone for granted as family, and then had a sick moment when all the foundations have given way and the roof is falling in, it is naturally helpful to find that the accustomed figure has survived the crash. There had been a moment—moments perhaps—when Terry had seen this figure in a nightmare, horribly transmuted into the image of murder. They were gone. This was Uncle Basil who had always been kind, even if he appeared to be more interested in stamps than in his ward. The rough chin and the untidy hair were most reassuring tributes. Terry found herself clinging to him and being very warmly kissed.

And then Scotland Yard. Statements. People who wanted to know all about everything. About the picture—James

Cresswell's Turner which was the apple of his eye. Last heard of, it had been in a garage, in the boot of Spike Reilly's car—only of course not really Spike Reilly but Peter Talbot. And then on Wednesday night James Cresswell had a mysterious telephone call telling him he would find his picture just inside his own gate. And he did. But no one seemed to know how it got there, and they all wanted to know very badly. Until suddenly Colonel Garrett chipped in and said in his most offhand voice,

"Lot of fuss about nothing. Thought he'd better have it back, so I took it back."

Someone with a very starchy voice said,

"Oh, you took it back? May I enquire how, Colonel Garrett?"

Garrett stuck his chin in the air. His eyes snapped.

"Easy as mud," he said. "I drove the car out of the garage—one-horse place, man and a boy doing something else—drove down to Heathacres, rang up from a call-box, drove back to town."

"And may I ask why?"

Garrett shrugged his shoulders.

"Valuable picture. Cresswell probably glad to get it back again. One-horse garage not the place for a Turner—definitely."

Terry's heart warmed—she could have kissed him. But you can't kiss people at Scotland Yard—"He didn't want Peter to get into trouble. He's a lamb."

Then more talk. Everyone wanted to know a lot of things which Terry would very much have liked to know herself—things about Maud Millicent, about Jake, about the Bruiser. And quite suddenly she thought about Alf, and broke in upon the grave-faced men and their statements.

"Oh, please, will someone find Alf. He's a bull-terrier—and an angel—and if they've all run away—and I expect they have—there won't be anyone to feed him, and he does so hate being shut out in the yard, poor lamb."

One of the men was rather nice. He had very blue eyes. He laughed and said that Alf had been found and they were very glad to know what his name was and that he was an angel, because he had bitten two policemen under the impression that they were burglars and it might soothe him to be properly addressed.

Terry relaxed. She produced her friendliest smile.

"Oh, do you think I might have him? He was the one bright spot." She was aware of Peter's eyes upon her, poignant with reproach, and blushed vividly as she stuck to her point. "He was—really. And of course he thought the policemen were burglars if they came breaking in. Do you think I might have him?"

"I daresay it might be arranged—with Jake. We haven't got him yet, but when we do he—er—won't be in a position to keep a dog for some time to come. By the way, Mr. Talbot—" he turned to Peter—"I think you were lucky to get away as you did last night. Your derelict house on the edge of the cliff is Lattersley Hall, Sir John Lake's property. When it had to be abandoned on account of the dangerous state of the cliff three years ago, he built again about a mile and a half inland. Well, his garage was broken into last night and his new Rolls taken. A very daring piece of work, and I daresay we can all make a guess at who was behind it. It was the only way they could have escaped. If they hadn't had a car, we'd have got them. And, considering the car they got, you were very lucky indeed not to be overtaken on the road. I see you took about ten minutes telephoning to Colonel Garrett."

Peter smiled engagingly.

"And then I took a wrong turning."

"By accident, or by design?"

"Well, I had an idea it might be safer. It made us a bit late getting to town, but Mrs. Simpson is a very enterprising woman, and I thought there had been enough shooting."

"Have you traced the car?" snapped Garrett.

The blue-eyed policeman smiled a thought grimly.

"Oh, they dropped it like a hot coal as soon as it had served their turn. It was found abandoned in a Chiswick by-road. We've got the Bruiser, and we shall probably pick up Jake and Bert in the course of the day, but I expect we can whistle for Maud Millicent Simpson. Unless one of them gives her away."

"They won't," said Garrett. "They won't know anything. That's why we've never got her. She'll change her skin and save her bacon. You won't see hair, hide or hoof of her, the she-devil. You'll get the others, and they won't know anything, any more than Fabian Roxley did."

"I wish he hadn't got away," said the man behind the desk.

Terry lifted startled eyes.

"Has he got away?"

The blue-eyed man nodded.

"For the moment. But we shall get him of course—we shall get him."

They signed their statements, and came out into bright sunshine, clouds rolling back and the sky blue overhead.

"I must go and see Aunt Fanny," said Peter. "After wasting a good wreath and lot of undeserved affection it's the least I can do. Terry—if I came and fetched you in an honest off-the-rank taxi, do you think you would come and have tea with her, and—er—with me?"

Terry looked at him, and looked away.

"I might."

"They don't seem to be going to arrest me or anything of that sort. Bygones, I gather, are going to be bygones. Spike Reilly is dead and buried, and nobody is going to cast stolen passports or pictures up at me. Frank, in fact, has squared the police. So what about it?"

"I'd like to."

"All right—half past three."

"Miss Talbot doesn't have tea at half past three!"

Peter grinned.

"Did I say half past three? I meant three o'clock."

"Peter, she doesn't—"

"My sweet, it's going to take us quite a long time to get there—quite a long time."

It did. The honest taxi wasted time in the most sympathetic manner. The blue went out of the sky, and the sun disappeared for good and all. It turned rather dark and very cold. If anyone had been looking for weather signs they might have prognosticated fog.

Peter and Terry were entirely disinterested in the weather. They sat side by side in the taxi and felt shy. They had known each other so short a time as time is measured by days and nights, and hours and minutes. They had been thrown so violently, so intimately together, and now just how did they stand? They didn't quite know. Emergency had given place to convention and the civilized life. They talked about everything and everyone except themselves. Frank Garrett. Fabian Roxley—poor Fabian, and how dreadful. The nice man with the blue eyes—he really was nice, wasn't he? And Alf—oh, Peter, I do want him so badly!

Peter laughed.

"You'll have to teach him not to bite policemen."

"He thought he was being a noble defender, poor angel. Do you think I'll be able to get him?"

"I should think so."

Alf had broken the ice. Terry came a little nearer.

"Peter, do you think they'll get Maud Millicent? I don't think I shall ever feel safe if they don't."

A hand was slipped inside her arm. It certainly made her feel safer. Peter said,

"They'll do their damnedest. The bother is no one knows what she looks like. Garrett says that's always been the trouble. When things get too hot she just turns into someone else and starts all over again. They don't know what they're looking for."

"We saw her," said Terry. "There ought to be something—something—"

Peter gave a short angry laugh.

"We saw a mask, and a wig, and some clothes, and a lot of make-up, and nobody's going to see those particular things any more. They weren't Maud Millicent—they were just things she was wearing, and she won't be wearing them again—you can bet your life on that."

Terry shivered.

"What does she look like really? Doesn't anyone know?"

"Louisa Spedding knew. And she's dead."

"Isn't there anything you'd know her by?"

"I don't know. I don't think so, unless—" He laughed

suddenly. "You know, when she was the old woman with the cough and I was in the taxi with her going to be gaoler to you, I thought about what I could do to have a chance of knowing her again, and I snipped some little holes in her dress."

"What with?"

"Just nail-scissors. I thought they might be handy—and they were. So there's a magnificent clue for the police. They've only got to find a black skirt with five little nicks cut out of it and they've got Maud Millicent. I've put it in my statement, so there they are—they've only got to find the black skirt."

There was a silence. The taxi pursued an even fifteen miles an hour. Peter put his arm round Terry and waited to see what she would say. She didn't say anything.

"Terry—"

She looked up, and down again very quickly.

"Terry—"

A dimple appeared in the cheek nearest to him—a first appearance as far as Peter was concerned.

"Peter—"

"Terry—"

Terry began to laugh.

"You go on saying it," she explained.

"I know I do. It's absolutely crass. I don't really want to say anything at all. I've always wondered how people manage to propose without making fools of themselves."

"They d-don't."

"You just let yourself go and don't care whether you're making a fool of yourself or not?"

"I think so."

"Terry—I'm doing it again, and I'm making a fool of myself all right—only I don't care if you don't. Do you? *Do you?*"

"No—I mean—Oh, Peter, you don't really, do you?"

The conversation became incoherent.

CHAPTER XLII

MISS Blanche Hollinger looked at her watch. She was going to have tea with her dear friend Miss Talbot, and Miss Talbot set great store on punctuality. Miss Hollinger set great store on it herself. She had been resting, and she wished to allow herself plenty of time to dress. Tea would be at a quarter past four, and owing to Miss Talbot's recent bereavement—very sad, very sad indeed—it was probable that her dear friend would be the only guest. But she must have plenty of time to dress.

She proceeded in a leisurely fashion, and it was astonishing how long it took. Nobody who knew Miss Blanche Hollinger would have supposed her toilet to have been a lengthy affair. The result hardly seemed commensurate with the time and care expended, yet she seemed abundantly satisfied herself. The tilted glass reflected a stooped, middle-aged figure in very middle-aged underwear of the solid, bulky sort which dressmakers deplore. The grizzled hair was twisted into a bun at the back, but there were a number of wispy ends which defied control. Tinted spectacles are not embellishing, nor was Miss Hollinger's countenance one which it would have been easy to embellish. The skin was sallow and shiny. There was an ugly droop of the mouth—Nevertheless the lady seemed pleased with herself. She donned grey Cashmere stockings and square-toed strap shoes, and then, throwing open a cupboard door, she stood hesitating between her best and her second-best dress. The second-best had it. Miss Fanny would certainly be alone, and after a bright interval the day was breaking down. Her old black would do very well indeed.

She put it on, a frumpy, old-maidish garment of a full and bundly cut. She added the cyclamen scarf, and fastened it at the neck with a pebble brooch.

The hat came next, and again she hesitated, deciding finally on a boat-shaped purple felt. Her old black coat would do, as she had only to run in next door, and she would be leaving it in the hall.

Owing to the fact that her bedroom was at the back of the house, Miss Hollinger missed the arrival of Peter and Terry in a taxi. It set them down and departed again whilst she was fastening her shoes. Terry was being embraced by Miss Talbot whilst Miss Talbot's dear friend was still undecided as to which of her two hats she should wear.

There was a second embrace.

"Oh, my dear child—what a joyful, joyful day!" Miss Talbot produced a handkerchief and dabbed her eyes. "After being so dreadfully, dreadfully unhappy—to have everything come right! It seems almost too much—exactly like the prodigal son. Only of course, my dear, I don't mean that Peter would ever have behaved like that, because he's always been the best of boys."

Peter put an arm about her.

"That's right, Aunt Fanny—speak up for me. You see, she met me in such bad company that it's going to take quite a lot of living down."

Miss Talbot looked fondly from one to the other.

"And I have so wanted you to be friends," she said. Then, with a simplicity which Terry found touching, "He *is* good, my dear—he really is. He has always been very good to his old aunt."

Peter's conscience gave him a sharp stab. He bent to kiss her, and at this affecting moment the door opened and Miller announced,

"Miss Hollinger—"

The little group broke up in inward if not outward confusion. Miss Hollinger stood just inside the door peering short-sightedly through her glasses. She couldn't believe her eyes—she really couldn't believe her eyes.

Miss Talbot rustled to meet her—not in black, not in mourning at all—in fact quite the contrary. The dress that rustled so imposingly was that rather bright blue silk which she had bought just before the sad news of her nephew's death. And she was wearing her best diamond brooch. No wonder Miss Hollinger blinked.

Miss Talbot took her by both hands and said in a warm, excited voice,

"Oh, my dear, come in, come in! Such wonderful news—you'll never guess—I don't see how anyone could! It's like the most joyful dream, and I'm only afraid that I may wake up! But no, no, it's true—oh, thank God, it's true! My dear, dear Peter whom I thought was dead! Oh, my dear, it is exactly like the prodigal son, except that he never was a *prodigal*. But he was dead and he is alive again, and he was lost and he is found!"

Miss Blanche Hollinger stood there peering and blinking, first at the ample figure, the bright blue dress, the large plump face and handsome white hair of her dearest friend, and then at the two young people by the tea-table. They were standing quite close together—that girl Terry Clive whom she had never really liked, and a young man with blunt features and fair hair who, astonishing though it seemed, must be dear, dear Peter.

Miller had turned on the light in the old-fashioned crystal chandelier. The drops dazzled with all the colours of the rainbow, and the light shone full upon Peter Talbot. Miss Hollinger gave a little gasp and pressed the hands which still grasped her own. She said in her high, toneless voice—a faded voice with no ring in it,

"Oh, my dear friend—" She paused, apparently to seek for words, and finding none, fell back on a fluttered repetition. "Oh, my *dear* friend—"

"Come and meet him," said Miss Talbot. She released her clasp, put an arm about Miss Hollinger's shoulders, and drew her forward. "You know my dear Terry, but you and Peter—I don't think you have ever met."

"Once in the dark." Peter came and shook hands. "And of course I know you by sight, Miss Hollinger—I've seen you from the windows here. But you wouldn't know me."

Miss Hollinger fluttered.

"No, no—of course not," she said. "And your aunt has no photograph, Mr. Talbot."

"He wouldn't be done," sighed Miss Talbot. "But you must now, my dear boy, for you know, when I thought you were dead and I hadn't even got a photograph—no, no, I don't want to think about that dreadful time. But it would have been a comfort—I did feel that, though of course no picture really does justice to someone you love."

"Oh, yes—that is so true," said Miss Hollinger. "How do you do, Miss Clive. And now you must not really let me intrude upon this family re-union. You should have put me off, my dear friend—I could come another day—"

But Miss Talbot held her firmly.

"Certainly not! Why, I wouldn't hear of it! I asked you to tea when I thought I was only going to have my own poor company to offer you, and now that Peter and Terry are here, it's the most delightful thing in the world, because I always like my friends to know and like each other, and I've wanted you to meet my dear Peter for so long. But that time you did meet—in the dark—he was just going abroad. Sit down here, my dear, between Peter and me. And, Terry dear, you come over here. . . . Yes, abroad, my dear, and that is how the stupid mistake arose about his being dead. . . . Yes, ring for the tea, Peter—and Miller can draw the curtains too. . . . They are so very careless abroad—really criminally so. You know, I always feel as if anything might happen there. And, you see, it *did*. That poor man with the very odd name—what was it, Peter?—Mr. Spike—yes, Spike Reilly—if it had happened in England, he might have died ten times over in the same hotel as Peter without such a disgraceful mistake being made. Because that is how it happened, my dear, though I shall never quite understand how it was possible, *even abroad*. That poor man died in the hotel, and by some disgracefully careless mistake he was buried as Peter Talbot."

The entrance of Miller with the tea-tray had by no means interrupted the flow of Miss Fanny's talk. Miss Hollinger said,

"Oh dear—what a terrible mistake!" and, "Oh, thank you," when she took a cup of tea.

Miller, at the window, released the rose-coloured curtains from the silk cords which held them back. The room was gay with a rose chintz, the gold of picture frames, and the smooth sheen of flower-patterned china under the sparkling chandelier. Miss Fanny Talbot sat behind a massive Victorian silver tray and dispensed tea from an immense bulbous teapot. Her white hair picked up the light and shimmered like frost. Her fine dark eyes were shining with excitement. Her really beautiful rings flashed with ruby—diamond—sapphire—

In this bright setting Miss Hollinger made a faded picture. The purple boater had seen better days, the cyclamen scarf was a wilted rag, and she was wearing her old black. She may have wished that she had not put it on. It is certain that she had no idea of the sound foundation on which such a wish might very well have rested.

Miss Talbot, pouring out tea and talking all the time, was a little chilled, a little disappointed. She expected more sympathy, more warmth from her dear friend. And perhaps Miss Hollinger realized this, for quite suddenly she was responding just as Miss Talbot would have wished her to respond. She could not stem the tide of talk—it would have been vain to attempt it—but she cast her offerings upon its tide—an "Oh, *yes*"; a "Yes, indeed"; an air of devout attention; short interjections expressing wonder, sympathy, interest, and thankfulness. Peter proffered cake. A small piece was taken, nibbled slightly, and crumbled on the plate. Miss Hollinger's attention was entirely taken up with what her dear friend was saying.

Peter, very much bored, caught Terry's eye. He was afraid he was going to laugh, and looked quickly away.

His glance fell by chance upon one of the breadths of

Miss Hollinger's bundly skirt. It was made very full after some archaic fashion, and as she sat turned towards Miss Talbot and away from him, the breadth of black stuff displayed a row of little holes. In other circumstances he might have thought that the moth had got into it, but the moment he saw those holes he knew that he had made them himself. With a pair of nail-scissors. In a taxi. With an old lady who had coughed and explained to him that he was to look after Terry Clive until she could safely and conveniently be murdered.

Peter felt himself turning cold. Ice-cold and steel-hard.

The old lady with the cough had been Maud Millicent Simpson.

She had sat beside him in a taxi.

He had cut those five nicks in her skirt.

It was Maud Millicent Simpson's skirt.

It was Miss Blanche Hollinger's skirt.

His thoughts raced, but neither his face nor his body moved. His eyes lifted to Miss Hollinger's face and dropped again. Maud Millicent's ears had been pierced. She had worn pearl studs in them. Miss Hollinger's ears were pierced. She wore small gold rings in them. Her grey, untidy hair hid all the ear except the pierced lobe, but as soon as Peter's eyes had rested upon that lobe his racing thoughts came to a sudden stop. They had reached certainty. They stayed upon it.

The lobe of an ear. Not much to go upon, but enough. No two lobes are alike in shape, in texture, in the way they join the line of the jaw. The lobe that had worn the pearl stud was the lobe that was wearing the gold ring. He was as sure of it as he had ever been of anything in all his life.

And so what?

Miss Talbot's voice broke in.

"Terry darling, you are eating nothing. Mrs. Grey will be seriously offended if nobody eats her cake. She has made a very special angel-cake for us. Cut it, Peter dear, and give Terry a piece—and then, I think, Miss Hollinger will be ready."

Peter got up. He stood there cutting the cake. What was

he going to do? Could he make an excuse to get out of the room and telephone to Garrett—to Scotland Yard? Garrett would be the quickest—half a dozen words would be enough. He had them all ready—"Maud Millicent here at Aunt Fanny's. Get Scotland Yard."

He took Terry her piece of cake. The plan was a washout. He simply did not dare leave Terry and Aunt Fanny alone with Maud Millicent, who might guess why he had left the room. That she was as cunning as she was ruthless he knew very well. The disturbance of his thought might have warned her already. She might be guessing *now*. Just what a facer it must have been to come into Aunt Fanny's drawing-room and meet him there, he could imagine.

He cut another piece of cake slowly. Thank heaven Aunt Fanny never stopped talking. He took off his hat to Maud Millicent's nerve, but it appalled him. Aunt Fanny's drawing-room and Spike Reilly—and she hadn't showed a thing! A woman with a nerve like that would take any desperate chance to get away. That bunchy skirt would easily accommodate the little pistol which she had pressed against Terry's neck only last night.

He carried the cake to Miss Hollinger. She helped herself, twittering excuses.

"Dear Miss Talbot—always so kind—but indeed I hardly ever eat cake—only—as you say—Mrs. Grey—such an excellent cook—and, I'm sure, such an excellent cake."

Peter turned away and set the plate down again. The plain fact was that she could shoot them all—if she chose to take a chance. Not such a desperate chance when all was said and done. Mrs. Grey was as deaf as a post, and Miller tolerably hard of hearing though she wouldn't admit it—and the two of them a couple of floors down in a basement kitchen. Not much risk there—an empty house on one side since old Mrs. Langley's death, and Miss Hollinger's own house on the other, empty too. He remembered Aunt Fanny saying that she only had a morning maid. If Maud Millicent could get ten minutes' start, the police would never lay hands on her. Wig, hat, and dress—it wouldn't take ten minutes to change these, and he would certainly have a bolt-hole where, as Frank Garrett said, she could change her skin.

It wasn't to be risked. If she was to be prevented from doing any more mischief, he must use every citizen's right in an emergency and make the arrest himself. As he turned from the table and walked back to his seat, he had made up his mind.

Miss Fanny was telling her favourite story. As a child of five she had presented a bouquet to Queen Victoria, and after a lapse of sixty years the incident had become garnished with a quantity of highly dramatic details. The momentary contact and the gracious smile on the one side, the much rehearsed embarrassed curtsey on the other, had become in retrospect quite a long conversation. Miss Fanny was well away with what she said to Queen Victoria and what Queen Victoria said to her. When very much exalted, she had been known to introduce the Prince Consort into her narration, regardless of the fact that he had died a good many years before she was born.

"She had so much dignity. I remember looking at her and thinking how wonderful it was. She seemed quite a rock. You couldn't imagine her being shaken by anything."

"Wonderful!" said Miss Hollinger. "Such an example to us all."

She set down her plate. Her hand moved towards the gathers of her skirt. And in that moment Peter leaned sideways and took her by the wrists. He said,

"The game is up. You are Maud Millicent Simpson. I'm holding you till the police get here."

Just for a fraction of a second there was a resistance. He had the sense of a violence that was checked even before Miss Fanny screamed and Terry started from her chair. It turned to a limpness, a look of confused terror, a faint bleating protest.

"Oh—oh! What is it? Pray let me go. I don't know what you mean."

"I think you do," said Peter.

Miss Fanny opened her mouth to scream again. She had

dropped her cup, and the tea was soaking destructively into the front breadth of her new blue silk.

"Oh!" fluttered Miss Hollinger. "Oh, Miss Talbot—oh, my dear friend—I don't know what he means—he must be out of his mind. Oh, tell him to let me go!"

"Peter!" said Miss Fanny. "Oh, my dear boy!"

"I'm sorry, Aunt Fanny, but this is Maud Millicent Simpson. Terry, go and call Scotland Yard—Whitehall one-two-one-two. Give them this address and tell them to hurry. Tell them I've got Maud Millicent Simpson here. Be as quick as you can. Call Frank Garrett as soon as you've done with the Yard. And then keep out of here—I don't want you."

Miss Hollinger began to cry in a feeble, choking manner. Miss Fanny couldn't bear it. She pushed back her chair and got up.

"Oh, my dear boy, you mustn't! I don't know what you're thinking about, but there's some dreadful mistake. This is my friend Blanche Hollinger—my dear friend—"

Miss Hollinger moaned. She slipped down in her chair. Her eyes closed. Her mouth sagged open.

"She's fainting," said Miss Fanny. "Oh, Peter! Peter, let *go!*"

Peter had the most dreadful moment of indecision. Five little nicks, and the lobe of an ear—not very much to go on after all. Coincidence. Things did happen like that. Suppose he had made a mistake. *Suppose he had made a mistake*. He would have made the world's fool of himself, and Miss Hollinger would probably bring one action against him for assault, and another for slander. There was no quarter of the habitable globe in which you could live down a thing like that.

But he kept his hold of Miss Blanche Hollinger's wrists.

Miss Fanny, shocked and concerned, thrust past him with a dumpy green glass bottle of aromatic salts. She had removed the stopper, and a powerful blast of ammonia and scent rushed forth. Even a genuine swoon would have been hard put to it to persist. Miss Hollinger's nostrils quivered, her face twitched. A wild, convulsive sneeze jerked her into an upright position. It was followed by others not much less violent.

"Oh, Peter, let her go!"

"A handkerchief—" sobbed the afflicted lady.

"Oh, *Peter!*"

Peter glanced back over his shoulder.

"I can't let her go, but you can get her handkerchief," he said. "I think you'll find she's got a pocket somewhere in this skirt, and I should like to know what she's got in it."

"No—no—*no!*" screamed Miss Hollinger. "Fanny—my dear friend—you can't—I forbid it!"

"Go on, Aunt Fanny—get out her handkerchief!"

Miss Hollinger sneezed again disastrously.

"Go on, Aunt Fanny!"

Miss Talbot dived reluctantly amongst the gathers. Her face changed from concern to horror. Her hand came up with the little pistol in it. She backed away and let it fall upon her flowery carpet.

Peter was conscious of an overpowering relief. Because he hadn't been sure. He—hadn't—been—sure. But he had no time for more than a single flash of thought. The limp wrists which he had been holding became most vehemently and furiously alive. They twisted, struck at him, struggled, wrenched in a wild effort to get free. It took him all he knew to hold a mad, writhing fury. There was none of Queen Victoria's admired dignity about the situation. It was completely horrible. And in the middle of it Terry came back into the room.

They tied her up with the rose-coloured cords which had looped Miss Fanny's curtains. Miss Fanny cried all the time, and never stopped talking. Terry went to and fro and did what she was told without a word.

Maud Millicent had no words either. There was something dreadful about her silence. She strained against the rose-coloured cords. Her eyes were fixed in a stare of hatred. Her lips were dumb.

When the police came, and Miller was ministering to Miss Talbot, Peter took Terry away into the little back room on the half landing and put his arms round her. They stayed like that for quite a long time.

Then Frank Garrett came and told them what had been found in the house next door—papers, letters, the mask which Maud Millicent had worn, the clothes they had described—

"We'll make a clean sweep this time," he said. "All right, I'm going. And you'll be wanted. To make another statement. Lord—what a life!"

They heard him stumping down the stairs. Peter said,

"You'll stay here with Aunt Fanny, won't you, till I get back. Hold her hand a little. You're good at holding hands, aren't you?"

"I don't feel good," said Terry in rather a tremulous voice.

Peter put his cheek hard against hers.

"Darling, it's been such a horrible beginning—for you. But I'll make it up to you—I swear I will."

Terry pushed him away until she could look at him. There were tears on her lashes, but she wasn't crying now. She didn't speak, but she nodded her head slowly and gravely.

Slowly and gravely they kissed.